CODENAME EDELWEISS

CODENAME EDELWEISS

THE SEARCH FOR HITLER'S SON

JUSTIN KERR-SMILEY

First published by Universe
an imprint of the Unicorn Publishing Group LLP 2022
5 Newburgh Street
London W1F 7RG

www.unicornpublishing.org

10 9 8 7 6 5 4 3 2 1

ISBN 978-1-914414-32-9

Typeset by Vivian Head

Printed Short Run Press, Exeter, UK

I am lied to on all sides. I can rely on no one, they all betray me. If anything happens to me Germany will be left without a leader. I have no successor ... rack your brains and tell me who my successor is to be.

Adolf Hitler, March 1945

Hell is empty and all the devils are here!

William Shakespeare, The Tempest

BUENOS AIRES–POSADAS

Thursday 12–Saturday 14 August 1976

Ariel Guzman makes sure he is alone. In these uncertain times it pays to be vigilant. It might be paranoia but recently he has had the feeling that he is being watched. It is strange and unnerving, like someone pointing a gun at you. As far as he can tell nothing appears to be out of place. There are no unusual vehicles parked nearby and nobody is lurking in the shadows. The journalist waits for a car to pass before he crosses the street and enters his apartment building. It is a solid block of brick and stone, functional and unassuming like many in the capital. He gets into the lift and when it arrives at his floor he opens the gate, walks down the passage and unlocks his door.

Ariel places his keys on the hall table and hangs up his jacket. He takes a bottle of beer from the fridge, flips the top and has a drink. He returns to the living-room with a packet of pistachios and switches on the television to watch the evening news. Ariel reclines on a sofa and eats the nuts, tossing the shells into a waste-paper basket as he sips his beer. The military junta has issued a decree banning any gathering of the political opposition. He has already covered the story for his newspaper La Nación and so he rises and opens a window and listens to the traffic going by. It is spring and the air is humid and filled with pollen.

Ariel lives in San Telmo near the church of the Inmaculada Concepción, although he never attends Mass. It is not because he is agnostic, which is true, it is because he is not Catholic. He is Jewish. His surname had been changed from Gottlieb to the Hispanic Guzman by his father Otto, an immigrant from Hamburg who arrived in Argentina on a packet steamer in the last days of 1938 with nothing but the clothes on his back and a suitcase filled with books. It was after Kristallnacht. The writing on the wall, if anyone needed it, that Jews were no longer safe in Hitler's Germany. Otto escaped in time but many of the Gottlieb family did not and perished in the camps of Auschwitz, Bergen-Belsen and Dachau. If Ariel had any faith at all he would have gone to the synagogue. In fact, he has not been inside a temple since his bar mitzvah despite Argentina being the largest and oldest concentration of South America's Jewish diaspora.

'To be a Jew is to walk the earth forever,' his old father used to say. He never explained why but Ariel knows what he meant.

He turns his attention back to the television and sees a priest being interviewed. The man is young and unmistakably Indian. From his accent Ariel supposes he is a Guaraní from the remote north, probably Misiones. The screen shows the city of Posadas which melds into jungle and the ruins of the abandoned mission at San Ignacio Miní, before returning to the priest. The camera cuts to his hands. He holds a rosary and massages the beads as he speaks.

'I pray for my family and my people every day. I hope there will be an answer. It has been a long time.'

'Thirty years.'

'Yes, but I shall never give up. One day the world will know the truth, I am certain of it ...' The priest falters as his voice begins to crack. 'I'm sorry,' he says. 'It's hard for me. I'm sure you understand.'

'Of course. Father Javier Ibarra, thank you for coming here and sharing your thoughts with us about this terrible event.'

'Thank you.'

The programme resumes with the presenters in the studio. Ariel picks up a pencil and writes the priest's name on a pad. He is sure it is the same man who was the sole survivor of the Misiones tragedy, when a village church in the jungle caught fire killing everyone inside. It was thought to have been the result of a catastrophic lightning strike. Some even suspected arson but most people dismissed the theory. Who would have done such a thing and what possible motive could there have been?

After the fire a tropical storm had swamped the area and for two months no one had been able to get near the village because the rivers were impassable. When the parish priest finally turned up all he found, besides the burnt-out wreck of the church, was an emaciated little boy living on roots and berries. The child had not been in church because he was isolated with measles; the condition was often fatal to the Guaraní who had no natural immunity to the virus. When the boy recovered from his illness he knew enough that he should stay in the village, with only pigs and chickens for company, until someone appeared.

Ariel is certain the priest and the Misiones survivor are the same person but there is another reason he has written the man's name in his notebook. He had noticed the cleric fingered his rosary as he spoke. It was an automatic gesture, seemingly one of stress. He appeared to be holding the rosary for reassurance. And yet he was not in church or at prayer. It was as if he were keeping something back and felt guilty about it. As though he had a secret which he would not, or could not, divulge.

The following morning Ariel takes the metro into work. He gets on at Independencia, changes at Diagonal Norte and alights at Lavalle. The newspaper premises are a short distance from the station, on the thoroughfare of San Martín. On the first floor he is greeted by the sights and sounds of colleagues hammering away on typewriters, making and answering phone calls and calling out across the room. In the street horns sound and traffic roars past. Amid this cacophony Ariel approaches the editor's office.

Through the glass-panelled door he sees a man in a chair with his back turned, feet resting on the window ledge. Mario Ovalle hears him and swivels round.

'You're meant to ask if you can come in.'

'Your new position has already gone to your head.'

'Everyone calls me Attila.'

'You're certainly tall enough.'

'Thanks.'

Despite the abruptness they are close friends. Ariel was best man at the editor's wedding and is a godfather to his eldest child. He does not resent Ovalle's promotion, the job had been offered to him, but he prefers to remain a reporter. He leaves the newsroom as often as he can and only returns to use the phone or pitch another story. It is because of the latter that he is in the editor's office.

'Did you see the priest on Canal 7 last night?'

'Father Javier?'

'That's right.'

'I did, and ... ?'

'It's the thirtieth anniversary of the Misiones tragedy.'

'So ... ?'

'I thought I'd do a story.'

'Old news, isn't it?'

'The fire is but not the priest.'

'What's so interesting about him?'

'He's the only survivor and has never spoken about it before.'

'I know that. He was three at the time and remembers zilch. Probably traumatised by it, hence the memory loss.'

'I think he knows more than he's letting on.'

'You do?'

'Yes. He just couldn't bring himself to say it, not on camera anyway.'

'And you want to go all the way to Posadas and spend lots of company time and money interviewing him.'

'Yes.'

'And when he says absolutely nothing newsworthy, you'll file a piece on him and expect me to run it.'

'Damn, you're good. You're wasted as an editor.'

'Thank you. Again.'

'Can I do it?'

'How much is it going to cost?'

'A plane fare. A couple of days in Posadas. Maybe longer, depending on what he says.'

'That's a lot for nothing.'

'It's not going to be for nothing.'

'What makes you so sure?'

'I've got a hunch ...' both men say.

Ovalle smiles. If anyone can draw a sword from a stone, it is this man who has had more scoops and won more prizes than any other journalist in Argentina. Ariel Guzman is a household name.

'Okay. But no more than a week. Make sure you're back by Friday.'

He has barely finished speaking before his colleague is out the door and at his desk. Ariel phones a travel agent and books a seat on the next flight to Posadas and a room at the Hotel Continental. The aeroplane is due to depart at noon, enough time to return to his apartment and pack before heading to the airport. He calls the mission and asks to speak to the priest. Father Javier is not available. Ariel leaves a message, giving his name and the phone number of the hotel. The secretary promises to relay the information and adds the priest is likely to grant him an interview, with permission from his superior.

Ariel returns home. He puts some clothes into a canvas holdall and packs his camera and several rolls of film. He looks out of the living-room window. The taxi rank is empty so he dials for a cab.

He waits in the sun-dappled street and sees the plane trees are almost in leaf. It will be summer soon. In the branches an oriole feeds his mate as she guards her brood in their nest. The long-tailed passerine pauses briefly at the entrance before dashing away again.

When the car arrives, Ariel tells the driver to head for Jorge Newbery Airport, the capital's smaller terminus located in the Palermo neighbourhood on the northern side of the city. The taxi makes the journey in good time. After a coffee and an empanada in the departure lounge, he boards a Fairchild FH-227. The aeroplane is turbo-propped and has a crew of four and a capacity of fifty, but it is half full.

Ariel selects a window seat near the front of the aircraft. He takes out his notebook and writes a list of questions for the priest, ignoring the flight attendant while she runs through the safety routine and only looks up when they are airborne. He puts his pen away and places the pad in the seat pouch. He catches the attendant's eye and she returns the look. Ariel is not classically handsome but his natural charisma makes him attractive to the opposite sex. He has dark hair and deep blue eyes and a prominent nose which complements his face. Apart from charm he has something else that is essential to his craft. It is unique and can neither be taught, nor learnt: the gift of trust.

The Fairchild reaches cruising altitude and the hostess

proceeds down the aisle with a tray. She stops by his seat.

'Good afternoon sir, would you like tea or coffee?'

'Coffee, please.'

'Milk and sugar?'

'No, just black.'

She pours a cup and hands it to him.

'Excuse me, but your face seems familiar.'

'I'm Ariel Guzman.'

'I thought so. I always read your articles.'

'Glad to hear it.'

'If there's anything else you need, let me know,' and with a swing of her hips she sashays down the gangway.

Ariel admires her catwalk before he sits back and drinks his coffee. Journalism certainly had its advantages.

The aeroplane descends through a layer of cloud and touches down at Posadas Airport. As Ariel leaves he gives the flight attendant a wink. Her name is Carmen and he has her phone number in his pocket. He crosses the asphalt. The place is no more than a runway with a control tower. A few military helicopters and light aircraft dot the apron but otherwise it is empty. It is noticeably warmer and Ariel is sweating when he enters the terminal. He walks past a dozing official onto the main concourse where a plump, middle-aged man with a moustache and wearing a Hawaiian shirt is waiting.

'Señor Guzman?' he asks. He has tobacco-stained teeth and a gold cap on his upper left canine.

'Yes.'

'I'm José. The hotel sent me.'

The driver takes his holdall. In the parking lot is a Chevrolet, its chrome shining in the sun. Ariel admires the veneered dashboard and leather trim on the steering wheel.

'Nice car.'

'Thank you. She's a lovely girl. Never lets me down.'

'Your wife must be jealous.'

José laughs and turns the key in the ignition. The Chevrolet shudders and a low purr comes from the engine. Leaving the airport, they take the highway to the city. Office buildings rise on either side as they make their way to the Hotel Continental on Plaza 9 de Julio. It is a pleasant square lined with palms and dominated by a Gothic cathedral. The car circles the plaza and comes to a halt in front of a 1960s concrete edifice. José removes his luggage and takes it into the hotel. In the lobby Ariel gives him a tip.

'I'll be in touch. I'm sure I'll need you again. I'm here for a few days.'

'Okay, *jefe*. Just ask for me at the desk,' and he departs through the revolving doors.

Ariel checks in, asking the concierge if he has any messages.

The clerk hands him a note.

It is from Father Javier. His superior has granted permission for the interview and the priest asks if Ariel can be at the Jesuit mission on Calle Cordoba at 11 am the next day. There is a phone number. He puts the note away and takes the lift to his room. It is on the top floor with a balcony overlooking the square. He slides open the patio door.

Below him is the cathedral and the surrounding park. In the distance the Parana shines like polished pewter and on the far bank is Paraguay. He admires the view before returning to his room to unpack and take a shower. In a clean shirt and a pair of jeans, his hair combed, Ariel leaves the hotel.

The plaza is filled with people making their evening promenade. He looks about and sees a bar. It is too early to eat and instead he asks for tequila.

'You on holiday?' says the proprietor as he picks up a bottle and pours a measure.

'Yes. I want to visit San Ignacio Miní.'

'People often come here but they rarely do so twice.'

'Why's that?'

The man gives an enigmatic look and pushes the glass towards him.

'Twenty pesos.'

Ariel pays and takes his drink to a table. An elderly couple are seated nearby. Neither looks at the other as the woman speaks. She speaks constantly, talking in a torrent, and only pauses to draw breath. Her partner is resigned to his fate and says, '*Si, mi cielo*' but nothing more. Anything else could be fatal. It is payback for all the dalliances the man has had, consummated or otherwise, all the times he came home late and drunk, all the times he blew a month's pay on the horses. He is old and he is unwell. There has been a paradigm shift in their relationship. If the man does not want to die penniless and alone, he must accept this. So he does.

Ariel leaves the old boy to his fate and watches the locals enjoy the balmy air. Everyone seemed content as they wandered to and fro, or chatted on the benches. The pace of life in Posadas was slower than the capital and all the better for it. If something could not be done today, then it could always be done tomorrow. But this lassitude in no way made people idle, or effete. Argentina's interior had been carved out by pioneers centuries ago and was where the true Latinos lived, not like the vain and entitled Atlanticos on the coast.

Ariel downs his tequila and takes a walk. In an alley he finds a restaurant that specialises in fish. The Parana is noted for the dorado which can grow up to thirty or forty pounds and is prized by anglers. He orders food and a carafe of Sauvignon. The wine is placed on the table and he fills his tumbler and has a drink.

When his meal arrives, Ariel takes a slice of lemon and squeezes it over the chargrilled fish and begins to eat. The flesh is white and succulent and has a delicate taste. Soon there is nothing left except skin and bones. He wipes a piece of bread around the plate and empties the carafe into his glass. The sun has set and a full moon ascends the heavens. Its light is luminous and the Cathedral of St Joseph glows like alabaster. A breeze comes from the river shaking the leaves of the tall trees and a solitary bell tolls the hour. Ariel finishes his wine and settles the bill. He walks back through the square, his heart trembling in anticipation. He has no idea what the priest is going say but he knows, whatever it is, it will be a revelation.

Javier Ibarra cannot sleep. In his hand is a rosary and he rolls the beads between forefinger and thumb. He has already recited the Joyful Mysteries and is now saying the first Sorrowful Mystery: the Agony of Jesus in the Garden. Prayer is sacred and cleanses his soul. In the darkness and solitude of his room he can sense the Holy Spirit. The priest is preparing for his own Calvary, which he believes to be close. The hour of death is approaching.

Dawn comes stealthily like a thief and the walls of the cell begin to pale. Later, a ray of sunlight penetrates the shutters. Javier finishes the last Sorrowful Mystery and ends the cycle with a Glory Be. He kisses his rosary, lays it upon the bedside table and gets out of bed.

The priest slips a cassock over his head and goes downstairs. In the church he enters one of the chapels which has already been prepared. His server is waiting for him. He greets the child and puts on his vestments and opens a leather-bound missal. He turns to the appropriate page and begins to celebrate Mass.

At the Eucharist Javier raises the host and his server rings a brass bell, its jangle reverberating in the vaulted room. He holds the wafer before him and prays.

'Lord, I am not worthy to receive you but only say the word and I shall be healed.'

He consumes the host, which has miraculously become the body of Christ, and closes his eyes as it dissolves in his mouth. Now he is at one with the Lord. He genuflects and takes up the chalice, puts it to his lips and drinks the precious blood. He sets it on the altar and wipes it clean with a purificator.

Javier bows and takes a host from the plate.

'The Body of Christ.'

'Amen,' the boy says and a wafer is placed on his tongue.

The priest faces the altar again and with a blessing concludes the Mass. He thanks the child and sends him on his way. The boy is an orphan just as he had been and Javier wonders if he too will hear the call and join the Church. Some did, some did not. But everyone who has been cared for by the mission is like a brother or a sister. There are no exceptions.

Javier has breakfast with his brethren before going back to his room to resume his studies. He is reading Thomas More's *Utopia* and finds it curious how the English martyr and saint developed the concept of a just and equal society similar to that of his own founder, Ignatius Loyola. They had never known each other and yet were almost exact contemporaries. The Spaniard had been a soldier and prisoner of war before founding the Society of Jesus, while the Englishman was a lawyer and politician who became Lord Chancellor and one of the most powerful men in the land. Even so, More's exalted position could not save him from his monarch's wrath and he was condemned to death for his loyalty to Rome. And yet Javier knows the sacrifice was worth paying. The man is seated at God's right hand with all the other saints and he hopes that one day he will join them.

There is a knock and Javier closes his book and tells the person to enter. The door opens revealing a young man wearing a linen jacket and an open-necked shirt. He rises.

'Welcome.'

'Thank you, Father.'

'Don't thank me, thank the Lord. It was He who brought you. And, please, call me Javier.'

He shows his guest a chair. Ariel takes a biro and notebook from his bag and a camera, an Olympus Trip.

'I hope you don't mind if I take a few pictures first?'

'Not at all.'

Ariel unscrews the lens cap and checks the light meter. He puts the camera to his eye and focuses on the man's face.

'You're in shadow. If you could turn towards the window.'

'Like this?'

A shaft of light falls across the priest's body, his features illuminated by the morning sun.

'Yes, that's great ... *click, click* ... Just a couple more ... *click, click* ... Now look the other way – over there ... Perfect ... *click, click, click* ... And another ... *click.* That's fine, thanks.' Ariel puts the camera down. 'I always take photos of a subject if I can. It helps me write the story.'

Javier nods and reaches into a pocket. He removes his rosary and runs the beads through his fingers.

'So, what brings you here?'

'As you've probably guessed ... the tragedy at Misiones.'

'I thought as much. Unfortunately, I have nothing to add to what I've said already.'

Ariel makes a sympathetic face. He knows the best way to approach a difficult subject is to be direct. There is no point pretending otherwise.

'What caused the fire?'

'I've no idea but fires happen in the jungle. Especially if

there's been a drought. It was just before the rainy season.'

'Do you recall anything in particular ... anything unusual about it?'

'I'm afraid not. It was a long time ago.'

'What did you actually see?'

'I saw the church burn down with everyone inside ... and I remember the screaming.'

'But you've no idea how it happened?'

Javier remains impassive. 'Absolutely none.'

'None at all?'

'Like I said, none.'

Ariel can feel blood pounding in his ears and his nerves are taut and stretched like the strings of a violin. A bow is drawn across and a chord echoes deep within the chambers of his heart.

'I'm sorry to say this Father, but I don't believe you.'

The other man is perplexed.

'You don't believe me?'

'No.'

'Why not?'

'I don't know why exactly but I'm sure you know more than you claim. A lot more.'

Javier tilts his head to one side like a bird which hears a new song. The journalist is able to read a person well. Unsurprising perhaps, given his profession. But there is something else about him, something unworldly and the priest wonders if he has studied theology.

'Were you ever a seminarian?'

'No. The opposite in fact.'

'You have no faith?'

'Not only that. I'm Jewish.'

At last Javier's prayers have been answered. Here is the prophet the Lord has sent, the man to whom he must divulge his secret. It is the Wandering Jew who shall know the truth.

'Your people were the first to hear the word of God. You are truly blessed.'

'My father might disagree with you. His family were killed in the Holocaust. He was the only one to survive.'

Now it all made sense. It is why the Lord has brought this man to him, to bear witness.

'Before I tell you anything I want to know if you are prepared to accept the consequences. The story is so incredible and, indeed, so awful that people may die, including you.'

'I understand.'

'I'm sure you understand in a literal sense but I don't think you can possibly comprehend the forces which will be unleashed by what I have to say. Are you prepared for this?'

'Yes.'

'Are you absolutely certain?'

'Yes, I am.'

Javier sighs and clasps his hands as if in prayer.

'Very well.'

The priest recounts what happened and explains why he has not spoken about it before. He had seen everything and forgotten nothing. One day a group of strangers arrived in his village and corralled everyone into the church and set it on fire. He was not among them as he was sick and so he hid under his bed and watched everything through a crack in the wall. He heard the cries and saw the flames consume the building until it collapsed in a pile of burning timber. When the parish priest found the lone survivor several weeks later, Javier told him exactly what had happened. The cleric took the boy back to the mission in Posadas and informed his superiors about the tragedy. They made him promise to keep silent, a promise which has been kept for all these years. Apart from the man who found him and the head of the mission, only the superior generals of the Society have ever known and they have been forbidden to speak out by successive popes. His Holiness Paul VI wants the knowledge buried deep within the Vatican and never to emerge.

'Why the secrecy?'

Javier raises his eyes to the crucifix on the wall before turning his gaze back to the journalist.

'Because the people who did this were Nazis. Some of them had been protected by the Church and some were helped by it to escape.'

Ariel wonders if he has heard correctly. Judging by the priest's expression, he can tell that he has.

'I'm sure you've heard of Odessa.'

'Yes. You think they were involved?'

'I don't think, I know. The organisation is still active, particularly in Argentina. They might appear to be dormant but they've never gone away.'

'How do you know it was them?'

'There was one other survivor from the village although she did not witness the fire.'

'Is she alive?'

'No. She was a nun here. Her name was Maria. She was also my cousin. She died recently from an aneurysm. It was she who confirmed what happened in the village. Naturally, the Church was sceptical about the witness of a three-year-old Guaraní boy but they had to believe her since she corroborated my story.'

'What did she tell them?'

'She said the men who did this were Nazis. Furthermore ...'

Javier pauses for a moment as though he cannot believe what he is about to say.

'... they had been ordered to do so by Adolf Hitler himself.'

Ariel ceases writing and puts down both pen and notebook.

'That's impossible! Hitler committed suicide in the bunker. Everyone knows that.'

'If only it were true. In the last days of the war Hitler and Eva Braun fled from Berlin with some followers and came here to Misiones where they made a secret camp in the jungle. Maria said she had worked for them. The Church asked her to prove it. She took them to the camp.'

'Where was it?' Ariel starts to write again.

'Some distance north of our village. Towards Iguaçu.'

'Does anything remain?'

'I believe so. The Nazis left in a hurry. They set fire to the place but they failed to destroy it because of the rains. It's probably jungle now.'

'What happened to Hitler and the others?'

'They escaped across the River Parana into Paraguay.'

'Are they alive?'

'No. Braun perished in the camp from a fever.'

'And Hitler?'

Javier shakes his head in bewilderment. 'He died of a broken heart, so I'm told. A man who killed six million Jews and shed not a tear, dies of grief.'

'Because of Braun's death.'

'No, not because of her.'

'Why, then?'

The priest again looks at the crucifix as if willing the figure to remove the tongue from his mouth.

'I'm afraid I cannot tell you because the information will surely be fatal. Not only to many, many people but also to yourself.'

'You said you would tell me everything you know.'

'About the tragedy, yes, but not this. Also, I can't tell you because I cannot break the seal of a sacrament. When Maria was dying she asked me to hear her last confession. What she told me could set the world alight and possibly start another war.'

'If you can't tell me, who can?'

'Nobody. No one else will speak.'

'But others know?'

'Yes, certainly there are others, including the Society's superior general and His Holiness the Pope.'

'How will I ever find out?'

Javier is silent. The man is brave and honourable but he realises such knowledge can only be the death of him.

'If anything happens to me, you shall know the truth.'

'You mean, if you die? I don't mean to be flip Father, but that could be a while.'

'I don't think so. I don't think so at all. In fact, I'm sure the time is very near.'

'I see,' says Ariel, trying not to appear incredulous and confused.

'If I die, a man's life will be in mortal danger. A wholly innocent man. A man the Church has a moral obligation to protect. And you must help him.'

'Who is he?'

'I can't say. But he has a codename. You must not reveal this to anyone.'

'Okay. I'll keep it off the record. What is it?'

Javier utters a single word: 'Edelweiss.'

The priest feels a gust of wind pass over him, like the giant sweep of an angel's wing, and he shudders. It is as if he is standing at his own grave. The wind increases and he gets up to close the window. The interview is over and Ariel rises.

'Father, I appreciate everything you've told me but there's one more thing. To verify the story, I need to find the camp. Will you help me?'

'I can put you in touch with a local guide. He'll know where it is ... if there's anything left.'

Javier pities the man before him. The journalist is unaware of what he is about to unleash and he feels guilty he has said so much, even though he knows he is right to have done so. He goes to a drawer in his desk and brings out a wooden box. Inside is a turquoise marble and, next to it, a silver medal the size of a large coin.

'I want you to have this. It is Our Lady of Guadeloupe. She will protect you.'

'Okay.' Ariel takes the medal and puts it in a pocket.

'Pray for me.'

'What kind of prayer? I only know how to say Kaddish.'

'That will do. That will do very well. And if I should die, do you promise to help this person?'

'Yes, I promise.'

'Thank you. I can see you're a man of your word.'

When his visitor has gone, Javier closes the door and returns to his desk.

'That is why they are called the chosen people.'

And the priest picks up his copy of *Utopia*, removes the marker and begins to read.

MISIONES–IGUAÇU–POSADAS

Sunday 15–Friday 20 August 1976

The Chevrolet travels along the narrow road. In the fields cows lie in the shade of eucalyptus chewing cud as they seek respite from the afternoon heat. The vehicle passes a lone gaucho on a horse, a cattle dog at heel. The land has been cleared of forest, which rises immense and green in the distance like a tide waiting to burst forth. The air is sultry and the grass is filled with the cry of crickets.

Ariel and his driver are on their way to an estancia near San Ignacio Miní, one of the last human habitations before the jungle. It is a two-day journey on horseback to Javier's village followed by a further ride to the camp. The guide is a Guaraní who worked on the farm and came from a hamlet not far from the priest's.

'Here we are, *jefe*.'

The car emerges from a bend in the road and there, encircled by pines, is the estancia. The house is built around a courtyard and has dark red adobe walls and a pantile roof. A grapevine winds its way around the eaves, its fruit ripening in clusters.

Beneath the vine is a hammock and the veranda is set with tables and chairs.

As the Chevrolet comes to a halt a trio of mastiffs bound towards it barking furiously. They are Dogos, a native breed noted for their brute strength and aggression and used to protect livestock. José is terrified. He winds up his window and cowers at the wheel. A man in a black *campero* strides towards them with a chainsaw in one hand. He shouts at his hellhounds which cease snarling and begin to whine and wag their tails.

'Hermann Mattei,' he announces as Ariel exits the car.

The rancher removes a protective glove and he winces at the man's grip. Mattei notices and apologises.

'Sorry, don't know my own strength. I've been cutting brushwood all day and my fingers are numb.'

Mattei is handsome, broad-shouldered and blond. His eyes are aquamarine and deepset, the sclera unusually white so that he has a penetrating, almost hypnotic stare. He looks Scandinavian rather than Hispanic, common enough in the capital and the surrounding countryside, which has all manner of European immigrants, but not in Misiones.

José revs the Chevrolet's engine and sounds his horn before passing through the open gates. He drives down the road and the car is consumed by a cloud of dirt. He has promised to return at the end of the week.

Mattei takes the visitor indoors and shows him to his quarters.

'I suggest an early night, you'll be riding out at dawn. We have kids, so we all eat together. Supper is at eight.'

‘Fine. See you later.’

Mattei departs and Ariel enters his room. He approaches the window and looks at the fields and the jungle beyond. The horizon is sombre and heavy with cloud. A storm is brewing and silent forks of lightning tear the lowering mass of cumulus. A deep rumble follows and wind flays the poplars, scattering leaves across the lawn. Spots of rain begin to splash the panes and he turns away. At the other end of the house he can hear a piano play and children’s voices. They are speaking German instead of Spanish and he realises that his host’s antecedents are not Scandinavian but Teutonic.

As the storm breaks Ariel joins the family for their evening meal. They dine on rare roast beef, boiled rice and runner beans, the food accompanied by a bottle of Malbec from their own vineyard. A servant ensures the adults’ wine glasses are always replenished. The children are blond like their father, polite and respectful. After supper is finished they kiss their parents goodnight and troop off to bed. When they have left Mattei’s wife, Soledad, offers their guest a nightcap.

‘A brandy, if you have one,’ says Ariel.

‘I’ll join you, we make our own batch here on the farm,’ and Mattei motions at the servant who has been standing unobserved in a corner. The man approaches a sideboard, opens a decanter and pours two glasses before returning to his position.

Mattei speaks over his shoulder.

‘Hector, you can go now.’

'Thank you sir, thank you ma'am,' and the servant retires.

'I'd better see if the children are doing what they're meant to be doing,' says Soledad, wishing her husband and guest good night and leaving them alone in the dining-room.

Mattei reaches for his brandy and Ariel does the same. The liquor is robust and a fiery essence flickers on the palate.

'Thanks for having me to stay.'

'Not at all. Always nice to see a new face. As you can imagine we don't get many visitors here,' and Mattei squints over the brim of his glass. 'Tell me, what's your impression of Misiones?'

'It's different from the east. Wild and open. Not many people either.'

'That's the way we like it. No one bothers us up here, we do our own thing.'

'Not even the junta?'

'No, not even the junta. We're like another country, we abide by our own laws.'

'Such as?'

'The laws of nature, not man.'

'Interesting. I wonder what Darwin would say.'

'I'm sure he'd agree. Just as different species are uniquely adapted to their habitat so is man. Take the Guaraní, for example. They're forest people, they wouldn't survive five minutes in the city and the same goes for the city dweller in the jungle. Each to their own.'

'Where do you fit in?'

Mattei laughs and has another sip of brandy, rolling the liquor around his mouth.

'Fair point. A bit of both I suppose.'

'And who's the apex predator?'

'We are, naturally.'

'We?'

'The white man.'

Ariel listens politely as his host expounds at length on his racial theories and eugenics. At last they finish their drinks and leave the table.

'See you in the morning,' says Mattei.

Ariel returns to his room. He sits at the desk and listens to the wind in the trees as he writes in his journal. He yawns. It has been a long day. He closes the book and undresses, climbs into bed and turns out the lamp. Soon he is asleep.

A blood-red sun rises above the land and swathes the estancia in light. Its rays penetrate the jalousies and wake Ariel. He lies in a daze for a moment before levering himself out of bed. He washes at the basin and puts on his gear. Then he loads a new cartridge in his camera and places a notebook and pencil in a pocket along with extra rolls of film. Ariel opens the louvre doors and steps onto the veranda.

The sky has cleared and the air is moist with a petrichor smell. Dew shimmers on the grass. Nearby a pair of horses are saddled, rolled mats and sleeping bags on their haunches. Ariel hears footsteps and sees Mattei approaching with the guide. The Indian carries a rucksack and also a rifle and a bandolier of ammunition as pumas roamed the forest. Ariel has not told the rancher the reason for his journey and claimed he was writing an article about the Guaraní for a scientific journal. Only the guide knows why he wants to visit the jungle and Javier has sworn him to silence.

'Hope you find what you're looking for,' says Mattei with a grin. 'The Indians don't always talk to strangers. But my man should help.'

'Okay. I should be back by Friday.'

Ariel puts a boot into a stirrup and mounts his steed and they set off beneath a tropical sun which hangs like a ripe fruit above the trees. In spite of the eucalyptus and thorn, shade is sparse and the horses toss their heads and flick their tails at the flies that follow. It is noon and the sun at its zenith when they reach San Ignacio Miní. The ruined arches and eroded stone columns are all that remain of a mission which once teemed with life and stand as mute witnesses to a tragic and violent era. The horses amble past and by evening they have ventured far into the forest. That night Ariel and his guide camp under the stars, the fire left burning to keep predators away.

The next morning they arrive at the village, or where it used to be. The clearing has been overtaken by jungle and the huts have collapsed. In the middle is the area where the church once stood. Saplings crowd each other and thrust their way towards the light. The only evidence of the conflagration are the charcoal timbers of the building now festooned with orchids. Glossy hummingbirds flit from flower to flower, their wings drumming the warm air.

Ariel dismounts, unstraps his camera and starts to take pictures.

'You ever been here?'

'No, boss.'

'I thought your village was close.'

'The place is haunted. No one comes here.'

'What do you think happened?'

'It was the devil. Vengeance.'

'Vengeance for what?'

'Don't ask questions boss. Best not to ask questions.'

Ariel slips the Olympus over his shoulder and smiles but the man looks scared.

'I don't care to stay, boss. We should leave now.'

'I've got all I need. Let's go.'

Ariel gets back onto his horse and they set off again along the trail. A lone toucan whistles as the riders leave the abandoned village to the forest and its ghosts.

After journeying further into the jungle they reach the camp the following day. It has not been destroyed, as Ariel had feared. Although draped with lianas and vines the place is well-preserved. The palisade and watchtower remain and the huts all have their shingle roofs. This time the guide refuses to enter and instead holds his companion's horse while Ariel approaches the compound. He brings out his notebook and begins to write. After a few minutes he replaces it in his jacket and starts to snap away with his camera, his heart quickening. He walks through the camp taking photos of everything he sees.

In a clearing a wooden cross is stuck into the ground. It is sturdy and covered in lichen. Ariel bends a knee and takes some pictures. He puts his camera aside, goes towards the cross and brushes away the vegetation. His fingers trace the surface. There seems to be an inscription. He rubs it clean and stoops to take a closer look. He reads and gasps as if he has snagged a finger on a thorn.

Hier ist Eva Braun Hitler
6 Februar 1912–2 Dezember 1945

So the priest was telling the truth. The *Führer* and his wife had escaped the bunker and fled to Argentina and she had died here. Ariel shivers. Beneath his boots the bones of Eva Braun crumbled into the earth. He raises his camera again, takes a close-up of the inscription and walks away.

Ariel goes towards the largest building in the compound. The doors sag on their hinges and he enters a long room with a hammer-beam roof. He stands in disbelief. It is a relic from the Nazi era. The walls are lined with moth-eaten flags emblazoned with swastikas and, at the far end, a swagger portrait of the *Führer* glared. Whoever was here seemed to have left in a hurry. Glass and cutlery lay strewn across tables and coats and jackets hung from hooks. Ariel takes more pictures before going back outside and wonders which were Hitler's quarters.

One of the huts has a veranda and is set apart. He climbs the wooden steps. The flyscreen is torn. He pushes it aside and enters what seems to be a study. There is a mahogany desk with tarnished brass handles. Above it is a portrait of

Hitler. The painting is mottled with damp but the face and bleak, staring eyes are unmistakable.

Ariel realises it must be the *Führer*'s residence. A suite of chairs is arranged around a table. A map of the region and another of the Americas are pinned on a wall. In the next room is a large bed with a carved headboard, the linen cobwebbed and mouldy. He sees his image reflected in a mirror. A door leads to an annexe with twin single beds and a secretaire. In a corner is a child's cradle. There is another picture of Hitler, the same expression of cold contempt in his eyes. Ariel approaches the wooden cot and wonders if a baby ever slept in it. He reaches out and his hand gently rocks the cradle.

The journalist and his guide return to the estancia two days later. The Indian takes the horses to the stables, while Ariel is served toasted avocado sandwiches and iced lemonade as he writes up his report.

A maid appears and clears the plates and cutlery.

'How was your meal, sir?'

'Very nice, thanks.'

The girl's hands shake as she gathers up the china and a knife falls with a clatter onto the tiled floor. She picks it up, raises her face and talks in a whisper.

'You must be careful, sir ...'

Ariel looks at her.

'What do you mean?'

She is about to speak when Mattei's wife appears.

'Josefina, was that you?'

'Yes, ma'am.'

'You're clumsy. What are you?'

'Clumsy, ma'am.'

'Go and clear-up the kitchen.'

'Yes, ma'am. Right away.'

The maid hurries off and Soledad shakes her head at the girl's retreating form.

'Sorry about that.'

'Not at all, it was an accident.'

'Hopeless staff. Barely human, some of them,' and she returns inside.

Ariel finishes the lemonade and checks his watch. José would be here soon. He puts the notebook in his bag and goes and sits in the hammock. He takes off his boots and swings back and forth, listening to finches twitter and spar in the vine above.

When José arrives he refuses to get out of the vehicle and Ariel has to put his own luggage in the boot. Mattei and his family gather on the porch to say goodbye and he thanks them for their hospitality.

'Come and stay with us anytime.'

'I will.'

José puts the Chevrolet into gear and turns the car. The family wave them off, the Dogos bounding after the vehicle until it passes through the gates and into the road. Before it has gone Mattei makes a mental note of the number plate.

The Chevrolet rumbles on down the track past a herd of longhorn browsing in the fields.

‘Good to see you, *jefe*. How’d it go?’

‘All right. Can’t say I’m sorry to leave. They’re an odd bunch.’

‘Not surprised. Everyone hates them round here.’

‘Why on earth didn’t you say?’

‘Sorry, *jefe*. You never asked. I thought they must be friends of yours.’

‘What else do you know about them?’

‘What don’t I know? The Matteis are one of the most powerful families in Misiones. They own, or run, just about everything including the police.’

‘Anything else?’

‘They’re all Nazis. Every damned one.’

Ariel curses inwardly. He has walked straight into a hunter’s trap. He can always back out, but it goes against every instinct. He will have to see it through to the end.

‘That figures,’ he says.

The other man does not respond. Good riddance to the Matteis and their like. It is the last he will ever see of them.

They arrive at the Continental and José promises to return and take Ariel to the airport in time to catch the last flight to Buenos Aires. Ariel asks for his key at reception and ascends in the lift. In his room he locks the door, picks up the phone and dials. He taps his foot impatiently while it rings. The call is answered.

‘La Nación, Ovalle speaking.’

‘It’s me, Ariel.’

'How'd it go?'

'You're not going to believe this but I've got the biggest story since Moses came down from the mountain. Clear tomorrow's front page and leave the next five blank.'

'You want six whole pages! Are you crazy?'

'Wait till you hear what I've got to say.'

Ariel describes what has happened since his arrival, starting with Javier's interview. He has the priest's testimony and photographs of the camp. More importantly he has discovered Eva Braun's grave, which proves beyond doubt that Hitler and his wife escaped the Führerbunker and ended up in Misiones.

'And to think I ever questioned you ... Get back here now.'

'I'm catching the next flight. I'll come straight to the newsroom. Make sure someone from the picture desk is there as well. I want to see the photos.'

'No problem. Nice work, *compadre*.'

'I'll be there soon as I can,' and Ariel hangs up.

He pauses before letting out a wild yell and punching the air in delight. He has the scoop of a lifetime. He takes his holdall and goes downstairs to check out. There is nothing else to do and he hangs around the lobby. Ariel is anxious and does not want to miss his plane. The next one did not leave until the following morning and he would be unable to make the deadline. He constantly checks his watch but the hands scarcely move.

At last the entrance door revolves and José appears.

'*Hola, jefe*. Sorry, got stuck in traffic. Ready?'

'Yes, let's go.'

They leave the hotel and descend the steps to the Chevrolet. As they drive out of the city, Ariel is elated and winds down the window. He lets his arm hang free and revels in the cooling breeze and laughs.

'You seem happy.'

'Just one of those times when everything falls into place,' he says, raising his voice above the buffeting wind. 'Get La Nación tomorrow and you'll see what I mean.'

'Never read anything else. It's my favourite paper.'

'Good for you.'

They arrive at the airport and the driver hands over the luggage.

'*Vaya con Dios.* And thanks for the business.'

'You've been great. Cheers, José.'

'If you ever need transport again just let me know.'

'Will do. Take care, *viejo*,' and Ariel walks away. 'Remember, tomorrow's paper!' he calls out as he heads towards the terminal.

José waves and watches Ariel depart. He returns to his car, guns the engine and takes the road back to Posadas. When he joins the highway, he switches on the radio. A folk song is playing and he increases the volume and taps his fingers on the steering wheel. The windows of the city are ablaze in the afternoon light and the driver's face creases into a smile.

BERLIN–FREDERICIA

Sunday 29–Monday 30 April 1945

The cold air is dead and no bird sings. Instead, there is a constant barrage of artillery which, day-by-day, creeps closer. Spring has abandoned Berlin. The only living creatures in the city are rats and people. The last cat and dog were eaten weeks ago. The people, like the rats, scavenge in the gutters and piles of rubbish, searching for anything that might sustain them. Some have taken to eating grass which grows between the shattered elms that line the streets and boulevards. It is only a matter of time. The regime, led by a maniac who has set half the world alight, will fall soon.

The burial party ascend the concrete steps of the bunker into the garden. Between them they carry the bodies of a middle-aged man and an attractive blonde. The man is in uniform and has leather boots, the toes of which are scuffed. The red-and-black ribbon of the Iron Cross adorns his jacket. The woman is dressed like a respectable *hausfrau* and wears a fox stole. One of her shoes is missing. Both have bullet holes in their temples.

The soldiers dig a shallow grave with picks and shovels

and dump the bodies in it. They would never have treated the corpses with this careless abandon even a few days ago, such was their reverence for the leader whom they have followed without question for more than a decade. Now it is every man for himself and they are desperate to get away. Jerrycans of kerosene appear and the contents are slopped over the bodies. The stench of fuel is powerful and, when the cans are empty, the men step away. Someone lights a rag and tosses it onto the corpses and the funeral pyre erupts in a roar. The heat is intense and the men drop further back as bright flames leap into the sky. The clothes on the bodies burn and blacken and the exposed flesh begins to split. There is the unmistakable smell of roasting meat. As the flames settle the soldiers descend into the bunker. Their job is done. The *Führer* is no more. All that remains is a pile of ashes to be scattered by the winds.

The moon bathes the ruined city in a spectral light. A group of people in Soviet army uniforms hurry through streets choked with rubble. The fighting has stopped for now. Even soldiers have to rest. But the people must be careful, there are patrols and the snipers are vigilant. They make it to the East-West axis which leads through the Tiergarten at the Brandenburg Gate, a short distance from the Chancellery.

In the shadows a Junkers JU-52 is guarded by a detachment of storm troopers. The soldiers stand to attention and salute before retreating as the five members of the group board the plane. They are Adolf Hitler, his wife Eva Braun, his aide

Martin Bormann, and SS-Obersturmbannführer Ludwig Stumpfegger, his physician. The pilot is the last to board. She is Hanna Reitsch. A devoted follower of the *Führer*, he has chosen above all others to effect his escape from Berlin. She had learnt about the mission the previous day. The plan has been devised by the propaganda minister, Joseph Goebbels, who has persuaded Hitler against making a futile last stand in the capital. The National Socialist project must continue. It does not have to be in Germany or even Europe, but another continent where they can rebuild the Third Reich far away from watchful eyes. Somewhere like South America.

Despite the situation, Hitler would have laughed at the idea and refused outright had his wife not come to him that morning with the most extraordinary news, a look of profound happiness on her face, the happiness of a woman who now carried a baby in her womb. A baby she had longed for and, after two miscarriages, had not thought possible. Doctor Stumpfegger had confirmed it. Eva Braun is pregnant. What is more, she is certain it is a boy. It has to be.

The news transformed the *Führer* in an instant. The change was complete and miraculous. The physical disabilities, psychological traumas and tics that had become manifest in recent months sloughed like a snake's skin. The Third Reich would continue into the next century and beyond, led by his very own son. His flesh and blood. Hitler has not known such joy since the fall of France but that undreamt of success pales into insignificance when compared to this.

Goebbels swore their close circle to secrecy as he worked

out the details of an escape plan. Apart from Reitsch, Bormann and Stumpfegger, the only other person in the Führerbunker who knows is General Ritter von Greim. He had flown in three days previously with Reitsch and is recovering from a wounded foot, shattered when their Storch was hit by Russian flak as they landed near the Tiergarten. Von Greim will ensure his fellow generals remain in the dark. To keep the plan secret Goebbels has elected to remain behind with his wife and children. They will commit suicide once the *Führer* has escaped. Hitler and Eva Braun would be replaced by their body doubles who, unknown to the others, have been kept apart in a secret annexe. They had no choice but to agree to the deception. As it was, both actors realised they had little chance of escaping, given their appearance after plastic surgery. They might as well die honourably for the Fatherland.

The passengers strap themselves into their seats as Reitsch switches on the magnetos and increases the throttle. She pumps the primer several times then presses and holds the ignition button. There is a cough and a splutter and the engine growls. The troop withdraws and the aeroplane taxies onto the deserted and bomb-blasted street. Reitsch opens the throttle fully and the JU-52 picks up speed and is soon airborne. Flying above the rooftops, the aeroplane soars across the ruins of one of Europe's grandest cities. The pilot sets the compass for north-north-west, checks the airspeed indicator and charts their course. The winds are moderate and the aeroplane starts to gain height as it heads for the clouds.

There is silence until Stumpfegger tries to make conversation. His excited babble fails to hide his relief. He cannot believe his luck. He had thought he was condemned to the same fate as the rest of Hitler's entourage: most likely a cyanide pill or a Soviet firing squad. Now, not only has he been saved, he has escaped. The doctor talks about the various stages of pregnancy and the methods of giving birth. A glare from the *Führer* stops his prattle. Conversation is not permitted.

Bormann turns and smiles coldly. He hates the doctor. He hates anyone who tries to get between him and his beloved leader. The aide has had a miraculous rise to power, from a foot soldier who started out in the lowest echelons of the Sturmabteilung, or SA, to the *Führer*'s right-hand man. Bormann has been there since the beginning. He joined the Freikorps in 1922 and later served a year in prison for the murder of a rival. He rose up the ranks, becoming chief-of-staff to Rudolf Hess. Since 1935 he has been the *Führer*'s personal secretary and is a man to be feared. His ruthlessness has been commented on by Hitler himself who once described his face as beyond cruel. Every emperor needs a lackey and the *Führer* is no different. It could have been anyone, it just happens to be Bormann. And, in his doglike devotion, he has never failed his master.

The JU-52 flies on as the wind whistles outside the fuselage. There is no heating and the occupants wrap their greatcoats more closely around their bodies. In the east the sky lightens and, one by one, the stars in the heavens dissolve. The aeroplane turns and drops beneath the cloud. Instead of a ruined and smoking city acres of green fields and forest spread out below. The country briefly becomes sea before it returns to country again. The JU-52 banks steeply and begins to descend. Out of the starboard window a concrete strip indicates a runway. It is Vandel airfield in southern Denmark.

The aeroplane lands and comes to a halt and the passengers disembark and get into a waiting Mercedes Tourer. Two motorcyclists with armoured sidecars lead the way followed by a half-track with a platoon of Waffen-SS. The vehicles head towards the port of Fredericia where a U-boat is waiting. Denmark has not yet fallen to the Allies who are concentrating their pincer movement on the enemy forces in and around the German capital. Compared to the rest of northern Europe, the Scandinavian country has been little troubled by the war. The Danish government has had an uneasy relationship with the Nazi occupiers since the invasion of 1940. As a result, many lives have been saved including the country's Jewish population who have not been transported to the death camps, unlike millions of others. But the antipathy between the occupied and their oppressors is real. The soldiers in the half-track scour the fields and hedgerows looking for any sign of movement that might indicate an ambush. With the war almost at an end, the Danish resistance have reasserted themselves and attack all German military.

The Mercedes and its escort arrive unscathed as dawn breaks over the naval port. Tall cranes stand as bleak silhouettes against a rose-coloured horizon. The air is fresh and carries a whiff of the cold, grey Baltic. Sandbagged anti-aircraft batteries guard the dock, their guns bristling at the sky. Moored to the quayside is a Type VIIC submarine its name, *U-977*, painted on the conning tower. As luck would have it the vessel has just been refitted before it departs on a last patrol. The crew are rested and ready to leave on what will be their most important mission of the war. The submarine's commander, Oberleutnant zur See Hans Schiller, has told them they will be carrying important passengers – they will find out who they are soon enough. It would be impossible to keep the identities of the *Führer* and his spouse secret in the restricted confines of a U-boat.

The submarine sits low in the water because its hold is full of gold bullion. The vaults of the National Bank of Denmark have been raided and its contents deposited in *U-977*. The torpedoes have all been removed and, in their place, bars of various weights and sizes have been stashed. There are many millions of Reichsmarks worth of gold, the combined weight of which is almost six metric tons. Whatever difficulties lie ahead for Hitler and his companions, a shortage of funds will not be one of them.

Schiller and his three officers wait on the dockside. The lieutenant looks smart in his naval uniform and peaked cap and has a raffish Van Dyke beard; like many U-boat commanders, he is decorated and has been awarded the Iron Cross, both first and second class, and the U-boat war badge. He has been on active service since December 1939. This is his fifth patrol and will be the longest and most perilous by far. As he stands in the chill early morning Schiller feels hungover. Yesterday was his twenty-fourth birthday and, at the urging of his crew, he had celebrated with rather too much abandon. He can still taste the schnapps in his mouth.

The Mercedes stops and the driver opens the door and salutes. Hitler gets out and is followed by the others. It is the first time Schiller has seen him in the flesh. He is surprised at how old and stooped he looks compared to the youthful and dynamic leader of the film reels. As the *Führer* approaches, the commander raises his right arm and shouts, *'Heil Hitler!'* and his fellow officers do the same.

'Welcome aboard, sir, it's an honour to have you and Frau Braun.'

'Thank you, Lieutenant.' The *Führer* notices the decorations on Schiller's uniform. 'Iron Cross, first class. What did you get it for?'

'North Atlantic patrol, sir. Last year.'

A ghost of a smile plays on the older man's face.

'Good. You will know the waters.'

'Yes, sir.'

And with that the commander escorts Hitler and his wife towards the submarine. The sailors are lined up along the hull and stand to attention as the pair are piped aboard. The honoured guests are led to an open hatch. Schiller goes first, helping them descend into the bowels of the vessel. He takes them to his own quarters and asks if there is anything they need.

'Coffee and pastries,' says Braun. 'The *Führer* requires breakfast. After that he must be allowed to rest. If we want anything else we shall let you know.'

'Ja, meine Dame.'

The curtain to the cabin is drawn and the commander tells Bormann and Stumpfegger to bivouac with the others. The space will be cramped, he tells them, as there are two extra men. He has taken over the chart room since his own berth now has Hitler and Braun. The doctor is content but Bormann protests.

'I'm the *Führer*'s private secretary. I should have the chart room!'

Schiller observes him contemptuously. The man's eyes are small and blue like a pig's, while his face is broad with the sheen of over-indulgence. He does not look as if he has ever suffered hardship in his life let alone seen action. It is staff officers like Bormann whom the commander really loathes.

'No. You shall be with my men. While on board this vessel you are subject to navy regulations at all times. That includes my commands.'

Now it is Stumpfegger's turn to smile. The *Führer*'s aide can whine and spit all he wants but he will have to sleep alongside the greasy sailors.

With the sun rising above the ocean there is no time to lose. The crew prepare the submarine for departure and soon it is cruising across the harbour. When it passes the breakwater the vessel expels air from its ballast tanks and begins to dive. In less than a minute it has disappeared beneath the waves. The choppy waters of the Baltic swirl above but there is no sign of the submarine. *U-977* has sunk without trace.

FREDERICIA–CAPE VERDE

Monday 30 April–Friday 22 June 1945

The submarine descends into the murk. When it has reached a depth of fifty fathoms the bow levels and it proceeds on its course, the diesel engines thrumming at a regular beat. The crew go about their duties and Bormann and Stumpfegger take to the bunks in the fo'c'sle to keep out of the way.

A sailor approaches with a pot of steaming coffee, a jug of milk, cups and a plate of freshly baked pastries. At the commander's cabin he calls out and a familiar voice tells him to enter. He opens the curtain, delivers the tray and returns to the galley where he and the cook are preparing breakfast for the rest of the company.

Stumpfegger cannot sleep. He hangs his legs over the side of the bunk and chats to a seaman who looks as though he has no need to shave. The doctor is correct in his assumption. Moses is the youngest on board and just sixteen. His father is a Lutheran pastor, hence the unusual moniker. The youth is flaxen-haired, gap-toothed and pale-eyed. He grins from ear to ear. It is his first patrol and his beloved *Führer* is on board. He tells the new arrival how he joined the Hitler Youth on his seventh birthday and has been in the *kriegsmarine* since he was fourteen. Beside them Bormann snores, his mouth agape, his thick tongue lolling.

'I hear we're going to South America.'

'You're remarkably well-informed for a rating.'

'There are no secrets on board a boat but that's what everyone's been saying. Besides, when I asked Warner, the senior watch, he didn't deny it and he should know.'

'Perhaps Herr Warner should do what he does best and stick to his sextant and compass.'

'Don't worry, he's a good chap, old Warner. He's a Saxon like me. I say old even though he's only thirty but he seems ancient. His hair's going grey.'

'Mine, too.'

'Really?' and Moses takes a closer look. 'So it is, by your temples. You'll be salt-and-pepper before long. How old are you?'

'Thirty-three.'

'Greybeard!'

Stumpfegger smiles. He is not offended. The youth's frankness is disarming and he feels as though he has already made a friend. He will need several more among the submarine's company if he is to keep his sanity on the long voyage beneath the oceans.

One of the petty officers appears and Moses goes back to work. The doctor lies down on the bunk and inspects the myriad of pipework above his face. The tubes gleam in the electric light and he feels as though he is floating in a coffin. A steel coffin which will take him all the way to South America.

In the control room Schiller has his eyes to the periscope as he directs the vessel through the straits. They are passing the Sound of Skagerrak and must proceed cautiously as the area is sown with mines. The 'rose garden', sailors liked to call it. After an hour he is satisfied the way is clear and gives the order to dive to eighty fathoms. Beyond the littoral shelf the water is deep. There is an optimum route that brings *U-977* close to the Norwegian coastline but not so near as to be hazardous to the vessel or in range of Allied warplanes that are hunting for the last Sea Wolves.

The commander raises the periscope handles and it slides into place with a hydraulic hiss. He gives orders to keep their course and maintain silent speed and goes to the chart room. He spreads several maps across the table and picking up a pencil and set-square, he starts to plot a route that will take *U-977* beyond Orkney, then due south past Ireland to the coast of Portugal. From there they will cross the Atlantic and head for the Cape Verde islands. After two days rest and recuperation they will sail west to Brazil before making their way towards Mar del Plata off the coast of Argentina. There is no question of entering the River Plate. It is a hundred miles up the estuary to Buenos Aires and the waters are too shallow to navigate without charts or a pilot. Instead, they will lie a mile offshore and signal the Querandí lighthouse on the promontory. A launch will be dispatched to collect the *Führer*.

Once Schiller has plotted *U-977*'s course he realises there is another problem and if it is not rectified soon the mission will have little chance of success. He had been told of the top-secret nature of his assignment by Admiral Doenitz the previous day but he had no idea of their actual destination until he received his orders from the fleet's high command shortly before they set sail.

Schiller returns the charts to their tubes and places them in their allocated compartments. He dons his cap and straightens his uniform and goes to his former quarters. He asks for permission to enter and is told to proceed and he pushes the curtain aside and draws it behind him. Eva Braun is lying on the bunk. It seems strange having a woman on board, even more that she is in his cabin. But the assignment is hardly normal either. She barely glances at Schiller as she files her nails, blowing at them occasionally.

The *Führer* is sitting in his chair and, since there is no other furniture in the cramped quarters, the commander remains standing.

'*Heil Hitler*!'

'What is it, Lieutenant?'

'Sir, owing to the extraordinary circumstances of this mission ...'

The commander pauses as he tries to find the right words. When he fails to speak the *Führer* prompts him.

'Tell me.'

'Sir, our journey is extremely perilous. The Allies have control of the skies and we cannot rely on any assistance from the surface fleet. We're on our own. But the real problem is resupply ... usually this would happen on patrol when we're far away from Allied shipping lanes. Then we could take on more fuel, water and food. This is now impossible.'

'Go on.'

'I have calculated that our passage to Argentina should take about eight weeks, all being well. We may have enough fuel if we conserve what we have and aren't forced to take evasive action. However, we can't survive with our current food reserves even if we were to go on half rations. A crew cannot function properly on such a meagre diet and it could very well jeopardise our mission.'

'What do you suggest?'

'Sir, to put it simply, there are too many of us on board. Since we're no longer a fighting vessel, we don't need such a large crew. With your permission, I shall ask for volunteers to leave and we can put them ashore off Bergen. Then there will be plenty of space for everyone and we need not concern ourselves about a lack of victuals.'

'How many do you propose?'

'Sixteen should do it, sir. I'll ask the married men to go first. They will understand.'

'Quite so. They should return to their families and be ready to build a new Germany when the time comes.'

'Yes, sir.'

'When do you have to do this?'

'Within the next twenty-four hours. I'll muster the men now.'

'Wish them good luck and God speed.'

'Yes, sir.' Schiller looks directly ahead, salutes and leaves.

The sailors stand by with their kitbags, each with a one-man inflatable dinghy strapped to his back. This is just a precaution in case the two dirigibles capsize or spring a leak. They have one week's rations. *U-977* is heading for an isolated stretch of coast not far from Norway's southern city where the men will disembark.

The commander peers through the periscope to see if any lights are shining onshore. There are none. The night is dark and fog drifts across the water like a wraith. The conditions are as perfect as can be for a clandestine landing. It is risky bringing the vessel so close to shore but necessary or the men will be carried out to sea by the wind and the tide. They are using the electric motors and travelling half-speed ahead. It is the slowest they can go. The diesel engines can only run at a minimum of six knots. Apart from Schiller's orders and the crew's staccato response, the men are silent. All they can hear is the ticking of the motors and, for those listening to the hydrophone, the ping of sonar. The tension is palpable.

'Four fathoms ... Three-and-a-half fathoms ... Three fathoms,' says a voice.

'Steady as she goes,' says the commander.

'Three fathoms ... Three ... Two-and-a-half ...'

The submarine carries on. They are about to stop engines and lower the anchor when the bow rears up and people grab onto whatever they can. Anything that is not secured falls off the desks and tables with a crash and slides across the floor. Schiller holds onto the periscope handles and he turns and swears.

'The gauge, helmsman, the gauge, blast you! What's it reading?'

'Sir, it says two-and-a-half fathoms.'

'It can't be right! We've run aground. Check again.'

The man does so and bangs the instrument with his fist.

'Depth reads two-and-a-half fathoms, sir!'

U-977 remains trapped at an angle of thirty degrees. It lies above the waterline as far as the for'ard hydroplanes. For five minutes the motors go at full speed astern but the vessel will not budge. The commander orders the engines to go ahead on one, astern on the other, to no effect. Schiller swears under his breath. There is nothing he can do but proceed with his plan to disembark the men. At least there will be less weight and, once they have gone, he can try again.

The for'ard hatch is opened and the crew say their goodbyes. The dirigibles are passed through and the last man salutes his commander.

'Bon voyage, sir.'

'All the best. And take care.'

'Thank you, sir. If we're captured we'll say our boat struck a mine and we are the only survivors.'

'Very well,' and Schiller returns the salute.

The man climbs the ladder and disappears. The hatch is closed. The commander can hear footsteps and voices on the hull then a clang on the ironwork – the signal the men have cast off. Schiller waits until they have had time to paddle clear.

'Every man to his station.'

The crew resume their positions and await orders.

'Pump out the levelling tanks.'

'Aye, aye, sir.'

The vessel hums into life and there is a rushing noise as seawater evacuates.

'Set the trim first to starboard, then to port.'

'Aye, aye, sir.'

Schiller hesitates. The manoeuvre is a last resort but he has little choice.

'Engines full speed!'

'Engines full speed!'

The submarine shudders as the turbines revolve at maximum. The propellers send geysers spewing across the stern and each crewman holds on. *U-977*'s hull creaks and groans with stress and the engines roar. In the control room the needles on the dials go into the red but everyone ignores them. In spite of the effort, the vessel refuses to move.

The commander looks at the row of compressed air cylinders. They are full, each showing a capacity of 205kg. As the motors race and the vessel shakes, he has an idea. It might be possible to raise the submarine off the rocks if they open all the blowing valves at once and let compressed air stream through the diving tanks beneath the keel.

'Cut the engines,' he tells the chief engineer.

'Aye, aye, sir ... Engines cut.'

The motors cease to whine and the submarine seems to sigh and settles. There is quiet and the men's faces relax.

'If we go on like this we'll split the hull. Let's see if we can shift her with compressed air. Open all the valves at the top and close those at the bottom.'

'Aye, aye, sir,' and a crewman pulls a series of levers.

'Ready?'

'Ready, sir.'

'Start the motors.'

'Aye, aye, sir ... Motors started.'

Once again the vessel comes alive and Schiller gives the order: 'Release the valves.'

'Aye, aye, sir ... Valves released.'

There is a whooshing sound and a loud rumble as compressed air is forced into the ballast tanks.

'Motors at maximum.'

'Motors at maximum.'

The engines run at their shrillest pitch and the faces of the crew are set once more.

'Full speed astern.'

'Full speed astern.'

There is a jarring sensation as the submarine shudders and moans.

'Hard a-starboard, hard a-port.'

The first officer repeats the command and U-977 rocks from side to side. There is a terrifying screeching noise as the keel scrapes on the rocks. At last she moves and the bow comes down. With a backward motion, finally, the submarine is free. The crew shout for joy and Schiller leans against a bulkhead in exhaustion. It had been touch-and-go but, once again, it appears the gods of Valhalla are with them.

'Well done, everyone,' he says as he turns and faces his comrades. 'Well done.'

The trip around Orkney and Ireland is uneventful until they pass the Portuguese coast and *U-977* finds itself in danger again. Although the war is over, the Allies have issued orders that all enemy submarines must surface and surrender. The point is to prevent any members of the Nazi high command from escaping. If they knew who was aboard this particular vessel, doubtless the entire Allied fleet would be despatched to sink it.

A Sutherland has spotted *U-977*'s shape beneath the surface and radios a message to a Royal Navy frigate patrolling off Gibraltar. Using its radar, the battleship pursues the submarine out to sea, straddling it with depth charges as the vessel dives to its furthest limit of 125 fathoms. With each explosion, steel splinters sheer off, valves are smashed, pipes burst and jets of water and steam pour out. The noise is enough to set the men's teeth on edge and crack their eardrums. There is a cry and the helmsman shouts the compass has been blown out of its frame. Everyone takes cover. The gyro wheel spins around the vessel at ten thousand revolutions a minute but fortunately no one is hit.

The frigate follows the submarine for forty-eight hours and the crew remain on constant watch, staying awake with Benzedrine and Pervitin tablets. No one leaves his station. For those who need to urinate, a bottle is passed around. With their pallid faces and blank, staring eyes, they look like dead men. At last the Royal Navy ship gives up the chase and the vessel is safe again. The damage is assessed and repaired and *U-977* resumes its course towards the equator.

As the temperature warms, the heat inside the hull increases. The air is fetid and the stench of sweat and oil pervasive. Mould covers everything and the bulkheads are washed down daily. Every night the garbage is fired from a single empty torpedo tube at the stern. Despite the effort, hygiene is almost impossible. The clothes stick to the men's bodies and since the crew has to wash with salt water they constantly itch and scratch. Almost everyone breaks out in a rash and some have boils.

One day the senior watch, Warner, approaches the commander and shows him his hand. He has cut it on a piece of machinery and it is swollen up to his wrist. Schiller puts him on light duties with instructions to bathe the wound regularly with soap and distilled water. If the injury gets any worse, Warner must consult him again. The following evening he returns. The swelling has spread along his forearm. There is nothing else to do except lance it. Stumpfegger is called, bunks are lowered to form a table and the senior watch lies down. There is no anaesthetic and the commander orders Warner to drink plenty of schnapps. If the situation were not so serious, the crew would fall about laughing. Imagine being ordered to get drunk by the chief while on patrol. But Schiller is right. If the operation is not performed correctly, sepsis could set in and, if it does, the man will almost certainly die.

The doctor uses the vessel's basic first-aid kit. He lays out the instruments and asks for ice. The cook brings a jug of frozen cubes and the arm is numbed. After Warner has taken several slugs from a bottle, Stumpfegger cleans the swollen limb with rubbing alcohol. He takes up a scalpel and makes an incision. A mass of fluid and matter pours out. He squeezes the arm firmly and Warner groans and faints. The doctor sutures the wound. When he has finished, the unconscious crewman is taken to a bunk to sleep off the effects of his ordeal. The rest of the company get back to work.

U-977 rises like a leviathan from the deep. Water is expelled from the ballast tanks and, as air rushes in, the commander can feel the vessel ascend. As it rises so does his heart and the hearts of his crew. There is an overwhelming sense of relief. Soon they will breathe fresh air and see the sky and feel the wind on their faces. The past weeks have put them under intolerable stress. Now the most perilous part of their voyage is over.

Schiller takes the periscope and scans the horizon. It is the dead of night but he can make out the islands of the Cape Verde archipelago. He has chosen to anchor off Maio, one of the remoter outcrops on the eastern side of the chain, a few miles from the larger mass of Boa Vista. Although the island is inhabited the main town of Porto Inglês lay further south, with only the odd hamlet clustering around a cove or isolated stretch of beach.

The commander lowers the periscope and watches the depth gauge fall until it reads zero.

'Hatchway free,' says the chief engineer. 'Pressure equalised.'

Schiller turns the securing wheel, opens the hatch

and climbs out. His first officer joins him on the bridge. Together, they stand in awe. The sea glints like broken glass in the moonlight and the heavens are awash with stars. They have not seen the night sky, or indeed any sky, since they left Denmark more than a month ago. All around rolls a vast expanse of water. The archipelago looms out of the darkness like mute, sleeping monoliths. Before them rises the island of Maio dominated by a rugged, indigo peak. A cool wind brings a scent of the seashore and the men breathe deeply, filling their lungs. They take in great breaths, again and again. The taste is like an elixir after the oil-laden atmosphere of their underwater prison. For a submariner air is the most precious of gifts. It is not drowning they fear but a slow death by asphyxiation. Every sailor knows his soul belongs to the sea.

The vessel rocks in the surf and waves slap its sides in an irregular beat.

'Congratulations, sir. We made it,' says the first officer.

Schiller permits himself a smile.

'We're not there yet but let's hope we're over the worst of it.'

The commander takes the communication pipe and orders everyone up on deck to see Cape Verde for themselves. The men muster below and a rating exits from the aft hatch followed by Hitler and Braun. Others emerge until the entire submarine's company is lined up on the sea-soaked hull. The *Führer* turns to the officers standing on the bridge. They salute him. He nods in approval before facing the assembled men.

'*Kameraden*, we have begun a remarkable journey and made great progress so far. We have succeeded solely through your diligence and your discipline. I am proud of you. You never wavered in your duty and, during the most testing times, you've acted like heroes. Because of this you shall not taste the bitter bread of defeat. Instead, men such as yourselves will form the vanguard of a new Reich. But there is one man above all others who deserves praise – three cheers for Lieutenant Schiller!'

The crew give a chorus of hurrahs and when they fall silent, the *Führer* speaks again.

'We shall build a new Germany in South America. National Socialism will rise again. A pure Aryan nation will thrive once more and rule the world!'

The men cheer and sing the national anthem, their voices ringing out clearly across the sea.

Early next morning the remaining dirigibles are assembled on deck and lowered into the water. In the first several crewmen get in. Others then lead Hitler and his spouse down the slippery iron rungs into the waiting boat. Bormann and Stumpfegger follow and the last places are taken by Schiller and his officers. Warner, his arm in a sling, gets into the next boat with Moses and the rest of the crew. When everyone is ready they cast off, the sailors paddling hard.

The water is limpid and the rocks and rippled bed clearly visible. Beneath the boats silvery shoals of fish swim past. There is barely a breath of wind and the ocean is calm. Amid the splash of oars comes the bark of sea lions, leaping and diving in the surf. An albatross circles and tilts its wings as it climbs a thermal stair.

When they strike sand the crew leap out and grab a rope, bracing themselves against the waves. A sailor takes Hitler by the arm and helps him off. The Nazi leader stumbles through the surf like a conquistador claiming a piece of the New World. While the rest of the company come ashore, the *Führer* stands on the beach. He shields his eyes and gazes across the water towards *U-977*. The submarine's paintwork is streaked with rust and pitted by corrosion as the sun beats down on its hull. In the distance the horizon trembles in the equatorial light and the sky is a washed-out blue.

Hitler finds it hard to believe he has made it this far. They have spent forty-six days under water with no resupply and have survived being depth charged. It is an unprecedented feat of seamanship. He knows how Cortez must have felt when he stood silent upon a peak in Darien. All the deprivations and terrors of his long journey have evaporated. He is free again. As he had told the men last night, this was just the beginning. There would be another Germany. They would build a glorious new Reich.

The *Führer* calls out to his wife.

'Come, join me,' he says. As they walk along the beach, the tide races in and recedes. Another wave rises and falls and the surf crashes and rushes in once more.

When Hitler and Braun return, a rough shelter has been made out of driftwood and they take refuge in its shade along with Stumpfegger, Bormann and the officers. Schiller has organised the crew into teams to fish for tuna and turtles, which they will cook on the beach. What is not eaten will be taken aboard and refrigerated for the onward voyage. A group of sailors set off for the nearby village and return carrying sacks of fresh fruit and vegetables. The locals were surprised to see such pale-skinned men so far from home but they were happy to take the matelots' money.

A fire is lit and there is a smell of burning wood and kelp. Turtles and tuna are gutted and filleted before being impaled on stakes. The pieces are held over the flames, blanching in the heat. The flesh is smoky and tender and the crew are encouraged to eat as much as they can. They have a long journey ahead. When everyone has had enough, the party takes a siesta while some sailors strip off and swim in the surf. Moses amuses his mates and plays the fool, pretending to be a seal as he barks and puts his hands together like flippers. He dives beneath the waves and holds his breath for as long as possible before he emerges, spluttering. Everyone is glad to feel the sun on their bones again after the grim confinement of the submarine.

The company spends the rest of the day on the beach until the sun starts to sink behind the mountain and shadows spread across the sand. They pack up the remaining food and return to the dirigibles and paddle through an opal sea towards the vessel. The *Führer* and his spouse are taken aboard while the crew collapse the boats and stow them in the hold. The last man to enter the submarine is the commander who closes the for'ard hatch, entombing everyone.

Schiller gives orders for *U-977* to get underway. As the sun sets beyond the island the engines are started and the vessel heads for the open sea. He had intended to remain an extra day and let the men rest a while longer. But Hitler insisted they leave immediately. Although the coast of Africa is hundreds of miles away, the attack by the frigate had shaken him. He fears being spotted by another Allied ship and wants to reach safety as soon as possible.

Dusk descends upon the ocean and the sky is a net crammed with shadowy fish. The contours of the archipelago fade in the evening light until, one by one, they disappear as night falls. *U-977* resumes its journey, the conning tower just visible above the rise and fall of the waves.

MAR DEL PLATA–BUENOS AIRES

Monday 15–Friday 27 July 1945

Across the inky expanse of water a light on the headland flashes in code. Everything is in place. The reception committee at Querandí is ready. A launch emerges from the gloom and draws alongside the submarine. Braun, Stumpfegger and Bormann are taken aboard while Hitler remains on deck with Schiller. The rest of the crew are down below. The *Führer* addresses the commander for the last time.

'You have served the fatherland way beyond the call of duty. I shall not forget you, Lieutenant.'

'It has been an honour, sir,' and the officer salutes.

'Farewell. You have your orders; you know what to do.'

'Yes, sir.'

Hitler removes his glove and extends a hand. Schiller hesitates to take it. No subordinate would ever dream of doing such a thing.

'This is the only way that I can thank you.'

Schiller takes the outstretched hand.

'Good luck, sir.'

The *Führer* releases his grip and replaces the glove.

'Thank you. I shall need it.'

Without another word Hitler turns away and is helped aboard the launch. He sits at the stern and a blanket is placed over his shoulders. The engines are throttled back and the boat moves off into the night leaving a luminous trail in its wake until it disappears into the darkness. Once again the Nazi leader has vanished into thin air.

As day broadens over Buenos Aires *U-977* enters the harbour. A pilot has guided them safely up the estuary and the Argentine coastguard has been alerted. The minesweeper, *PY10*, draws alongside and a gangplank is placed between the vessels. The crew of the submarine are assembled on deck dressed in their navy blue uniforms, the officers wearing white caps. They have all washed and shaved and their newly polished boots gleam in the sunshine.

Lieutenant Emilio Cosmelli of the Argentine navy exchanges salutes with his German counterpart and is taken onto the U-boat and descends a ladder into the control room. He looks about and is impressed by the state of *U-977*. In spite of the long journey it has undertaken, everything is spick and span. The officer is led past the wardroom towards the for'ard torpedo tubes. Schiller takes hold of a wheel and opens one of the compartments. Cosmelli's admiration turns into wide-eyed astonishment. The tube gleams with gold. There are piles upon piles of bullion reaching as far back as the eye can see.

Schiller picks up a solid, shiny ingot and hands it to him.

'This one is for you,' he says. 'I would like to open a bank account.'

The Reich gold is placed in several depositories in the capital, including the Heinrich Dörge Central Bank of Argentina and the Banco Alemán Transatlántico. Many of the accounts are opened in the name of Eva Duarte, more commonly known as Evita – the beautiful wife of the vice president, General Juan Peron, the country's de facto leader. Only he and a select few know who was on board *U-977*. Argentina had been Germany's ally throughout the war and even before. The general considers Hitler to be a fellow head of state and also a personal friend. At heart they are both National Socialists. It is he who has facilitated the *Führer*'s escape. Germany's former leader is now staying at the secluded ranch of Villa Garay, thirty kilometres north of Querandí, and owned by the wealthy Nazi, Max Garay. When Hitler has recuperated he will be taken to a camp that is being built near the Iguaçu Falls where he will be safe and far beyond reach.

The crew of *U-977* are detained and interrogated by the authorities but Peron orders their release, leaving the commander under arrest. Later, he is brought aboard the cruiser *Belgrano* where he is kept in isolation. The Argentine vice president is playing a double game and has allowed the Americans to question him. The CIA in particular want to know why Schiller has taken his submarine on such a long voyage after Germany's capitulation, suspecting that a senior figure, or figures, may have been aboard and escaped. They have no idea that it is Adolf Hitler. Everyone knows both he and Braun committed suicide in the bunker. The charred remains were discovered by the Russians and dental records have proven their identity, or so they have been led to believe.

Schiller's years as a submariner serve him well. Although he is threatened and cajoled and deprived of sleep and food for days, he does not break. Eventually his interrogators give up. The war is over. A single U-boat commander is of little importance to them.

As Schiller lies despondently on his bunk the cabin door opens. The guard stands aside and Lieutenant Cosmelli enters. In his hands are a bottle of whisky and a pair of glasses. He seems happy.

Schiller gets off the bunk. 'What's this about?'

'Sit down. I've good news.'

Cosmelli opens the bottle and pours a measure into each tumbler and gives one to his guest. The men raise their glasses and drink.

'You're going to be released. The order comes from on high. The Yankees have given up – you're no use to them anymore.'

Schiller is relieved. He has no love for the Americans, particularly after his interrogation. In fact, he views them with contempt. Their arrogance and stupidity had been breathtaking at times. Apart from the possibility of having stowed a high-ranking official on board, they were keen to know about the V-2 rocket programme. It did not matter that their prisoner was a U-boat commander who knew even less than they did.

'Thank God for that.'

'What will you do?'

Schiller pauses and takes another drink.

'I haven't given it much thought. I don't want to go back to Germany. The fatherland is in ruins. I wonder if I'd be able to stay here?'

'Really, you'd like to live in Buenos Aires?'

'Why not? I've heard it's a beautiful city and the summers are warm and the winters mild.'

'If that's what you want, I'm sure it can be arranged. I'll have a word and let you know. In the meantime, is there anything else I can do for you?'

The commander looks at the bottle before them.

'Perhaps you can leave me the whisky.'

And they laugh and clink glasses.

Schiller stands alone on the pier and watches as *U-977* is towed out to sea. It is the end. The United States Navy is going to sink his beloved submarine. Cables are dropped into the water and the vessel is cast adrift by tugs. In the distance the battleship USS *Phoenix* lurks. Its armament is ranged against the submarine which looks miniscule in comparison to the floating behemoth. But, just as an insect with a fatal sting, the vessel has proved her worth against much bigger prey. The tenders withdraw and, like a condemned prisoner, *U-977* awaits her fate.

The air is rent by a barrage of explosions as the cruiser's main guns open up and water around the vessel erupts in pale fountains. There is a brief silence before the shriek and crash of another salvo splits the air and the sky shakes with its force. This time the shells find their target, striking the hull as flames burst and smoke pours. The submarine lists and sinks sternwards into the sea. Its bow rises in a last salute and *U-977* slips beneath the waves. A foaming ring of surf remains. Then it, too, disappears.

'Farewell, little boat,' says the commander.

Schiller remains on the jetty, lost in thought. The war is over and his country is no more. Everything that he admired and fought for has perished. With a leaden heart he turns and walks away.

The sailors wander from bar to bar singing, their wallets stuffed with cash. Each crewman has been rewarded for his endeavours and, like all matelots ashore, the money burns a hole in their pockets. Among the group are Warner and Moses who have become inseparable since the voyage. The senior watch had lost his younger brother earlier in the conflict, when his submarine was sunk off Scapa Flow, and *U-977*'s youngest recruit has taken his place.

They enter another dive and Moses insists on buying the next round. He has already bought several and, although his comrades protest, the youth throws his money on the bar.

'Drinks for everyone!' he says and the other sailors do not know whether to laugh or weep.

Bottles and glasses appear and more alcohol is consumed. Moses goes from table to table introducing himself and flirting and kissing the women. When a fiddler strikes up he dances about like a dervish. The whole bar claps along as they watch him spin around the room. The music stops and he falls down in a heap and everyone applauds. The rating jumps onto a chair and fulminates: 'We are the vanguard! We're going to build a new Germany! The glorious Third Reich shall rise again! *Deutschland uber alles*!' he says, and starts to sing.

His comrades try to shut him up but the youth will not listen.

'Let us drink the health of Adolf Hitler. To our beloved *Führer* – long may he live!'

He grabs a bottle of rum off the bar and starts gulping it down. Warner takes his friend by the arm and pleads with him.

'For God's sake, Moses. Enough!'

The young sailor refuses to be silenced.

'Away with you, greybeard! You heard what the *Führer* said,' and he calls out to his fellow patrons once more. 'Yes, ladies and gentlemen, Adolf Hitler is alive and well, you can be sure of that ...'

He is cut short by a sharp blow across his face.

'Shut up, damn you!' and the senior watch hoists him from the chair.

Moses glares at the older man as his cheek burns and his eyes water.

'No, greybeard! I won't shut up. I won't!'

The bar has gone quiet. The rating looks at his comrades who sit silently before him.

'Have you forgotten the *Führer*'s words already? You're cowards, the lot of you, cowards!'

He staggers towards the door, turns and raises an arm.

'*Heil Hitler*!' he cries and is gone.

In the thin light of early morning a fisherman rows his caïque across the harbour. The sea is glassy and the air soft. Above the boat gulls mew. He stops by the breakwater and begins to throw pieces of bread. Fish appear and the surface churns with their bodies. The man gathers his net and throws it in an arc and it lands with a splash. He waits for the net to sink before he takes it up again and starts to haul it in. It is heavier than usual and he assumes that among the fish is a piece of flotsam, usually old rope or a rotten lump of wood.

As the man draws the net towards his boat he is surprised by the weight. Whatever it is, it is heavy. He heaves the net against the caïque and amid the thrashing fish he can see a mannequin. The man is surprised. People threw all sorts of things into the harbour these days, although he has never seen a tailor's dummy before. This one is even wearing clothes. He turns the object over with a boat hook and springs back in shock. It is not a mannequin but the body of a youth. His skin is mottled and flaxen hair is plastered to his head. The sockets are empty because the fish have already eaten Moses' eyes.

VILLA GARAY

Saturday 28 July 1945

The sound of the aircraft can be heard long before it is seen. The distinct drone of a DC-3 rises and falls on the wind but there is nothing on the horizon except a bank of clouds, ascending in a procession of pale whorls. Then a lone speck appears. As it increases in size, the markings of the Fuerza Aérea Argentina become visible on the wings and fuselage. The *Führer* has an honoured guest. The nation's *caudillo*, Juan Peron, and his wife, Evita, have flown from Buenos Aires to join him at Villa Garay. The mission is confidential and, despite his wife's pleas and protestations, Peron had refused to be dissuaded. He has never met Hitler and is intrigued. He is delighted the plan to rescue the former German leader has gone so well. There is much to discuss, particularly money. Peron needs the Nazi gold to finance his ambitious social welfare and construction projects, which he hopes will propel him to the presidency and overall power. The general has told Evita the *Führer* is a colossus, a veritable giant among men. His wife remains unconvinced but he is sure that she will understand once she has met him.

The aeroplane lowers its undercarriage and descends. As

it approaches, a Mercedes drives across a field raising a thick cloud of dust. The Dakota touches down and taxies to a stop. A door opens and steps are lowered. A military aide emerges and angles an arm in salute. The general and his wife appear and walk towards the car. He is in full military regalia while she wears a blue polka-dot dress, sunglasses and a yellow silk scarf. The vehicle sets off towards an estancia, shaded by mimosa and winter bark, a few hundred metres away. The Mercedes draws up at the house and Peron and his wife alight.

Evita is as glamorous in real life as she is in photographs. With her bleached blonde hair, peerless smile and pale skin, she looks and acts just like a movie star. Her appearance and elegant persona belie her humble background. She was born in Los Toldos, an impoverished village in the Pampas, and is the youngest of five children. They were all illegitimate as her father, Juan Duarte, a local landowner, had another legal family. When Evita was a year old, Duarte abandoned his mistress and their children and returned home, condemning them to a life of penury. Her mother worked as a seamstress to make ends meet, although she and her children were ostracised. Duarte then died unexpectedly, but the family was refused permission to attend his funeral and were thrown out of the church when they tried to pay their respects. It left Evita with a lifelong sense of injustice and a desire to right wrongs. For this reason, she has an iconic status among ordinary Argentineans. It has also made her a shrewd judge of character. She is certain the *Führer* is a fraud and a chimera. He was nothing more than a mythical beast. Evita actually used this word to describe him to her husband and, when Peron pretended not to know what it meant, she replied: 'a fire-breathing goat!'

The ranch owner, Max Garay, stands on the porch. He has acted as the go-between for Peron and the Nazi high command. He is bald and bearded, dressed in a cream linen suit, and exudes the easy bonhomie of the monied elite. Gathered around him are various flunkies and bodyguards but there is no sign of Hitler and Braun or their entourage. Normally, protocol would dictate that they meet their visitors in person. But the fewer people who see them the better and so the couple remain indoors.

'Welcome to my humble abode,' says Garay in a voice that rings like a cash register. He embraces the *caudillo*. 'What an historic day this is!'

Peron laughs, revealing shark-like teeth.

'The hard part may be over but there's much more we have to do.'

'I know, I know. We can deal with that later. Time for a celebration, don't you think? I've raided the cellar and opened my best wine,' says Garay, winking at Evita. 'All work and no play, your husband. Now come inside and let me introduce you to our guests.'

The *caudillo* and his wife enter the house. Waiting in the hall are Hitler and Braun and their coterie. The *Führer* is in uniform and appears transformed. He is unrecognisable from the forlorn ghost who arrived at the ranch just over a week ago. He has a tan and the vitality, which had been missing for so long, has returned. There is a spark and he seems like the leader of old. In contrast, Braun is demure, although there is a motherly glow about her and she holds her hands meekly, as if cradling an infant. Bormann and Stumpfegger stand to one side, also in uniform. Evita notices Hitler's aide grinning at her like a hyena and gives an involuntary shudder. The doctor has a puckish face and looks kind, if careworn.

After introductions, Garay leads the group to a spacious dining-room. The mahogany table has been laid with the family silver, and crystal goblets, tumblers and jugs of water glitter in the light. A vase filled with lilies decorates the centre. The wine has been decanted and placed on a marble-topped sideboard. Servants pull out chairs and the guests are seated, linen napkins removed from rings and placed on their laps. Wine is poured and the first course of gazpacho is served from a tureen. The meal will be without meat in deference to Hitler's vegetarianism. This is hard for most of them, particularly the Argentineans, who relish a rare steak even at breakfast, but the *Führer*'s habits must be accommodated wherever possible. His meat-free diet does not preclude wine and he has already developed a taste for the Tempranillo that his host cultivates on the estate. The group relaxes and the lunch is a convivial affair, conducted in a mixture of German and Spanish, with the host acting as translator for Peron and Hitler who occupy one end of the table.

When the meal is finished the last course is cleared and coffee is served. Unusually, no one lights up a cigar or even a cigarette. The *Führer* cannot abide smoking in his presence.

Garay rises and takes Hitler and Peron to the library and the doors are closed while they discuss affairs of state. His wife, Gertrud, leads Evita and Braun to the drawing-room. The hostess's mother was born in England and, when she was a girl, had lived in Hampshire and socialised with the county set, playing tennis tournaments, going to black-tie balls and attending house parties at the weekends. Along with her sensibility for fine art and antiques, Gertrud has inherited her mother's taste for afternoon tea, which is served in porcelain cups, with a variety of sandwiches and cake.

The women sit and make polite conversation and the hostess turns to Evita.

'Did you know Frau Braun is expecting?'

Evita is astonished. It is the first indication she has had that Braun is pregnant. Hitler's wife gives an indulgent look and places a hand upon her belly.

'When is it due?' asks Evita.

'In November. I can hardly wait.'

'So, you're four months gone?'

'A little more – almost nineteen weeks. The baby's not kicking yet but at least the morning sickness has stopped.'

'Ah, yes, the trials of the early trimesters,' affirms Gertrud.

'How many children do you have?' asks Braun.

'Six. They're grown up now.'

'Girls and boys?'

'Yes. Three of each. All happy and healthy. I'm very fortunate.'

Six? Evita says to herself. She longs for a child. So far,

she has only ever miscarried. It pains her beyond belief and she hopes and prays that one day it might happen but she is not sure it ever will. She fears that her inability to carry to full term is because of the backstreet abortion she had at fifteen. She had been working as a chorus girl in Buenos Aires and was raped repeatedly by the theatre's impresario. It was either that or destitution. So she put up with his jealousy and violence, and his foul breath as he screwed her backstage, night after night, following every performance.

The conversation changes course and Peron's wife listens as Braun chatters away. She pities her. This poor woman, who has no more charm or wit than a dairymaid, is carrying the progeny of the world's most dangerous criminal. It simply beggars belief. She is nothing more than a brood mare for Beelzebub.

After an hour the men emerge from the library. Garay expounds loudly on their recent discussion and places an avuncular hand on his guests' backs. The meeting has been a success. The *Führer* has promised to bankroll Peron's next election campaign, and even beyond, saying he looks forward to seeing him in power. The *caudillo* is delighted to have such resources at his disposal and believes he has absolute control over Germany's former leader. The man is in the country as his guest, after all. But he is unaware Hitler is simply waiting for the right moment to assume power. Evita is correct in her appraisal. The *Führer* and his cohort cannot be trusted. The *caudillo* does not have a loyal satrap, as he supposes, but a Trojan horse.

IGUAÇU

Wednesday 29 August–Monday 17 September 1945

The camp lies deep in the heart of the jungle. The fortress is encircled by a ditch and protected with a palisade. At the entrance is a watchtower. The layout is much the same as the Wolf's Lair at Rastenburg in eastern Prussia, where Hitler was so nearly assassinated by Von Stauffenberg's bomb. The *Führer*'s resilience to the blast astonished his staff and the bomb plotters. But it did not amaze the man himself. He knew, as he had always known, that the Almighty had saved him for greater things. Just as He had preserved his life on the Western Front, when the British sergeant had refused to finish him off as he lay wounded in a muddy shell hole at Ypres, or when he had been blinded by mustard gas in the last weeks of the war. Incredibly, his sight was restored after a few days. The doctors said his blindness must have been hysterical. Hitler knew differently. It was not hysteria but a miracle. God had determined he should survive so that he could eradicate the two great evils of the world: European Jewry and Bolshevism. As far as he is concerned, the first has already been accomplished. Now it is Russia's turn.

Across the compound the *Führer* can hear the voices of

other followers who have fled to the jungle to be with him. They are a disparate group but all are dedicated Nazis. They include Walter Rauff, who designed the mobile gas chamber and was later involved in the extermination of Jews and partisans in Italy. In this work, he was aided by SS Captain Erich Priebke, one of those responsible for the massacre at the Ardeatine caves in Rome. After the war, both men were hidden by the Austrian bishop, Alois Hudal, a Nazi sympathiser based in the Vatican. In 1938 the cleric had sent Hitler a book he had written on the rise of National Socialism and signed it with a personal dedication. The *Führer* was charmed but thought no more about it until a steady trickle of senior officials began to appear in Argentina. All of them have used the escape line established by Hudal. Hitler is impressed that those who have managed to flee have espoused Nazism in its purest form: the annihilation of all enemies everywhere.

There are about fifty people in total. Most are other Nazis who have arrived via the Odessa network as well as local sympathisers, many of whom are of German descent. Each one has been vetted by Bormann before being allowed to learn the real identity of Grey Wolf, the codename for Hitler. The aide has refused at least a dozen people on the grounds that fanaticism alone is not enough. They must be prepared to die for the *Führer* and they must be discreet. Above all, they must be able to keep a secret. It is not only about Hitler but also Eva Braun. At five-and-a-half months her pregnancy can no longer be hidden.

The *Führer* sits in a rattan chair on his veranda and enjoys the last rays of the evening sun, listening to the sounds of the forest as the animals settle down for the night. Brightly feathered parakeets line the branches and whistle and chirp as they preen themselves. High up in the canopy howler monkeys chatter and hoot. Amid their echoes comes the sound of music. Braun's favourite song is playing on the gramophone as she flicks through the pages of a faded fashion magazine. Hitler would prefer something classical, like *Parsifal* or *Lohengrin*, but for once he has indulged his wife's tastes and can hear Marlene Dietrich singing. He forgives the German-born star's treachery for serving the Allied cause, because her dusky voice is as rich and lustrous as the Viennese coffee in his cup. He is sure that in her heart Dietrich was a National Socialist even if she did not know it. Hitler has never failed to convince anyone of the rightness of his thinking. He is like the patient soldier of the song, knowing that, whatever happens, his lover in the lamplight will always be waiting for him, just as Germany was.

Aus dem stillen Raume, aus der Erde Grund
Hebt mich wie im Traume Dein verliebter Mund
Wenn sich die späten Nebel drehn
Werd ich bei der Laterne steh'n
Wie einst Lili Marleen
Wie einst Lili Marleen

As the day ends and darkness falls, the *Führer* philosophises. Nietzsche was right. Man is a god. But first he has to go through the cleansing fire of war. Without war, man is nothing. War is the ultimate purifier. All corporeal matter incinerated until only the soul remains. As he had written many years ago in *Mein Kampf*: 'If you want to shine like the sun, first you have to burn like it.'

As the expected birth date draws closer a festive atmosphere fills the camp. All are glad there will soon be a new and important addition to their number. None more so than the *Führer*, who acts as doting husband and would-be parent rather than the embittered leader of a lost empire. He knows, with the birth of his son, a new Reich will rise like a phoenix from the ashes of the old. And this Fourth Reich will be more magnificent and awe-inspiring than its predecessor. It will unite and dominate the world, because the world now has a new enemy. One that is even greater than the Jews; a cancer called Communism. A disease that must be eradicated at all costs.

A horseman rides through the emerald forest. Blades of light penetrate the canopy and illuminate the boughs as they descend to the jungle floor. He is so exhausted that sometimes he falls asleep in the saddle, waking when his steed stumbles or hears an unexpected sound. But the rider must go on. He is almost there. It has been a long and desperate journey that began several months ago on the snowbound steppes of the Ukraine, then Poland, as the Wehrmacht retreated in the face of the Soviet onslaught. Many of his comrades froze to death during the long march back to Berlin. Those who were captured by the Russians and spared the firing squad were taken eastwards to prison camps in the Urals. Most will never return.

He is one of the lucky ones. Using an Argentinean passport and wearing civilian clothes, he had slipped through the dragnet cast by the Allies for officers of the Waffen-SS. He had made his way to Switzerland where, with the help of Odessa, he obtained Red Cross documents stating he was a non-combatant. He travelled to France, crossing the Pyrenees into Spain and continuing his journey to Portugal. In Lisbon he boarded a freighter and a month later the vessel reached the mouth of the River Plate and cruised up the estuary to Buenos Aires. He was home after five long years of war.

The rider approaches the gates of the camp and asks to see Reichsleiter Bormann.

'Your papers,' says the guard.

The visitor hands over his SS identification disc and as soon as the soldier sees it he salutes abruptly.

'Yes, sir! Come this way please.'

The new arrival gets off his horse and loops the reins around a post and follows the guard into the camp. He is taken to a large wooden building in the centre of the compound. Bormann is seated at the head of a table surrounded by lackeys playing drinking games and slaps his thigh and laughs uproariously. He looks up as the weary and mud-spattered visitor approaches, his face flushed, his eyes glazed.

The man stands to attention and raises an arm.

'*Heil Hitler*!'

'Who the hell are you?'

'My name is Tiago Hecht.'

IGUAÇU

Tuesday 6 November–Sunday 30 December 1945

The woman's screams fill the cabin, frightening the animals in the forest and scattering them through the trees. Eva Braun has been in labour for several hours and there is still no sign of the baby. A sense of panic invades the room and fear is etched on everyone's faces. In particular the *Führer*'s. He is mad with worry and, in turn, encourages and curses Stumpfegger while trying to comfort his wife who, with no pain relief, is in agony. There are no epidurals in the jungle.

The doctor has rolled up his shirtsleeves and his face is pale and sweating despite the efforts of a propeller fan, which spins above his head and casts flickering shadows across the room. It is years since he attended a birth let alone actually oversaw one. The last time was shortly after he graduated from medical school. He knows next to nothing about obstetrics. He also knows the best thing is to stay calm and not distress either the mother or the baby in her womb, which is almost impossible amid the febrile atmosphere and the swirl of people around him. Stumpfegger cannot concentrate in this maelstrom. It is driving him mad.

'Everyone out!' he says. 'Everyone!'

There is silence. At first no one moves. The doctor looks up and his eyes tell them he is close to despair.

'I said, out!'

Those present depart until only Hitler and Bormann remain.

'*Mein Führer*, you can stay, but you,' he says to the aide, 'you must leave.'

Hitler nods at his secretary who reluctantly obeys. At last they are alone. Braun is delirious and murmurs repeatedly about her baby.

'Sir, may I have a word?' Stumpfegger glances across the room to indicate that he wishes to speak out of earshot.

They move away and the doctor explains the problem.

'The baby's head is too big for the birth canal. If it enters, I will have to use forceps for delivery.'

'Then do so.'

'It's risky in these conditions. There is no guarantee it will fit and the umbilical cord could get wrapped around its neck – I need to perform a Caesarean. I must do so soon otherwise your wife could start haemorrhaging and I doubt I'll be able to stop the bleeding. Not here.'

The *Führer* realises the gravity of the situation. It had been his decision Braun should give birth in the camp and not at the hospital in Posadas, which Stumpfegger had suggested. It is unlikely anyone would ever have learnt about her identity, yet Hitler had refused to consider it. Now both wife and child are in mortal danger.

'Is there any other way?'

'I don't think so.'

'What about infection?'

'There's a possibility but it's a small one. The risk of further complications, if we continue with a natural birth, is far greater.'

'Have you ever performed a Caesarean?'

The doctor shakes his head and looks at the patient. Braun is moaning on the bed, the sheets twisted and drenched in her waters.

'No, sir, but I've seen it done several times. It's very simple. You just make an incision across the abdomen and afterwards you put in some stitches. I can administer local anaesthetic. She won't feel a thing and it will be over in minutes.'

The *Führer* remembers the doctor's operation on the crewman's poisoned arm in the submarine and decides to go ahead.

'Very well then, do it.'

Stumpfegger gathers the implements he needs from his medical bag while Hitler tells his spouse what is about to happen. She smiles, showing she understands. All she wants is for the birth to be over and to hold the infant in her arms. The *Führer* kisses her forehead and leaves, and the wives of two local Nazis return to act as nurses.

The doctor swabs up again and the women wash Braun and change the bed linen. He approaches with a syringe and injects the expectant mother on both sides of her belly. After a while he takes a scalpel and taps it lightly on her stomach.

'Can you feel anything?'

'No,' murmurs the patient.

‘Here?’

‘No.’

‘Here?’

Braun wags her head.

Stumpfegger makes an incision. The surgical knife pierces the flesh and a mixture of blood and amniotic fluid flows as he draws the blade across her abdomen. He puts the scalpel aside and places a hand in the wound. Reaching into the uterus he grasps a slippery, purple mass and carefully brings it out. It weighs less than he thought and seems so small and vulnerable. He turns the baby upside down and, holding it by the ankles, he slaps its bottom. The newborn opens its mouth wide. At first there is no sound. Then it begins to bawl. The doctor cuts and ties the umbilical cord and hands the mucus-covered infant to one of the women. While she cleans the child he starts to stitch the wound in his patient’s stomach. The baby’s cries bring Hitler and others rushing into the hut, their faces shining and glad.

‘It’s a boy,’ the doctor says.

‘I knew it!’ cries the *Führer* and he goes to his wife who is now cradling the newborn. He caresses both woman and child and begins to weep, scarcely able to believe that this has actually happened. The Reich has a son.

In the first few days after the baby’s arrival everything goes well. Braun soon recovers from the ordeal and is able to breastfeed without any complications. The infant is healthy and, when it is not crying or feeding, it sleeps. Stumpfegger is the hero of the camp and Hitler jokes that he should be decorated. Even Bormann is pleasant to him.

A fortnight later things begin to go wrong. One morning Braun wakes with a fever and the doctor is summoned. They wonder if it is malaria but Stumpfegger thinks it unlikely. The bed is made from camphor wood and the lamps in the huts burn eucalyptus oil at night to keep insects away. He washes his hands in a basin, dries them and removes the dressing to check for inflammation. He had taken the stitches out a couple of days ago. It is exactly as the doctor fears. The cut is raw and inflamed. There should be dry skin and scabs by now. Instead, septicaemia has set in. There is nothing that can be done in the camp. The patient has to go to hospital.

'Frau Braun has sepsis,' he says. 'She needs penicillin.'

'Don't you have any?' Hitler looks at him in consternation.

'*Ja, mein Führer*. But only pills. In this state it will be difficult for her to take them orally. Also, she needs far more than I can provide. Your wife should be on a drip.'

'Do it!'

'Sir, we do not have the equipment here. We have no facilities. Frau Braun must go to a proper clinic.'

'That is out of the question!' Hitler shouts and the others in the room turn to blocks of stone. 'Absolutely and incontrovertibly out of the question!'

Hitler paces up and down, putting his left arm behind his back as it begins to shake. He stops and turns on Stumpfegger, jabbing a finger at him, his eyes bulging with rage. His face is puce and the corners of his mouth are flecked with spittle. 'You will administer penicillin and you will do so here!'

The doctor is terrified. Standing ramrod straight, he nods vigorously.

'Yes, sir. Right away, sir.'

The *Führer*'s anger passes with the violence of a hailstorm and he gathers himself.

'Good,' is all he says.

Stumpfegger takes a pestle and mortar and crushes the tablets. When they are ground to a powder, he sweeps the penicillin into a glass and adds water. He tries to get the patient to drink the liquid, tipping the glass and pouring the contents into her mouth. But Braun shakes her head at the bitter taste and half the medicine spills down her chin and neck. The doctor lays her back on the pillow and puts a damp cloth on her forehead. In a cot in the corner, the baby gurgles and kicks its little legs.

Day turns into night and Braun's condition worsens. In the early hours a meeting is held in the mess hall and Stumpfegger addresses Hitler and the other senior Nazis. He tells them she must be taken to hospital. He simply does not have enough penicillin to treat her and it cannot be administered orally. It has to be done intravenously. The others understand but are powerless. The decision is the *Führer*'s and his alone. He refuses to consider the risk of his wife going to hospital, instead declaring that a team will be dispatched to Posadas to bring the liquid penicillin and the medical equipment back to the camp. The doctor protests, the city is at least a week's journey away. The patient cannot wait that long. It is no good. The *Führer* has made up his mind.

The next morning Bormann, Priebke and Rauff set off on horseback. The man called Hecht would have joined them since he knows the area well, having been born in the region, but he is recovering from a bout of malaria contracted during his journey through the jungle, and is confined to bed.

The group head down the trail carrying enough food and water to sustain them for the outward trip. They barely sleep and ride day and night, fording rivers and avoiding lethal pits of quicksand. After six days of almost constant travel they arrive at Posadas and obtain the necessary supplies. But they are worn out and, despite fresh horses, the journey back into the forest takes even longer. A thorn pierces the hoof of Priebke's mount and the captain is left behind as Bormann and Rauff continue.

Eight days after setting out from Posadas the men enter the camp, their clothes filthy and torn, their faces drenched in sweat and grime. It is too late. Eva Braun is dead.

The *Führer*'s spouse is buried the same day. She is given a simple ceremony and a Nazi flag is draped over the coffin. After a few brief words she is lowered into the earth. Hitler throws soil into the grave and, as he walks away, others do the same. The last person to do so is Stumpfegger. He is baffled at the sheer waste of life. Her death was wholly avoidable. The doctor, like countless other Nazi generals, cannot understand why the *Führer* had refused to listen to reason. Only the souls of the German soldiers who fought and died in their thousands know why and they cannot speak.

Braun's death brings another problem. The child is being fed on milk powder and is losing weight. If he does not have a wet nurse soon, he will also die. Although there are a dozen women in the compound, only four are young enough and none has been able to breastfeed the child. Again, it is the doctor who alerts the *Führer* to the problem. Their leader seems little affected by Braun's death, while he stands at the baby's cot cooing over it. This time he agrees to Stumpfegger's suggestion and orders him to find someone suitable. There must be a girl in a nearby village. The younger and simpler she is, the better.

The doctor prepares to leave with Tiago Hecht, who has recovered from his fever. The Argentinean is a useful addition to the camp as he can speak both Spanish and Guaraní. He had joined the Nazi Party while studying in Berlin before the war and, during the conflict, had served with distinction on the Eastern Front. Before they set out, he disguises himself as a priest to allay any suspicions. Everyone trusts a man of the cloth.

The next day Stumpfegger and Hecht return with a local Indian girl. They have paid her father a lot of money and he has promised them his silence. He has been told that after six months the girl will return and he will be given a further sum. It is not true, of course. When the child has been weaned the girl will be killed. Both Bormann and Rauff have insisted on this and have volunteered to do it.

The girl breastfeeds the child, which soon recovers and starts to puts on weight. In the weeks that follow the baby is able to sit up unaided and observe his surroundings. The boy is curious and seems to take in everything. His hair is dark, his eyes the same pale blue as his father's. In fact, they are the same colour as his Austrian grandmother's Klara, who died of breast cancer when the *Führer* was just eighteen.

Hitler had been devastated by her death and some in his family believed he never fully recovered. It was the reason he had wandered aimlessly through the streets of Vienna, vainly trying to be an artist and refusing to work until the small legacy from her will ran out and only then by doing the most menial jobs. He was desperate to study at the academy but was refused twice and so he lay in his bug-ridden lodgings in a perpetual funk, railing at the injustice of the world. From time to time he would stir himself and paint but the pictures rarely sold and, when they did, it was for pittance. The problem was that Hitler had never learnt to draw, he could only copy postcards and was unable to master perspective. The buildings he painted were too big, the people too small, or else it was the other way around. Either way it was not his fault, it was always someone else's. One day the world would understand and everyone would be sorry they had ever doubted his genius.

Stumpfegger and the girl are most involved in the infant's

care and soon become close. Her name is Maria and like most Guaraní she is illiterate but she has an innate intelligence. She is also pretty and the reason the doctor chose her. He begins to teach her German which she picks up quickly since she can speak some Spanish as well as her own native language. Although the girl has had no formal education, every month a priest from the parish came to hear confession and say Mass in her village. He also provided news from the outside world. The church was the only one in the vicinity and could accommodate more than a hundred people.

Hecht is playing cards with his cronies in the mess hall when a guard appears at the door.

'The *Führer* wants to see you.'

'Me?'

'Yes, now.'

The lieutenant is nervous. He is one of the youngest members of the camp and has only been there three months. He hopes he is not in trouble. He does up his tunic and puts on his cap, then crosses the compound and presents himself at the quarters. Bormann shows him to the study and the Argentinean stands to attention and salutes.

'*Heil Hitler*!'

The *Führer* asks his aide to leave. Bormann bows respectfully but as he departs he scowls at the lieutenant, letting him know his place.

When he has gone, the Nazi leader motions at a chair.

'Sit down,' he tells his visitor.

Hecht perches on the edge of the seat, his back straight and shoulders square. He has never had a personal audience with the *Führer* before. Hitler observes the earnest young man before him with his smooth skin and saturnine good looks.

'I've had my eye on you, Hecht, since you arrived at the camp. You have natural leadership qualities.'

'Thank you, sir.'

'They tell me you were in the Waffen-SS.'

'Yes, sir. I joined the party in '38, when I was a student in Berlin, and volunteered as soon as war was declared.'

'And you served on the Eastern Front ...'

'Yes, sir, almost a year, from '42 to'43.'

'Were you at Stalingrad?'

'Yes, sir. I was wounded. A sniper shot me but he failed to finish me off. I pretended to be dead and waited until he fired again. Then I got him.'

'And because of this, you were decorated?'

'That's right, sir. A Knight's Cross with oak leaves,' and the Argentinean feels a glow of pride.

'A tough battle, was it not?'

'Yes, sir. It was the cold which was the worst. The Russians didn't seem to be affected at all, even when the diesel in the engines froze. Sometimes it was minus twenty degrees Celsius during the day but they would laugh and eat ice cream ...'

Hitler cuts him off.

'I know. I saw the reports.'

'Yes, sir.'

There is silence. The *Führer* appears pensive. He is thinking about those far-off days, when his desk was covered with maps and the whole of Europe lay at his feet. Then, anything seemed possible. Now, the Reich was no more and he was a fugitive hiding out in the Amazon jungle.

'I have asked to see you because there is a dilemma and it is this: while my son and heir is still an infant, I am getting older. Also, I'm not in the best of health.'

'But, sir, you're in wonderful condition for a man of your age!'

The *Führer* raises an admonishing hand.

'There's no need to flatter.'

'Sorry, sir.'

'If anything should happen to me, my son will need a guardian. I have chosen you. You're young, brave and intelligent.'

'Sir, it would be a great honour but what about Bormann, or Priebke, or Rauff? They have much more experience than me.'

'Bormann has no brains and the other two have no courage, whereas you have plenty of both. If I die, my son shall be your responsibility. You must act as regent and prepare him for the task to which he has been born and which is the world's destiny. Is that clear?'

'Yes, sir. I will do everything I can.'

'Naturally, I hope to live long enough to see him become an adult. But – who knows? I shall inform Bormann and the others in due course. However, for the moment, let us keep this between ourselves ...'

The *Führer*'s voice fades and he looks at Hecht as if to indicate his audience is over. The Argentinean takes the hint and jumps to his feet. He salutes and turns on his heel, marching out of the room.

Bormann lies on his bed in a fever. He is burning hot and his clothes are damp with sweat. But he is not sick, or at least he is not ill. What Hitler's aide needs most, and is desperate for, is a woman. He has not had sex in months and the lack of any physical relationship consumes him daily. In Berlin, even in the darkest days of the bunker, there was always plenty of skirt to go round; the secretaries and copytakers were renowned for it. Some were little better than prostitutes except you did not have to pay to get their knickers off. Perhaps it was the aphrodisiac of power or the uniform. Whatever it was, the *Führer*'s aura rubbed off on his male staff and made them irresistible to women. Out here in the forest it is different. The few females present are either too old or unavailable. Hitler's aide has tried to relieve the urge with masturbation although he finds it deeply unsatisfactory, like being a teenager again. He has the occasional wet dream but that is all.

Bormann thinks of the girl. She would be perfect. In fact, she is probably a virgin. Surely he would be able to have his way with her? All he has to do is wait for the right moment and strike. He doubts the *Führer* would mind; he would probably insist on it. The aide remembers that she often bathes in the river in the afternoon. The camp is quiet at that time of day as everyone takes a siesta or plays cards or reads in the mess hall. No one is about. The girl is usually accompanied by one of the women but not always. She has gained the ruling committee's trust and there is nowhere for her to go apart from back to her village.

Bormann gets up from the bed and puts on his boots. He leaves the hut and walks through the compound to the entrance. A guard salutes and he continues along a trail towards the river. As he descends the path, he can hear water rushing through the ravine. The noise becomes louder and he goes in a crouch towards a rocky outcrop. He squats and peers over a boulder and to his delight sees that he is in luck. The girl is alone. She is bathing in a pool, her clothes folded on the shore, her back to him. He reaches for a pebble and throws it into the water. His quarry hears the splash and turns round with a look of confusion on her face. But she can see nobody and resumes her ablutions.

Bormann rises from his hiding place and approaches the river. The girl hears footsteps and screams when she sees him. He stops and stands at the water's edge, grinning. He beckons her forward but the girl crouches lower and covers herself.

'Come here.'

Maria is terrified and moves further out into the river. The man standing before her smiles a death's head smile.

'Come on, I won't hurt you.' He takes up her dress and holds it out to her.

The girl refuses to leave the water and begins to shiver, not from cold but fear.

Bormann flaps the garment in encouragement. When this does not work he drops it to the ground and pulls out his revolver, pointing it at the girl.

'Now, my little chick. Now you will come.'

Maria emerges from the water, her arms shielding her body. She has barely put her foot on the bank when Bormann grabs her and throws her to the ground. The girl screams and he slaps her across the face. She screams again and he slaps her even harder until she sobs. Her attacker drops his gun and tears off his jacket and slips the braces over his shoulders. He pushes the girl down and slumps on top of her one hand holding her wrists above her head, the other fumbling at his flies. He grabs his cock and tries to penetrate her but she is too tight. He licks his forefinger and rams it into her vagina. She cries out in pain and Bormann laughs. Most definitely, she is a virgin. He cannot wait to make her bleed.

The aide takes hold of his engorged penis and is about to thrust it into his wailing victim when a bullet hisses past his ear. He freezes and rolls off. Standing there with a gun is Stumpfegger. Bormann reaches for his own weapon but the doctor kicks it away.

'Leave her alone!'

The aide looks at the man with the gun.

'Do you want some, Stumpfegger?'

The doctor is appalled but his voice remains firm.

'I said leave her alone, you psychopath!'

Bormann laughs.

'Come on, Doctor! I know you want some, too. She's a

virgin, for sure. You can go first if you like. I don't mind – we can take turns.'

'You make me sick!'

'Aw, poor you. It must be hard to be a saint.'

Bormann gets to his feet. He puts the braces over his shoulders, fastens his flies and buttons his tunic. All the time Stumpfegger keeps his gun on him. He bends down and retrieves the other weapon.

'You can have this back at the camp. Now get going.'

The aide snorts and gives a contemptuous flick of his head. He dusts his forage cap on his britches, puts it on and saunters up the path towards the compound. Stumpfegger has made a big mistake. Nobody crosses Reichsleiter Bormann and survives. The man has just signed his own death warrant.

The doctor replaces his pistol in its holster and puts the other gun in a pocket. He turns his back as the girl starts to dress. He had been right in his assumption about the *Führer*'s secretary. He had noticed how the man leered at Maria whenever she was in his presence and had kept a close watch on him. That afternoon he had seen Bormann leave the camp and followed him down to the river. He is very glad he did.

The girl quietly weeps and it seems to Stumpfegger his heart is going to break. He wants to place his arm around her and comfort her but right now he feels it would do more harm than good. Bormann is a beast. How could he think of doing such a thing? He is tempted to tell the *Führer* but thinks better of it. The aide is not a man to forget a wrong even if it is his own fault. No, he will just have to pretend it never happened.

Maria is dressed and Stumpfegger smiles. The girl returns the smile and looks relieved. It is all the doctor could have hoped for. Together, they walk back to the compound. Not a word passes between them.

IGUAÇU

Friday 9–Saturday 10 August 1946

After nine months the child is crawling and able to eat puréed foods. Maria continues to suckle the boy, more for his comfort than sustenance. Since she is the surrogate mother the baby sleeps with her but there is always a guard: at night, one of the women, by day, a man. She is never left alone with the child. As the girl sits on the veranda breastfeeding, she worries. Her friend, the doctor, has not been himself recently. He seems distracted and refuses to look her in the eye. She knows something is wrong.

There is a good reason Stumpfegger is perturbed; he is wracked with guilt. He has been informed by the ruling committee that it is time to move on, which means the girl has served her purpose and must be eliminated. This was first mooted three months ago but the doctor had urged caution and successfully argued that, while the child could be weaned, it must continue to be breastfed. The doctor was desperate to save the girl – this stay of execution was all he could propose while he thought of a way out. When the committee met again their decision was final. The girl would be shot the following morning.

That night, as the bullfrogs burp and bellow, Maria hears a sound outside the cabin. There is a tap at her shutter and she hears the doctor's voice calling her name. She opens the window, careful not to wake her guard. But the woman is not only asleep she is unconscious. Stumpfegger has drugged her coffee.

'Go!' he whispers. 'Go now!'

The girl is confused.

'You must leave – *fuera*,' he says, '*Vaya, vaya ahora*!'

Maria understands why the doctor has been acting so strangely. He is helping her escape. At last she can go home to her family. She starts to climb out of the window but a soldier appears and she ducks back again. The man stops and turns towards the *Führer*'s quarters. He sees movement in the shadows and unstraps his carbine.

'*Halt*! *Wer da*?'

A man emerges from the gloom.

'Just me – Colonel Stumpfegger. I couldn't sleep so I thought I'd take a walk. Lovely night, isn't it?' and he looks up at the waxing moon. He lights a cigarette and offers one to the soldier. The men smoke their cigarettes, the ash glowing in the darkness as they gaze at the night sky.

'There are so many shooting stars,' says the guard.

'It's because the atmosphere is clear.'

'You an astronomer as well?'

'No, but I studied some physics at university.'

'Where was that?'

'Munich.'

'Ah Munich, the forests and the mountains. Never been there myself.'

'Really? You must go.'

'I will one day, I hope.'

'Where are you from?'

'Leipzig. I miss it.'

'Are you married?'

'No. And yourself?'

'Me neither. I'd like to settle down with a good woman.'

'That would be nice, to have a family.'

The fatherland is a long way off. Indeed, it seems to belong not just to another world but another universe. Each man wonders if he will ever return. They smoke and chat and the doctor leads the guard away from the *Führer*'s quarters towards his own cabin, which he shares with Bormann and two others. The soldier and Stumpfegger put out their cigarettes and wish each other goodnight and the doctor enters his hut. He hears his companions snoring and assumes they are asleep. They are, except for one. Bormann opens an eye and watches him get into bed.

The girl waits. Her own guard has not stirred. The woman breathes low and deep. Maria looks at the baby in his cradle then at the portrait. She has heard about this man. The priests have told her in their sermons. They have spoken about a war waged by him on the other side of the world: a war in which millions died. This man they call *Führer* is the devil incarnate.

Below the portrait the child moves and sighs in his sleep. The girl picks him up and holds him close. He is beautiful and she loves him. The baby does not belong here or to the blue-eyed fiend who stares unblinkingly at them. She will take him with her.

Maria wraps the unprotesting bundle in a blanket and ties it across her shoulders. She is about to leave when she remembers the piece of paper which the doctor said was important and must be kept safe. He had shown her its hiding place in the secretaire. She finds the paper and puts it in a pocket and closes the drawer, being careful not to wake her guard. Maria climbs through the window onto the veranda. She creeps down the stairs and into the camp. Only the bullfrogs disturb the stillness. The girl keeps to the shadows and heads towards the perimeter fence. She walks along the palisade until she finds a ladder leading up to an observation platform. The compound has been built to keep people out rather than in and she ascends the rungs until she reaches the parapet. The girl pulls the ladder up and lowers it on the other side. She slips to the ground, pushes the ladder away and runs. She runs along the trail in the opposite direction of her village. Maria keeps on running, the branches and vines lashing her face, the precious bundle on her back.

When the empty cot is discovered the following morning and the girl and child are nowhere to be found, there is pandemonium in the camp. Hitler is deranged with fury and the female guard is summoned to his quarters to explain herself. Of course she cannot and the woman cries and screams to no avail as she is taken outside and shot. But her death does not solve the problem of the baby's disappearance. The *Führer* sits at his desk weeping. His chest heaves in agony and he can barely breathe he is so upset. It feels as though he is suffocating. He gasps and chokes for air and Bormann fetches a glass of water and urges him to drink. Hitler does so and having drained the glass, he feels better. He tells his aide to summon Priebke and Rauff. When they appear he orders them to take a troop of men and raze the girl's village to the ground.

'No one!' he says, banging his fist upon the table. 'No one must live!'

And he breaks down and sobs again.

'Oh, my boy, my boy, my boy ...'

Nobody says a word as the *Führer* moans. His hands are bent like claws and he tears his nails across the desk. He looks up and sees the officers standing there.

'What are you waiting for? I gave orders!'

Rauff clears his throat and ventures to speak.

'Sir, may I suggest that Oberleutnant Hecht comes with us. The villagers have seen him before and trust him. He'll be able to get them into the church. Then it will be easy.'

Hitler hardly cares. He flaps his arms as if to say, 'Do whatever you like, just kill them!'

The death squad saddle their horses and set off. This time Hecht is not only dressed in black he also has a missal in his hand. There are thirty men, each with a jerrycan of fuel tied across his mount's haunches. The weather is fine and they make good progress. After a day's ride, the group enters the village and pile their packs in the middle of the clearing. They look around, amazed at how impoverished the place is. The huts are made from mud and thatched with plantain leaves. The only building of any size is the church which rises above the other dwellings, its bell tower framing the tropical sky. Chickens peck and scratch the dirt while pigs doze in the shade, twitching spasmodically and flapping an ear. A dog barks a gruff warning but that is all. Neither the people, nor the village, appear to have changed since the Stone Age. They are the epitome of *untermensch,* serfs whose purpose is to be enslaved or killed.

The curious inhabitants emerge from their huts and gather round. Some recognise the man in black from his previous visit. Hecht tells them he has wonderful news. A local benefactor has granted a bequest to build a school. After it is finished, a teacher will come from Posadas and the children will learn how to read and write. He tells everyone to gather in the church so they can praise God for his munificence. The villagers are delighted and cheer and clap. Among them is Maria's father. He alone neither speaks nor applauds. He wonders what has happened to his girl. She should be home by now. He approaches the man in black.

'Where is my daughter?'

The Indian has slanted eyes, brown skin and tattoos. Hecht cannot hide his revulsion at this half-naked man standing before him and instinctively his lip curls, which he tries to conceal by smiling.

'Don't worry, my son. Your child is coming home soon.'

'You said it would be six months.'

'I know but the baby was poorly. Now he is healthy ...' and Hecht's face tightens at the thought of the infant's disappearance. He checks his emotions and places a hand on the doubting Indian as he addresses the others.

'Let us go to the church and worship the Lord.'

Maria's father moves away. He does not trust the man in black and, what is more, he cannot understand why these foreigners are here. But the people have no reason to be suspicious. They file faithfully into the church and he follows. The building is made entirely from wood and has a shingle roof. Not a single nail holds the place together. Hecht stands before the altar and watches as the villagers gather and sit on the benches. When everyone is present the church doors are closed. Some people turn and wonder why, but no one gets up. A heavy beam is placed across the entrance. The only other access is through the sacristy.

Hecht calls for servers and a group of children come shyly forward. He leads the prayers and the congregation join in. When he stumbles halfway through the Gloria, they look curiously at each other and so he opens his missal. He chooses a psalm and the church is filled with voices, joyous and strong, praising God. Even Hecht looks moved as he stands in contemplation, his hands steepled in prayer.

Outside, the death squad open the jerrycans and begin to pour petrol onto the church.

The villagers sing and lift their arms in supplication. Hecht reverently closes his missal and walks to the sacristy. People assume he is going to put on vestments before returning to say Mass. Everyone, that is, except Maria's father who knows something is wrong. The man cannot even recite the Gloria properly and is certainly no priest. Determined to find out what is going on, he goes to the annexe. He opens the door and sees Hecht walk away. The villager is amazed at what is happening. The church is covered in fuel and men are lighting torches. He tries to go back inside and warn the others but a shot rings out and he falls down, dead.

The sacristy is secured and torches ignite the wooden walls. Flames rise and soon reach the roof. Inside the church voices turn to cries then screams as the building catches fire and fills with smoke. People rush to the entrance and clamour to be set free. When nothing happens, they pound on the doors as they shout and curse and plead. The roar of combustion drowns them out and soon the only sound is the spit and crackle of flames. The conflagration shoots sparks into the sky and a bitter pall of smoke drifts through the empty village. The blaze reaches higher and higher until the bell tower topples and the roof collapses in a convulsion of flame, showering sparks in a fiery rain. After a while the death squad moves off knowing their work is done. There will be no survivors. Nothing stirs amid the burning timbers.

Stumpfegger is alone in the hut. He sits on a narrow bed and clasps his head in his hands. He cannot believe the girl has taken the child. If the guard had not appeared he would have escorted her to the perimeter and watched her vanish. All would have been well. No one would have been any the wiser. Now she has taken the boy. The doctor is at a complete loss. Only he knows what really happened but he cannot say anything. He would be shot just like the guard.

'My God!' he says. 'What have I done?'

'Yes, Stumpfegger, what have you done?'

The doctor starts in fright and sees Bormann standing in the doorway with a pistol in his hand.

'Let's go for a walk.'

'You don't understand, it's not my fault. I didn't do anything.'

Bormann remains at the entrance, his weapon pointing at the other man.

'Move it.'

Stumpfegger gets up with a groan, his shoulders slumped.

'I can explain everything ...'

'That's good. Very good. The *Führer* will be glad.'

He leads the doctor out of the camp at gunpoint and marches him down the trail to the river. It is one of the many tributaries that flow from the falls and its waters crash and boil through the mossy gorge. A mist ascends and is transfigured by a shaft of sunlight breaking through lichen-shrouded trees. They reach a bank beside a pool which swirls away from the river. It is the same place Maria bathed and where she was so nearly raped. This time it is Bormann who has the gun. He motions at the doctor to kneel.

'Please, you must believe me. It's not my fault ...'

'Talk.'

'I didn't do anything. I promise you. It was the girl.' His voice is high-pitched and tremulous and rises above the sound of water.

'Talk.'

'The girl took the boy. I don't know why ...'

A shot is fired and tears into the doctor's shoulder. He stretches his eyes in astonishment and grips the wound. There is an agonising burning sensation and blood seeps through his fingers. He is so stunned he cannot speak.

'Talk.'

Stumpfegger opens his mouth but no words come.

'I said, talk, damn you!'

The man kneeling before him swallows hard and finds his voice.

'Have you gone mad?'

Another shot is fired. This time it strikes the doctor in the leg. He chokes and rolls on the ground clutching his thigh and begins to weep.

'Please! I beg you. Please!'

'Talk, you rotten piece of garbage! Tell me what you did!'

Stumpfegger writhes in pain and twists like an eel upon the sand.

'It wasn't me. The girl – the girl took him ...'

'You let the girl go!'

'No, no – I didn't do anything. It was her.'

A third shot is fired. This time it hits the doctor's other shoulder.

'God! Please, no!'

'You helped the girl. You were out that night. I saw you.'

'I didn't help her. I promise!'

'I saw you leave the cabin and return.'

'I ... I had to go to the latrine ...'

'Don't lie to me!'

Stumpfegger turns away. He cannot bear to look at the man with the gun.

'Tell me exactly what happened or I'll put the next one in your balls!'

The doctor lifts his head and gazes at his adversary. The man's face is drawn and his lips are pale. He knows he is staring at death. He might as well speak the truth and be put out of his misery. Bormann is not the sort of person to let him live. Not after what happened with the girl.

'It wasn't my fault, I promise. She didn't deserve to die. All I did was tell her to leave. Then a guard appeared so I had to walk away. I swear that's what happened – I never thought she would take the boy!'

Bormann is satisfied. At last he has the truth. That is all he wanted. The man has served his purpose. He can go now.

'I believe you,' and the aide pulls the trigger and blows away the top of Stumpfegger's cranium. The doctor pitches forward and his brains spill onto the sand. Bormann puts the pistol in its holster and bends down and drags his victim to the water. A bloody pool marks the place where he fell and his body leaves a trail upon the ground. The other man pushes him in and watches as the current draws him away. Soon the corpse reaches the middle of the river and is buoyed and bumped along by the rapids and carried downstream. Bormann waits until it is out of sight then makes his way back to the camp.

On his return he goes straight to Hitler's quarters. The *Führer* is seated at his desk paralysed by misery. He looks up hopelessly as his secretary enters.

'Where have you been?'

'I went to see Stumpfegger.'

'Where is he?'

'He has gone for a swim,' Bormann says. 'A very long swim.'

The aide explains what has happened and his leader accepts it. He hardly cares about the doctor. The problem is that Stumpfegger's death will do nothing to hasten the child's return.

'Don't despair, *mein Führer*. We will find him. We will find your son.'

Hitler looks at Bormann, eyes raw and brimming with tears. His voice is filled with an unutterable sorrow and his body quakes as he speaks.

'My boy ... My boy ... My boy ...' is all he can say.

IGUAÇU–BELLA VISTA

Monday 12–Wednesday 23 August 1946

Grim-faced, the *Führer* sits astride a horse as the storm breaks and thunder echoes through the forest. A gabardine covers his shoulders and rain pours off the fabric in rivulets, running down his hands onto the flanks of his steed. He has given the order to abandon camp. Once again he is forced, like Napoleon, to retreat with only his baggage train. Unlike the emperor, he does not have the remnants of a vanquished army to protect him, just a few devoted, if bedraggled followers. The tropical storms have come early and with a ferocity unseen in years. Hitler has also demanded the camp be destroyed. Pyres have been built and the huts doused with kerosene, while torches are lit and placed in bonfires. Flames begin to rise but the *Führer* and his cohort cannot wait. They must leave before the rivers become impassable.

Since the girl escaped, the ruling committee has decided that remaining at the Wolf's Lair is not an option. Even though it is far from civilisation everyone fears that it is not far enough. Oberleutnant Hecht has recommended they cross the Parana into Paraguay, which lies in the heart of the Amazon basin. The others on the committee agree. The search for the boy will continue but the *Führer*'s safety is paramount. It does not take much to persuade Hitler and within a day they have gathered up the essential items, ready to leave the camp.

The group makes it way along jungle trails crossing tributaries, usually no more than streams, which have become raging torrents. Hecht grips the reins of Hitler's mount and leads it through the swollen rivers. Sometimes the water is so deep the animals lose their footing and have to swim but the Argentinean's horsemanship is such that they never panic.

After three days hard riding, they reach the shores of the Parana and the horses are set loose. An advance party led by Hecht has secured several motorboats capable of crossing the broad stretch of river. The ex-stormtrooper and Stalingrad veteran has now become the group's leader, supplanting Bormann as the *Führer*'s trusted aide. The German is furious but there is nothing he can do about it. Hecht has a toughness and intelligence none of the other Nazis can match, least of all a rapist.

Under cover of darkness they board the boats at Puerto España. Hitler watches as rain lashes the river, making the water seethe and tremble with its force. The steady chug of the vessel's engine soothes him. It is a long time since he has heard such a sound and it reminds him of better days. He wraps the gabardine more closely around his shoulders and stares at the approaching shore. The jungle seems impenetrable. He shivers and feels cold. Much colder than he ever thought was possible in the tropics. It penetrates to his marrow.

'Won't be long now, sir,' says Hecht above the throb of the boat's motor. 'We have accommodation in the nearest village.'

The *Führer* nods but makes no answer. Nevertheless he is impressed by the young man. In recent days the former soldier has proved to be indispensable. His commitment and endeavour remind Hitler of Reinhard Heydrich, the Protector of Bohemia assassinated by Allied agents during the war and, like Heydrich, he is sure Tiago Hecht will go far. Hitler is glad to have a man of his abilities at his side.

The boats arrive at a wooden jetty and the group disembark and step onto Paraguayan soil. A troop of horses await and the *Führer* is helped into the saddle. They set off for the village, less than a mile from the river. But the road is a torrent of mud and the horses make heavy going. The downpour does not let up and, when dawn comes, the world turns from black to grey.

The riders enter the village and dismount. The place is no more than a hamlet but at least it will give them shelter. Hitler is taken into a house and helped to undress. Towels and hot water are provided. He lowers his pale, naked form into a tin bath and sighs with relief.

'Cold. Cold,' he says.

Hecht stands on the porch smoking a cigarette. A hard rain falls as he looks down the road which has turned into a muddy river. He is waiting for the local doctor and wishes Stumpfegger were alive. But the idiot Bormann had decided otherwise. It is too bad.

The Argentinean hears the rattle of a motor and, peering through the bars of rain, sees a Model-T Ford approach, its wheels churning through the clay. The car pulls up at the house and a man gets out carrying a Gladstone in one hand and an umbrella in the other. He trots up the steps and stops in the porch, closes the umbrella and shakes himself like a wet dog.

'Awful weather, never known it as bad as this!'

Hecht stubs out his cigarette and shows the visitor inside.

'Thanks for coming.'

They enter a room and the doctor sees a middle-aged man in bed, the blankets rolled up to his chin. He is barely conscious. His breathing is shallow and his chest wheezes. There is no need to do an examination, the doctor can see the man has a fever and is suffering from influenza. Usually that would not be a problem. A few days in bed, keeping warm with plenty of fluids, should be enough to cure it. But 'flu in the elderly and frail could be fatal. And the man before him looks very sick indeed.

The doctor puts his bag down on a table and opens it.

'How long's he been like this?'

'Since he arrived. We crossed the Parana yesterday.'

The visitor looks at his host in amazement. What sort of people would cross the river in such weather? They must be out of their minds. But he does not mention it and takes out a syringe.

'As I'm sure you realise, the patient has 'flu so I'm going to give him an injection. The virus is already in his system – unfortunately there's not much else I can do.' He pulls the blanket aside and takes one of Hitler's arms and pushes up the shirtsleeve and gives him a jab. Then he releases the arm and puts the cover back. In all this time the *Führer* has not moved, his breathing unchanged.

The doctor places the empty syringe in his Gladstone and closes it with a snap.

'Keep the patient in bed and make sure he's warm and give him plenty of fluids to drink.'

'Is that all we can do?'

'I'm afraid so.'

Hecht looks at the doctor. There is one thing he has to know.

'Will he live?'

The visitor sighs. He hates this question, because the answer is almost always negative.

'That is entirely up to him ...'

The Argentinean escorts the doctor out and tries to pay him but the man refuses. He does not expect the patient to survive. Hecht thanks him. The man raises his umbrella and descends the steps to his car. The doctor starts the engine and travels off down the road. Hecht watches until the vehicle disappears in the swirling rain. He takes out a cigarette packet and lights one. He remains on the veranda smoking and listening to the endless patter on the tin roof.

Hitler lingers for another week and is mostly delirious. He raves about the hopelessness of his generals and the advancing Russians and accuses everyone around him of treachery. There are brief moments of lucidity when he stops shouting and surveys those surrounding his bed as if they were perfect strangers and wonders what they are doing there. Then he sees a face he recognises and seems relieved. It is Tiago Hecht. But the relief turns to desperation as the *Führer* grips him by the arm with a force that belies his frailty and utters his last words.

'For God's sake, find him!'

POSADAS

Thursday 19 September–Monday 22 November 1946

The girl hurries barefoot through muddy streets in the pouring rain. In her arms she carries a baby wrapped in a blanket. It is dark and cold and no moon shines. The only light comes from the street lamps along the pavement, each shivering in its own damp halo. She ignores the catcalls and whistles from the pimps and drug dealers who stand in doorways and under awnings as they shelter from the deluge. They wonder why a girl like her should be out so late and on her own. Only the desperate inhabit a night as foul as this. Everyone else has a place of safety.

Maria walks on down the rainswept street. She stops outside a building with a solid oak door. She tucks the bundle under an arm and firmly raps the iron handle. There is no answer and she knocks again, this time with greater urgency. She stands there in the chill and clutches the babe to her breast. He is warm and burbles in his half-sleep. The girl rocks him and kisses him. She sees the handle turn and the door opens. A woman's face appears, haggard from lack of sleep. She gives the girl a stern look.

'Why are you disturbing us at this time of night?'

Maria says nothing and shows her the bundle. The woman's face softens.

'You have a child?'

She nods.

'Is he yours?'

She lowers her eyes.

'Yes. He is my son.'

'Holy Mary Mother of God! Come in, for heaven's sake! Come in, out of the storm!'

The door opens wide and Maria enters the mission with the infant in her arms. After days of travelling and at the end of her strength, she has now reached her own place of safety. She hands the baby to the nun and collapses in a faint.

The shutters are opened and a damburst of light floods the room. The noise and sunshine wake the baby in the cot and he starts crying. Maria picks up the boy and consoles him. She raises her shirt and the infant quietens as he sucks on her nipple, his fists kneading her breast. It has been a week since she arrived at the Jesuit mission in Posadas. Maria has yet to tell the mission's superior Father Bartolomeo the truth about the child, although she knows she must do so soon.

She will have to reveal the identity of his parents since the child is plainly not Indian. But, for the moment, the boy is out of danger. She understands that when the superior learns the child is not hers, he will be adopted by the Carmelites who run the mission's orphanage. An unmarried Guaraní girl would never be allowed to keep a baby, especially one that did not belong to her. For this reason, Maria has decided to join the order, so she will always be near the boy and can act as his surrogate mother.

A few days later Maria tells Father Bartolomeo the truth about the child's identity and is sworn to secrecy both by him and the Jesuit principal of Argentina, who has travelled from Buenos Aires to see for himself. The superior general of the Society and Pope Pius XII in Rome have also been informed. Apart from them no one else knows. It is a secret as hermetic and hidden as a holy vow.

Maria is accepted as a novice by the Carmelites and clothed the same week. She asks to keep her baptismal name and this is permitted. The boy is christened shortly afterwards and the girl acts as one of his godparents. He is called Ignacio, after the Society's founding father, and given the surname 'Cruz' for the simple reason that nobody can think of a better one.

The infant grows quickly and, when he is old enough, he joins the crèche along with the other toddlers. They eat and sleep and play together, like any other group of children. Except that Ignacio is pale rather than olive-skinned, and his eyes ... his eyes are blue, like the heavens.

'He looks like an angel!' the mother superior once declared in one of her more effusive moments.

'Or the devil,' said Father Bartolomeo as he stuffed tobacco into his pipe and tamped it down with his thumb.

The visitor can hear the happy sound of children playing but the noise does nothing to alleviate his sombre mood. If anything, it exacerbates it. The young man is with Father Bartolomeo in his office and they are discussing the mission and, in particular, its charges. He is looking for a missing child and has been scouring the hospitals and orphanages in the region. So far he has drawn a blank. But he refuses to give up. The man knows the boy must be around somewhere and is prepared to pay a king's ransom to find him.

'I understand your concern, Señor ... ?'

'Szell, Cristian Szell.'

'Señor Szell. But, you see, it is not simply a question of money. There is no one of that description here, believe me. Almost all our orphans are from the city with just one or two from the countryside. But that's it. I'm sure you understand. I would certainly know about someone if they were blue-eyed and fair-skinned. However, you're welcome to come and see for yourself.'

'I'd appreciate it, Father. My poor sister is beyond despair and cannot face leaving the house. She weeps day and night and we don't know what to do. She tried so hard to have that baby and after my brother-in-law's unfortunate accident the boy was all she had. Why our maid took him we'll never know. We always suspected she was jealous ... Really, it's beyond belief. She had worked for our family for many years. But the most important thing now is to find him.'

'I'm sorry to hear that. Anyway, come with me to the yard and you'll see.'

They leave the office and enter the sunlit playground. The

man called Szell looks about. The children running here and there are too old but in a corner there are toddlers in a crèche being supervised by a nun. The visitor goes over and introduces himself. The sister in charge of the brood beams at him and is as proud as a mother hen.

The man crouches at the wooden gate and the children venture towards him, their curiosity piqued by the new face. He can see that they are, as the superior insisted, all Indian. And yet he inspects each one, looking in particular at their eyes. Some are light brown or even green but none are pale blue. He smiles and gets to his feet.

'They're very beautiful.'

'Yes they are. The mission is truly blessed to have them.'

'And they are truly blessed to have you, Sister,' says the visitor and the woman blushes.

He returns to the superior who is playing ball with some children.

'I know what you mean, Father. They're definitely all Indian.'

'As I said. At least you saw for yourself.' He hurls the ball away and the children surrounding him scream in delight and run after it. 'I'll keep a look out for anyone of your description and if there's even a remote possibility, I'll call you right away.'

'Thank you, Father. You've been a great help.'

'I wish I could do more.'

The superior takes the visitor back inside and they walk through the hall to the entrance. He opens the door and the man goes out onto the street.

'I'm very grateful,' Szell says.

'I'll be in touch if I hear of anything.'

Father Bartolomeo watches him depart before closing the door. As soon as it is shut he exhales and puts a hand to his chest in relief. As it happens, Maria has taken Ignacio to the hospital that morning for a check-up. They are due back shortly. The mission will have to be more careful when it comes to screening potential parents, including those who claim to have lost a child.

The man who calls himself Cristian Szell walks on down the street. It is one of several aliases Tiago Hecht has been using as he searches high and low for the *Führer*'s son. But he will not give up. He will not rest until he has found the boy.

BUENOS AIRES

Wednesday 23 July–Sunday 3 August 1952

Eva Peron is dying. The cancer, which first appeared in her cervix, has now metastasized to her bones. In spite of the revolutionary chemotherapy which she has been receiving, Argentina's first lady has only days to live. All the doctors can do is give her morphine to relieve the pain that flares and burns like hellfire through her body. As Evita drifts in and out of consciousness the medical staff surrounding her deathbed attend to her physical needs and try and make her comfortable. In one corner a group of nuns pray the rosary and permeate the air with murmured incantations.

The ailing first lady is being treated at the presidential palace, the Casa Rosada. As she awaits the inevitable, a multitude fills the capital's main square, the Plaza de Mayo. In the Metropolitan Cathedral facing the plaza a vigil is held for the Mother of the Nation, as Evita has become known. Meanwhile, the *caudillo* visits at all hours, unable to be away from his wife's side for any length of time despite the burdens of office. When it is necessary to leave the room, he stalks the corridors half-blind with despair. Nothing anyone says can comfort him. He knows the love of his life will soon be no more. The irony is that he is almost certainly the cause of his spouse's illness. The *caudillo*'s first wife also died of cervical cancer due to a venereal disease caused by the human papillomavirus, unwittingly given to her by her husband. Now the same has happened to Evita.

Evita makes a death rattle as she succumbs to the carcinoma which ravages her body. Peron is at her bedside and clasps her hand in his. He thought he had no more to tears to shed but he weeps constantly. He has never known such grief. It is all-consuming. In her altered state, Evita mumbles and her husband tries to catch the words but they are incoherent. In her last moments Peron's wife opens her eyes and looks at the man beside her. She seems at peace, as if she has already departed this mortal coil and is about to make her final journey.

'The child ...' she says. 'The child ...'

'What child?' asks Peron, who does not understand. 'What child do you mean?'

He wonders if she is thinking about one of her miscarriages. He knows that she considers each one has a soul and is waiting for her in heaven.

'The boy. The little boy – pray for him.'

'What boy, my love? Tell me ...'

Evita makes no reply. Instead she turns and faces the wall and breathes her last. Peron cries out in agony and kisses his wife one more time. Then he bows his head and lays it on her breast and sobs, his tears soaking her camisole. The Mother of the Nation has gone.

The death of Eva Peron is announced and a great cry rises from the crowds gathered in the Plaza de Mayo. Men weep openly and women scream and tear their hair while others collapse onto the pavement. As the news spreads more people arrive, filling the streets for ten blocks in each direction. Never before has the nation witnessed such a public outpouring of grief. The first lady represented everything that was noble and selfless about Argentina. Her death is nothing short of a catastrophe.

The government orders official activities to be suspended for two days and flags flown at half-mast for a further ten days. The following morning, as the first lady's body is being moved from the presidential residence to the Ministry of Labour, a massive surge crushes several people to death. Within a day the flower shops in Buenos Aires run out of stock. Blooms are flown from all over the country, some as far away as Chile, to replenish the supply. The streets of the capital are awash with bouquets and every corner has a makeshift shrine where votive candles burn constantly.

The first lady's sarcophagus is transferred to Congress for a final public viewing and a memorial service attended by the entire legislative body. The following day Evita, although she has never held public office, is given a state funeral together with a Requiem Mass. The bier is laid on a gun carriage pulled by members of the General Confederation of Labour, the nation's largest union. Peron and his cabinet proceed in its wake, followed by members of her family and friends and thousands upon thousands of mourners. People throw flowers from balconies and Evita's smiling image hangs everywhere. There is even a petition to make her a saint.

A week after Eva Peron's funeral, Argentina continues to mourn its loss, otherwise life has returned to its usual cycles and rhythms. The following Sunday, church bells ring out and Masses and prayers for her soul are said up and down the country, while the petition calling for her sainthood has already garnered over a million signatures. Whether she is beatified or not is superfluous. As far as Argentina is concerned, Evita is revered almost as much as the Virgin. And yet, despite the affection in which the former first lady is held, her memory is already beginning to fade. Soon she will become just another historical figure, adored by her acolytes and forgotten by almost everyone else.

BUENOS AIRES–POSADAS

Sunday 17 August 1952

In a city park the almond trees are in blossom. A wind blows and petals fall in a blizzard, scattering pale confetti across the lake. Otto Guzman is sitting on a bench watching his wife and child play hide-and-seek. He is writing in his journal and looks up from time to time as mother and son run through the trees and shadows, laughing. It is all a man could ever want. A family. Nothing else in the world is so important. He cannot contemplate what would happen if he lost them. He has already had one family taken away and could not bear to lose another.

Otto knows such thoughts are futile. Their destiny is out of his hands. All he has is the moment. He gazes at the wind-ruffled water and feels an abiding sense of calm. He realises he has never been so content. He finishes what he has been writing, reads it through and, finally, puts pen and notebook away. It does not say what he wants to say, nothing ever did. That is the problem with poetry. But it is a memory he will never forget.

We catch the leaves of falling hours

in our hands and crumble them to pieces,
watching our child hide behind the great figs
playing out his life.

The bandstand is alone and silent,
birdsong fills the air
with the thrill of spring
and my love takes the shape of a poem.

At the Jesuit mission two boys stand in the shadow of a high wall in the yard. They make an unlikely pair, which is why Father Bartolomeo calls them the heavenly twins. The elder is short and dark, like all Guaraní. The other is a couple of years younger but already a head taller than his companion. They have been close ever since Javier Ibarra arrived at the orphanage as a three-year-old and instantly took to the infant, Ignacio, becoming his adoptive brother and protector.

Now they are vying for the younger boy's prize turquoise marble, which shines like a coral sea when held up to the light. It is easily worth the price of all the other marbles and Ignacio refuses to part with it. But he cannot resist Javier's offer of his entire collection if Ignacio allows him just one chance. Winner takes all and the younger boy has agreed. The only snag is that the narrow-eyed Guaraní is the best marble player in the school. Even so, Ignacio is certain the odds are stacked in his favour. How could his friend win with a single shot? It is impossible.

The boys leave the cool of the shade and walk to the centre of the playground. They agree on the length of the throw and together they measure out a full five metres, where a line is drawn in the dirt. The marble is placed ceremoniously on the ground and sparkles like a jewel in the morning sun. Other children gather. At last Ignacio Cruz is going to let someone play for his marble. Bets are taken to cries of: 'He'll never do it!' ... 'Of course he will!' ... 'Go on, Javier!' ... 'You'll lose everything, you idiot!'

Ignacio pushes the crowd back behind the line and asks them to give his friend space as they chant 'Javier! Javier! Javier!' The Guaraní puts a finger to his lips to quieten them. This is serious. He needs to concentrate. He takes out his lucky marble and makes a fist which he kisses. He shakes it up and down and repeats his secret mantra. Then he puts the glass ball on top of his thumb, his forefinger protecting it like a trigger guard. There is silence. Every child holds their breath. Ignacio looks on with folded arms. Soon Javier's marbles will be his.

The Guaraní frowns in concentration. He flicks his marble and it rises in an arc, turning through the air. The whole world is still. The group watches in awe as it lands with a crack on Ignacio's prize and they erupt in a cheer. Javier faces them and raises his arms in glorious victory. He has won. Ignacio says nothing. Instead he marches to the glass balls lying side by side and picks up his own.

'Hey! That's mine!' says his friend. 'Give it here!'

'No it it's not! You cheated. Your foot crossed the line!'

'It didn't!'

'Yes it did. You cheated!'

Ignacio pushes past but Javier grabs him and tries to take his marble.

'Give it to me! It's mine now.'

They wrestle together and after a brief struggle, the taller boy extricates himself, steps back and strikes his friend in the face. Javier staggers and holds his nose. Blood drips from his fingers and his eyes smart with pain.

'You son of a bitch!' He hurls himself at his antagonist and they roll in the dust, arms and legs flailing.

The others circle and start to chant: 'Fight! Fight! Fight!'

Soon the taller boy is astride his victim and begins to pound him. Javier squirms trying vainly to ward off the blows.

'Stop that right now!' says a woman's voice and the children scatter like a flock of sparrows.

The two friends rise sheepishly. Javier has come off much worse and now has a black eye while his nose and mouth are covered with blood. Ignacio has a couple of bruises and a cut lip but otherwise looks unharmed. Shamefaced they stand before Maria, who is incensed.

'You're a disgrace, the pair of you!' she says. 'Fighting like a couple of tinkers over what exactly might I ask?'

'Marbles, Sister ...' they say.

'You boys and your blessed marbles. I'd ban the lot of them if I could! Go on, clean yourselves up and report to the superior's office. He'll be wanting a word with both of you.'

And with that the nun storms off.

The sounds of Father Bartolomeo's ferule can be heard all the way down the passage as the culprits are given six of the best. *Whack*! *Whack*! *Whack*! it goes, while a gaggle of onlookers listen from a safe distance and flinch with each blow. First one and then the other boy emerges from the superior's office, their faces flushed, hands clutching backsides. The pair are taken to the lavatories and trousers are lowered and buttocks inspected. A verdict is solemnly pronounced. They both got a right hiding. Old Barty did not spare them the rod. No, sir! Handshakes are exchanged and all is forgiven. Everyone agrees there is nothing like a scrap to enliven a dull day.

That night in the dormitory Ignacio wakes. He can hear sounds of distress from the adjacent bed and realises Javier is crying.

'What's up? Are you still hurting?'

'No, I'm okay.'

'What then?'

'I had a nightmare.'

'What about?'

'I can't tell you.'

'Why?'

'I can't tell anyone.'

'Why not?'

'Because I'm not allowed to.'

And the boy turns away and sniffles. Ignacio thinks for a moment then reaches for his clothes on the chair and rummages in a pocket. He removes his prized possession and holds it out to his friend.

'Here, take this.'

'What is it?'

'My marble.'

'It's okay. I don't want it.'

'Go one have it. It's yours. You won fair and square.'

'You sure?'

'As sure as you're my best mate.'

A hand darts and grabs the glass ball.

'Thanks!'

'You're welcome and by the way I'm sorry about this morning.'

'Me, too.'

A voice calls out in the dark.

'You two quit talking or you'll be seeing Barty for another beating!'

The friends chuckle and wish each other good night and settle down to sleep once more.

CAMPO DE MAYO

Monday 23 March–Friday 11 December 1964

The soldiers wear olive fatigues and stand in serried ranks on the parade ground beneath the glare of the midday sun. There are 500 virtually identical young men, most of them in their teens. One of the few who is not is Javier who has been able to defer call-up because of his studies. Now he has finished his degree and stands to attention alongside Ignacio, who is aged eighteen like the majority of his fellow conscripts. His friend is one of the tallest among them. He is also one of the fittest and has taken to basic training as if it were no more arduous than the rock climbing and kayak expeditions he made during school holidays. Consequently, he is one of the favoured recruits and already wears a team leader's brassard. The opposite is true of Javier, a chubby, bookish youth who abhors the petty rules, profanity and shouting. He also has flat feet and cannot march properly. This marks him out as a potential victim and no one victimises him more than Staff Sergeant Hugo Moya.

There are several reasons why the NCO picks on the youth. There is his apparent lack of soldierly qualities, from kit inspection and drill to making his laboured way around an assault course. But the reason he hates Javier most is because of his ethnicity, which is not so different from his own. Moya is part Guaraní and conceals this from his fellow NCOs and officers, who are mostly of Latino descent. In Argentinean society as a whole, and in the military in particular, the indigenous are considered lesser mortals and the sergeant feels he has a point to prove. And who better to make it for him than the awkward, shuffling boy from Misiones?

On their first day at the shooting range Javier had failed to hit the mark. His friend, who lay beside him, noticed and fired the remainder of his ammunition clip at Javier's target. When the scores were compared, Moya saw the discrepancy in the number of holes. Each man had been given ten rounds. Ignacio had seven shots in and around the bull's eye, while his friend, somehow, had three. It did not fool the sergeant and both recruits were given a dressing-down by their platoon commander and ordered to do double fatigues. From that day Moya has had Javier in his sights and is prepared to do everything in his power to back-squad him. If he could, he would have the clod-footed Indian running around the parade ground for the rest of his life.

It is night and a wind knifes in from the estuary. Javier lies staked out in the middle of the football pitch. A recruit has been ordered to throw a bucket of water over him regularly. Yet again, Sergeant Moya has singled out the Guaraní for special treatment. His particular crime is irrelevant. If he cannot break his spirit then he will break him physically.

Whatever happens, the sergeant intends to fail him.

When dawn comes Javier is unconscious. His comrades look on in horror and disbelief and wonder if he is dead. He has not moved or cried out for an hour. Ignacio is outraged but can do nothing. As a winter sun rises above the camp Moya appears and struts towards his charges.

'Time to fetch your fat friend.'

Along with another youth, Ignacio runs onto the field and unties the stakes. They rub Javier's hands and limbs and carry him back to the barracks where they attempt to revive him with a hot bath, towels and massages. After a while he moans and regains consciousness. Somehow, he has survived.

'Seems like he's made it,' says Moya, standing in the doorway. 'Ah, well, there's always next time,' and he walks away.

Ignacio simmers with cold fury. The man is a psychopath. At some point, he does not know when, or even how, he will take his revenge.

In the before dawn dark the reveille bell rings, bringing a litany of sighs and groans as the dormitory lights are switched on. The youths rise sleepily and put on their uniforms and lace their boots. A voice barks as they finish dressing and stand by their bunks.

'Listen up,' says Moya. 'I want all of you outside with a full pack in one minute. You'll be doing a thirty-six-hour day-night-day exercise at the end of which you'll be split into two groups, red and blue. Red are the attackers, blue will defend. Whichever team wins will have the weekend off. The losers will be confined to barracks and scrub floors. Is that clear?'

'Yes, Staff!' they chorus.

'All right, let's do it!'

Moya departs and there is a scramble as the recruits grab their kit bags and fill them with the essentials they need for the exercise then dash for the door. All but one leave within the allocated time. Javier is the last to appear on the square nearly a full minute after the others. He lines up beside Ignacio at the end of the first rank, sweating and breathing heavily. He stares at the ground hoping the sergeant will ignore what has happened but he can hear the tread of boots approach and fears the worst.

Moya stops in front of him and smiles curiously like a cat that has caught a mouse and wonders how to prolong its agony before it dies.

'I knew you wouldn't make it, monkey boy.'

'Yes, Staff.'

'You know why you're a monkey?'

'No, Staff.'

'It's because you're mother fucked one in the jungle and you're the result.'

A ripple of laughter emanates from the assembled recruits.

'You know what monkeys eat, don't you?'

'Yes, Staff.'

'They eat bananas, don't they?'

'Yes, Staff.'

Moya reaches into a pocket and produces the fruit.

'Here you go, monkey boy. Have a banana,' and he hands it to his victim. 'Now stand over there and eat.'

Javier does as he is told. Leaving the row, he turns to face the company. Moya joins him and addresses them once more.

'Since you think this comedian is so damned funny, you can all do fifty press-ups while Cheetah has his breakfast. Now!'

As Javier peels and eats the banana, his comrades get down to do press-ups, their bodies undulating in a khaki wave. They are strong and fit and the exercise does not take long but time enough for every man to curse and resent the Guaraní, which is what Moya wants. After they have completed the punishment the recruits are ordered to their feet and they go at a trot to the canteen. The last to enter are the youths from Posadas. They line up for a breakfast of scrambled eggs and beans and take their food to one of the tables. No one wants to sit next to Javier in case they become infected with whatever disease it is that makes him so hopeless as a soldier. The only person with him is his friend. They eat their food in silence.

It is the final day of the exercise. The soldiers have been beasted by the NCOs in a way that none has ever experienced and some have ended up in the sanatorium and certain back-squadding. Javier has avoided such a fate. He knows that if he drops out, he will have to endure another three months of basic training before he can resume the course again. And yet, he realises he is grasping the end of a rope, the cords of which are slowly, but inexorably, unravelling. He is poised over a gorge and below are the rocks upon which he will break his bones and be his death. There is only one way to survive. It is either him, or Moya.

Javier and Ignacio have been assigned to the attacking red team. All of them have been issued with American M-16 carbines, along with one hundred rounds of blank ammunition and two smoke grenades. They have worked their way towards a well-defended redoubt which is occupied by the blue team. The air is filled with the sound of gunfire, smoke, and the bark of NCOs using bullhorns and who are acting as marshals.

Sergeant Moya is pacing up and down in the open, urging the red team on. The end is in sight. One last push and they will take the stockade. The company are wearing full combat gear and have been fighting since first light. It is midsummer and the intense heat makes their heads spin and dust catches in the backs of their throats. Each man has a raging thirst having emptied their water bottles long ago.

As the sergeant stands and bellows, Javier reaches into a pocket and retrieves the small, metallic object which will solve his problems. He has a single live round, discovered on the firing range weeks ago. If the bullet had ever been found during a locker search he would have been court-martialled. It is hardly a keepsake, let alone a souvenir. It it is more a fetish, an idol that wards off evil spirits and gives him strength, like the indigenous tribes who kept the shrunken heads of their victims as trophies, the spirit of the dead warrior being subsumed into their own. At night, when everyone was asleep, Javier would inspect the round beneath his bedclothes. It is his magic bullet.

Javier opens the breech of his carbine and slots in the round. The recoil and retort of either a blank, or a real bullet is the same, only the sound a bullet makes as it travels through the air is different. Moya is on his own and with all the noise and fury around them, nobody will hear it. The M16 has a muzzle velocity of 3,000 feet per second and a maximum range of 550 metres. The sergeant is less than a tennis court away. Even Javier cannot miss such a target. At this range, the man's death will be instantaneous and no one would ever know who fired the fatal shot since all muzzles would be dirty from shooting blanks.

The weapon is firm in Javier's grip, his cheek resting on the stock. Everything slows as he draws a bead on his nemesis. He takes a deep breath and exhales until his lungs are almost empty. A sense of weightlessness descends and he feels calm as his finger squeezes the trigger. At the moment he fires the M16 jumps and the bullet sails harmlessly through the air. He has missed. Sergeant Moya is very much alive.

Javier turns to the youth whose hand is on his weapon and responsible for its sudden movement.

'What did you do that for?'

'He's not worth it.'

'How did you know the round was live?

'Why else would you line him up in your sights?'

'Why indeed?'

'And, besides, you're not a killer.'

'And you are?'

'I could be.'

Moya turns and sees them talking and yells.

'Get going, you cowardly sons of bitches!'

'Come on,' says Ignacio. 'We're almost there.'

Firing the last of their blanks, the friends charge past the sergeant, screaming like lunatics as they storm the stockade. A white flag is raised and flutters on the battlement. The red team has won.

Ignacio stands to attention in front of his company commander Lieutenant Alfredo Saavedra. The officer affects an aristocratic languor and smiles as though privy to a joke which he alone knows. He sits in his chair idly smoking a cheroot, like some nineteenth century hussar. The only things that are missing are a cuirassier and a pair of spurs.

'At ease, Private Cruz.'

The youth relaxes and places his feet square and his hands behind his back. He is neatly turned out, as always, with shined boots and a freshly blancoed belt. He has passed each section of the course with distinction. The lieutenant has summoned Ignacio because he wants him to consider a commission. They need men of his calibre in the armed forces and he tells him this.

The recruit looks bewildered even though he knows he has heard correctly.

'A commission, sir? I hadn't thought about it.'

'Most don't until they complete national service. You're the best I've seen in a long time. I don't say this lightly but you have what it takes – the right stuff. As I'm sure you're aware, the military runs this country. Sometimes we have civilian governments but democracy here is a fiction. They receive their orders from us and they always will. It's how things are.'

Ignacio thinks of the end-of-term parades at the academy, with the top brass taking the salute. If what Saavedra said is true, and there is no reason why it should not be, then one day it might be him standing on the rostrum as newly minted soldiers march past to the sound of trumpet, fife and drum. The implication is clear: if he really is made of the right stuff, as the lieutenant claims, he could become chief of the armed forces and, perhaps, even head of state. President Ignacio Cruz. It is a heady thought.

'So, what do you reckon?'

'I'm not sure.'

'Think about it.'

'I certainly will.'

'I'll put your name forward anyway,' says Saavedra. He signs some forms on the desk, marking the last with a flourish, then shuffles the papers and puts them to one side. 'The colonel will rubber stamp it and we'll take it from there. I've also recommended you for the helicopter course. It's four weeks and, if you make the grade, you'll go on to flight school. Apart from anything else, it's a lot better than square-bashing and will look good on your CV.'

'Thank you, sir.'

'No need. Dismissed.'

Ignacio raises a boot, stands to attention, salutes and leaves. The lieutenant watches him go. The youth would make a fine officer. Perhaps he will end up under his command. The matter for the time being is academic. Whatever the outcome, it does not change the fact that, almost two decades later, Saavedra will die in agony from a bayonet wound to the stomach as his men fight for their lives, defending a rocky outcrop in the South Atlantic.

'You what?' says Javier. 'Have you lost your freaking mind?' The friends face each other sitting on neighbouring bunks in the dormitory.

'What's wrong? It's a career. You know I've excelled in training. I'll make a good soldier.'

'You said you wanted to be a doctor.'

'So? Perhaps I can be a military one.'

'It's not the same.'

'Soldiers need doctors, too.'

'Don't be obtuse!' says Javier, his voice rising in anger. 'You know it's not. Seriously, if you join the military, I'll never speak to you again.'

'Come on!'

'*Ay Dios...*' mumbles Javier and he distractedly picks at the edge of a blanket. He loves his friend and cannot bear the thought of him in uniform. It goes against everything the Jesuits taught them. Ignacio is right about one thing.

He would be a good soldier, very good. And that is the problem. Everyone knows power corrupts and he fears what might happen to his friend if he joins the military. The signs were there at the orphanage. Ignacio, the alpha male, who dominated the other boys and always got his way. Fortunately, the nuns and priests had instilled a sense of decency and humility in the child. But the army could, and most likely would, take that away. It would be the end of their relationship.

'Please, I beg you. Don't.'

Ignacio realises he has come to a crossroads in his life. There are two paths in the forest and it is up to him which one to take. His friend has made up his mind for him. He will take the one less travelled. Any power or glory will have to wait for the afterlife.

'You win. I won't do it. But I'm going to take the chopper course. I've always wanted to fly.'

Javier beams and hugs his companion.

The next day Ignacio packs his kit bag and joins the elite who have been assigned to the helicopter squadron. The flight school is on the same campus, a short distance from its military counterpart. As they line up for registration, Ignacio surveys the aircraft assembled on the asphalt. They are US-made Bell UH-1 Iroquois, commonly known as Hueys and the workhorse of the West's airborne forces. Poised, with Perspex canopies and drooping blades, they look like dragonflies in the morning light. Ignacio feels a pang, as if he has met the love of his life. But he has made a promise and that is that.

It is over. The months of marching, boot polishing and obeying orders are finished. Everyone in the barracks is demob happy, especially Javier. Despite expectations, and the best efforts of Sergeant Moya, he has passed out thanks to the efforts of his only friend, who has recently completed flight school. Once again, Ignacio is top of the class.

The youths whoop with joy as they board the buses that will take them into the city and later disperse them to their homes. But first, they are going to celebrate in the Plaza de Mayo.

As Javier climbs the steps of one of the vehicles his friend pauses.

'You go on. I'll join you later.'

'What's up?'

'Sorry, I forgot. I have to make a call.'

'Make it in town.'

'The pay phones there never work. It won't take long. I'll see you in the plaza.'

'Okay. Catch you later.'

Ignacio lets him go and Javier waves as the bus pulls away to shouts and cries from the occupants. When the square is silent the youth returns to the main building. There is one more thing he has to do. It is not a phone call. He needs to see a person about unfinished business. As he walks, his footsteps echo through the empty drill hall at the end of which is an office. A man sits alone at a desk. It is the duty sergeant.

Moya wonders why the recruit is still here. He should have left along with the others.

'What do you want?'

Ignacio says nothing and closes the door. The sergeant is no fool. He knows what is about to happen. He can tell from the coldness in the young man's eyes. Moya is about to get the beating of a lifetime and there is nothing he can do about it.

POSADAS

Saturday 9–Tuesday 19 December 1967

The Summer of Love is in full swing. Freedom fills the air and flower power is blooming. For Argentina and, indeed, the whole world, the city of Posadas is no more than a sleepy Latin American backwater, famed for absolutely nothing. But for its residents, especially the youth, it is the centre of the universe.

Ignacio and Javier intend to make the most of this historic opportunity of sex and liberation and set about trying to seduce as many women as possible. Both are now students at the university. Ignacio has passed the first stage of his medical degree and has two more years of clinical practice and further examinations before he can qualify as a doctor. Javier has a master's in literature and is now studying pedagogy.

Even so, the dusty confines of the university library and lecture hall could not be further from their minds as they trawl the bars and clubs of the city in search of women, who rarely refuse their attentions. Ignacio is the more approachable with his playboy looks and easy charm but Javier makes up for any plainness with his winsome smile and inimitable wit. The taller, paler youth usually gets the prettier girl, while his darker companion settles for the homely, mothering type.

'Besides,' Javier would say. 'They're always grateful and never hassle you afterwards.'

The friends are in a bar downtown when they spot two girls at a table. They are attractive and look like they are out for a good time. Ignacio orders beers and they advance towards their intended partners. The girls see them approach, the taller and better-looking man carrying the drinks, his companion following.

'Ladies, you look lovely but thirsty,' and Ignacio places the bottles on the table. 'I would like to make an offer – drinks in exchange for your company.'

'Sounds good to me,' says the girl closest to him. 'Come and join us. I'm Jimena and this is Juanita.'

The men sit and bottles are raised. Everyone says, '*Salud*,' and takes a swig of beer.

'Jimena and Juanita?' Javier says. 'Wonderful! Are you twins?'

The girls laugh.

'No, but most people think we're sisters,' says Jimena.

'Actually, we're nurses,' adds Juanita.

'Nurses! Man, I love nurses!' says Ignacio.

The girl opposite scowls.

'What is it with guys and nurses? You think we're easy. It's so childish.'

There is silence and a frost descends before Javier comes to the rescue.

'What do you mean, easy?' he says, looking aghast. 'How dare you say such a thing! My mother's a nurse, my sister's a nurse ...'

His deadpanning is timely and effective.

'Really?'

'As God is my witness!'

'I guess that's okay then,' and the girl called Juanita cosies up to him.

The evening progresses and they move on from beer to tequila shots. Glasses are filled, lemons sliced, salt savoured and drinks slammed on the table and downed. Someone puts a coin in the jukebox and music plays. It is the song of the summer and those who are not standing already get up to dance.

'Come on,' says Ignacio and he takes Jimena by the hand and leads her onto the floor.

'How about it?' says Javier to Juanita and they join the other couple. The music blares from the speakers and people stamp their feet as they move and shake, everyone singing along to the chorus.

You know that it would be untrue
You know that I would be a liar
If I was to say to you
Girl, we couldn't get much higher!

Come on baby, light my fire
Come on baby, light my fire
Try to set the night on ... fire!

The friends dance and drink the night away. When the bar closes they wander arm-in-arm back to the men's lodgings, singing as they go. At the house Ignacio searches in his pockets for his keys. He finds them and tries to insert one in the lock but he is too inebriated and drops the keys. The others say, 'Shhh,' and laugh while he stoops and picks them up and tries again. This time the door opens and they enter. There is more tittering and further drunken admonitions for quiet.

An elderly voice calls out from a room.

'Who's that?'

'Sorry, Señora Bustos. It's just me and Ignacio.'

'I can hear others. I hope you haven't brought women back! You know the rules.'

'No, ma'am. Would we ever do such a thing? Sorry for disturbing you.'

'Go to bed!'

'Go to hell!' whispers Ignacio and the others clap hands to their mouths and almost faint with mirth.

'Yes, ma'am, right away,' says Javier.

They move on down the hall and creep up the stairs trying not to laugh. There are goodnight hugs and each girl goes to her partner's room and doors are closed.

Javier sits on his bed as the morning sun streams through his open window. He strikes a match, lights a cigarette and reflects. The girl who was with him had left as dawn rose over the rooftops. Juanita was a remarkable woman. She had taught him many things that night and would no doubt make someone a wonderful wife but it would not be him. No, she was the sort of woman who needed to find a good husband and have plenty of kids.

As Javier thinks about his date he hears a voice.

'You awake?'

'Sure. Come in.'

Ignacio enters. He has showered and shaved and looks refreshed. He wears a cotton dressing gown which ends above his knees and pads barefoot across the floor. He sits on a wicker chair, stretches his arms above his head and yawns. He cannot wait to hear the details about Javier's night.

'How was it, Don Juan?'

'Strange ... Beautiful, really,' says his friend, the smoke from his cigarette coiling above his head.

'One of the best?'

'Oh, sure.' Javier flicks the burning end into an ashtray. 'Juanita's certainly that – a lovely woman. But we didn't sleep together.'

The other man is shocked.

'You didn't?'

'No. We just talked. We talked a lot.'

'What about?'

'Everything. Life. What we wanted to do. That sort of thing.'

'And then?'

'Then I asked her if she wanted to pray.'

Ignacio bursts out laughing but stops when he sees his friend is serious. He sits there dumbfounded and realises

Javier is not joking.

'You ... prayed together?'

'Yes.'

'Why?'

'Because I told her I want to become a priest.'

Father Bartolomeo and Sister Maria are in his office deep in conversation. They cannot agree about what should happen next and there appears to be no solution, so contradictory are their views. The discussion is not about the mission or its work or, indeed, the Church. It is more important than that. It is about Ignacio or, to be more precise, it is about his parents. The boy has now come of age. Ever since he attained his majority he has asked, and is entitled to know, who his biological parents were. Usually it was not a problem. There was rarely any surprise. More often than not, it was a matter of class and money or, indeed, the lack of it: a case of the rich son seducing the family maid or the village bike who could not keep her legs together. Some ex-pupils wanted to discover the truth and others did not. It was entirely their decision.

But Ignacio is different and, because of this, Maria has been adamant. He must never know that he is the natural son of Adolf Hitler and Eva Braun. The nun possesses the protective instincts of a mother. After all, she had nursed him since he was a baby. He had sucked the milk from her own breasts. The superior knows this and sympathises but the law is clear and Ignacio has the right to know who his antecedents were, no matter how terrible the truth might be. The Church should not stand in his way.

Maria pleads once more. Her voice is thick with emotion as she twists a sodden handkerchief in her hands.

'Father, it will destroy him. It would destroy anyone. He has a right to his own life – to be his own man. Please, I beg you, leave him be!'

'Sister, I understand. You've always been like a mother to Ignacio and you saved his life, indeed his soul, all those years ago when you fled from the camp with him in your arms. But we cannot ignore Canon Law and an Act of Congress.'

'I know, Father, but these are made by men. There is a higher law.'

'You're right, there is. However, we have taken a vow of obedience and both the Society's superior general and His Holiness Pope Paul have decreed that we must follow the law as it stands, both the religious and the judicial. It is our sacred duty to obey. The Holy Father is God's representative on earth. In his wisdom, he has made his decision. We must accept it humbly and with good grace.'

'No!' cries the nun. 'No! It will kill him!' and she breaks down again in tears.

Father Bartolomeo's voice is filled with compassion and he lays a comforting hand upon her.

'Let us trust in the Lord ...'

Maria weeps and has not yet dried her eyes when a young man appears in the doorway.

'Sorry, I didn't mean to interrupt. I can come back another time.'

'Not at all, please join us,' says the superior.

Ignacio enters the room and shuts the door. He had only expected to see Father Bartolomeo. Maria looks at her former charge and tries to smile and he notices her eyes are red from crying. He had thought this meeting would be little more than a formality but he can tell it will be more than that. Much more. From their expressions it seems it might even be fatal. Ignacio feels like a man about to face a firing squad.

Javier runs as fast as he can back to his lodgings. It is only a few blocks from the university but he has sprinted so hard that he is out of breath when he arrives and sees his landlady waiting at the door. He had been given an urgent message while at a lecture telling him to come home immediately. He has no idea what it could be about but it must be an emergency. Señora Bustos was not one for histrionics.

'Thank God you're here! I don't know what's happened. Ignacio's locked himself in the bathroom and there's water pouring down the stairs. He won't answer and ... I really don't know what to do!'

'Don't worry. I'm sure everything's fine. The idiot has probably fallen asleep.'

Javier ascends the staircase as water falls in a cascade and spreads in a pool across the hall. He reaches the landing and pounds on the bathroom door.

'Ignacio! Open up. You're flooding the place ... Come on, open up!'

When there is no answer, he puts his shoulder to the door and throws his weight behind it. After a couple of hefty shoves the lock gives and Javier enters. He stops and stares. Ignacio is lying unconscious in the bath with the tap running. On the edge is a cutthroat razor, its blade gleaming in the light. His wrists have been slashed and blood is everywhere.

Javier rushes to turn off the taps and drags his friend's body from the bath. Señora Bustos hovers in the doorway, the water sloshing around her feet as she wrings her hands hopelessly. Her lodger shouts at her in desperation.

'Don't just stand and gawp, woman! Call an ambulance!'

The hospital is hushed and the room is white. The walls, the sheets and the bed: all white. A man stares at the ceiling. It, too, is white. So are the windows and blinds. And so are the nurses and doctors who come and go at all hours of the day and night. Everyone dressed in white. The patient wonders if white is the colour of life or perhaps it is death. Yes, it must be death. Death is white. Death is a ghost. He is dead.

Ignacio tries to move to a more comfortable position but can only shift his weight upon the bed. His hands and forearms are swathed in bandages and suspended by wires. He looks like a man who wants to fly and instead is pinioned like a lepidopteran to a board.

A nurse appears at his side.

'A visitor is here to see you,' she says and draws the curtain back.

A young man approaches holding a bunch of chrysanthemums and a box of chocolates.

'You asking me out on a date?'

'No. Although I realise I shall have to feed you.'

'Like a small child.'

'Or a duck.'

Javier puts the flowers in an empty vase, which he fills at the sink and places on the bedside table. He draws up a chair, opens the box of chocolates and offers it to the patient.

'Any preferences?'

'Nope. I love them all.'

Javier selects one and pops it into his friend's open mouth and takes another for himself. They spend the morning chatting and eating chocolates. After a couple of hours the nurse appears and tells them visiting time is over. Javier is about to leave but he has a question which, while on his mind throughout his visit, has remained unspoken and therefore unanswered. If he does not ask now, he never will.

'By the way, there's something I'd like to know. You don't have to say if you don't want to but I just can't understand why you did it. I mean of all the people I could imagine...'

Ignacio lies impassively, his arms akimbo, like a man on a cross.

'I'm sorry. Honestly, I am. But I can't tell you.'

'It's okay. You don't have to.' Javier turns to go.

'Listen, I know what you're thinking: I saved your life, I'm your best pal, surely I have the right to know ...'

'I said, you don't have to tell me.'

'You're at least entitled to an explanation. Do you remember that time in the dormitory when I heard you crying and you said you'd had a nightmare?'

'Yes.'

'And you wouldn't tell me what it was about?'

'No.'

'You said something like, 'I'm not allowed to.' I always wondered why but I've never asked. It's the same for me.'

'I understand.'

'I knew you would.'

Javier leans across and embraces his friend.

'See you soon. And keep your hands off those nurses.'

'Ha! I wish ...'

The visitor leaves the patient to convalesce, the open box of chocolates on his bed, the chrysanthemums in a vase beside him. When he has gone Ignacio lays his head upon the pillow and cries out in despair.

POSADAS–EL DORADO

Sunday 21–Monday 22 October 1973

The young man wears a white cassock and lies prostrate in front of the altar. Eleven others are with him on the flagstone floor of St Joseph's Cathedral. They are about to be ordained priests after an hour-long ceremony, which included a celebration of the Eucharist. The organist plays a fanfare and the candidates rise. An acolyte hands the Bishop of Posadas a silver ciborium. He dips his thumb into the bowl and anoints each man with chrism while the choir sings *Alleluia*. Javier and the other ordinands bow their heads for a final blessing and the bishop congratulates them. Now they will venture into the world and do Christ's bidding, just as the apostles had done almost two millennia ago.

The cathedral bells peal and the newly ordained priests process down the nave and gather outside on the sunny steps for an official photograph. Among the onlookers is Ignacio whose heart is filled with joy at his friend's spiritual transformation. Nobody would make a better disciple than the humble Guaraní with the shy smile and saintly disposition.

When the official photo has been taken the group

breaks up and the young priests are surrounded by their families. All except Javier who, as an orphan, has nobody except the handsome, bearded man who approaches. Father Bartolomeo and Sister Maria are among those who have sent their best wishes as well as their commiserations. They have been unable to attend the ceremony, as it coincided with the Society's annual retreat and both are confined to the mission.

Ignacio stands before Javier and folds his arms across his chest.

'May I have a blessing, Father?'

Javier says a prayer and makes the sign of the cross.

'May God always protect you and assist you in your work, in the name of the Father and of the Son and of the Holy Spirit.'

The friends laugh and hug each other. It seems hard to believe that just a few years ago they were boys at the orphanage. Now they have realised their vocations and are about to go their separate ways. Ignacio has spent the past few years working as a surgeon in the city hospital and has accepted a job at a remote clinic near the Iguaçu Falls. His companion has been teaching him the local language and the doctor is proficient enough to get by.

'You sure you can't stay longer?'

'I'd like to. But I should be on my way or I won't make Iguaçu by tomorrow. I've a meeting with the registrar in the morning.'

'Okay. Safe trip and look after yourself.'

'I will. Take care.'

'Write when you have an address.'

'You bet.'

They walk to Ignacio's motorbike, parked beneath the leafy spread of an ombú tree. All the doctor's worldly possessions fill the twin saddlebags astride the rear wheel of the Norton Triumph. The men have been on many expeditions in the surrounding wilderness of lakes and forests, with Javier riding pillion. This time his friend would be alone.

Ignacio straddles the machine and puts on a pair of sunglasses and dons his helmet. He ties the strap under his chin and kick-starts the bike. It makes a throaty roar and he grips the throttle and revs the 500cc engine. He waves and sets off along the road. Javier watches him travel down the main street. Neither man knows they will never see the other again.

The doctor weaves in and out of the busy traffic and is soon speeding along the highway. The city recedes, replaced by suburbs of concrete and brick. Before long even these modest homes are taken over by those of adobe and wood. On the outskirts the inhabitants eke out a living as sharecroppers and smallholders, working all day in the fields. At weekends and on public holidays they stood outside their homes holding up sides of pork, having slaughtered and cooked the family pig, and passers-by would stop to pick up their roast. After an hour's ride Ignacio pulls into a cafe to have lunch. He parks his bike in the shade and walks to a table beneath a bamboo awning. A girl asks him what he wants and he enquires if they have any grilled pork.

'Yes, sir, and *cui*, too.'

Cui is the Guaraní word for guinea pig and considered a delicacy by Indians. It is skinned and skewered then barbecued over charcoal. It tastes sweet, like rabbit but not as strong – more like chicken, which is why the locals refer to them as four-footed hens.

'Thanks, I'll have the pork and a Sprite.'

The doctor waits for his food and watches traffic thunder up and down the road. It feels as though he has turned a page and is embarking on a new journey. Ever since he learnt about the circumstances of his birth and who his biological parents were, he has wanted to escape. He wishes he could disappear off the face of the earth but since that is not feasible he wants to be as far away as possible. And Iguaçu is about as far as it gets.

Lunch arrives and Ignacio takes up his knife and fork. The dish comes with roast potatoes, boiled maize and a tomato and onion salad. He puts a dollop of chilli sauce on the corn and eats, washing the food down with the soda. When the doctor has finished his meal he places a handful of coins on the table. He walks to the Triumph and puts on his helmet then starts the machine, twists the throttle and joins the highway once more.

Ignacio motors along and the forest flashes by in shades of green and gold. The route cuts through an escarpment and a parade of ponderosa line its banks for miles. Above the trees the sky is a cloudless blue. Apart from a brief stop to fill up with petrol, he continues his journey and revels in the freedom of the open road.

The sun is sinking beyond the horizon when the doctor enters the town of El Dorado. He slows and cruises up the main street. None of the buildings, apart from the church, is higher than two storeys and plaster peels from the walls. A few citrus trees with white-painted trunks spring from concrete pavements but are the only signs of vegetation. And yet, he has visited worse places. There are a variety of bars and hotels. He sees one named Bavaria and decides to take a room for the night. The Germans had a reputation for cleanliness and the sheets would be washed and, hopefully, the mattress bug-free.

Ignacio idles up to the entrance and cuts the engine. He removes his helmet and runs a hand through his hair. It is a relief to be able to stretch his legs again. He takes his travel kit from a saddlebag and replaces it with the helmet. Inside, the hostelry is dimly lit and constructed from pine logs, like a mountain chalet. The walls are decorated with posters of hearty youths either skiing or kayaking or climbing mountains. There is even a set of wooden skis and a pair of snowshoes. Fairy lights festoon the bar despite Christmas being weeks away and the doctor realises the twinkling decorations must be a permanent feature. If kitsch is a place then it is here. He rings a bell on the bar and a man who looks like he might be the owner appears. He is about sixty and has the faded aura of a once-gilded youth. He is tanned, with sandy hair turning silver at the temples. Although his freckled face is lined, the man's eyes are clear and sharp and blue.

'*Guten Abend. Wie kann ich Ihnen helfen*?'

'Hi, I'd like a room please.'

'Oh, you're local. I thought you must be a gringo,' he says. The proprietor's Spanish is good, with just a slight accent.

'That's right, I'm from Posadas.'

'Your family's German, surely?'

The words cut the doctor to the quick, although his face remains blank.

'No, but they're gringos, like you said. My parents are English.'

'*Ach, ja*! Anglo-Saxons, of course. We have much in common, the German race and the English. Only a small stretch of water separates our countries. It's always a pleasure to see a European in this Godforsaken place.'

'I wouldn't go so far as to describe myself as European.'

The proprietor fixes him with his flinty eyes.

'You're mistaken, sir. You have Aryan blood – the best! You must never forget that. Now, as for a room tonight, there's a nice double at the front but I will only charge you for a single. It's early in the season and we're not too busy at this time of year. Do you have any other bags?'

'No, just this.'

'Then, let me show you the room.' The man takes a key from a hook and beckons his guest to follow. They climb the wooden stairs and proceed down a passage with a row of doors, one of which he opens. The room is clean and spacious and dominated by a bed with a brass frame. Its windows face the street and a tiled roof covers the terrace.

'This looks fine.'

'*Gut*! I will see you downstairs. You're the only guest here. A family just left this morning. I could do with company.'

The man straightens, makes a curt bow and leaves.

Ignacio freshens up and is soon drinking beer with the proprietor, Klaus, at the bar. The German influence in Misiones extends to more than just the nation's progeny and includes brewing, particularly the local ale, Von Hafen, which everyone drinks ice-cold. The doctor is glad he claimed his parents were English as his host cannot speak a word of the language and has never visited the country. Nevertheless, he more than makes up for this with nostalgia for his own, in particular Berlin and the 1930s.

'*Ja*, they were good times. Everyone was happy. There was so much joy and optimism after the awful Weimar era. And the Jews and Commies knew their place. By God, they did!'

The doctor does not respond and wishes they could talk about something else but the proprietor is just beginning.

'Here, listen to this. It's my favourite song and takes me back to those bygone days. Sometimes it even makes me weep.' He goes to an antique gramophone and puts a record on the turntable. He winds the handle and music plays. The German returns to his stool.

Die sonnige Wiese ist sommerlich warm
Der Hisch läuft in Freiheit waldein.
Doch sammelt Euch alle, der Sturm ist nah
Der morgige Tag ist mein.

When the last verse begins Klaus rises from his seat and

starts to sing. He has a fine voice and his soaring tenor fills the room. It is as though the years have been stripped away and once again he is alongside his comrades in a beer cellar, wearing a brown shirt with a swastika brassard.

O Vaterland, Vaterland, zeig uns den Weg,
Dein Gruss soll das Wegzeichen sein,
Der Morgen kommt wenn der Welt ist mein
Der morgige Tag ist mein.

The song ceases and the last chord dissipates in the evening air. All is quiet except for the scratch of the needle as it circles the vinyl. Klaus lifts the gramophone arm and the record stops and he puts it back in its sleeve.

'Beautiful isn't it?'

'Tomorrow Belongs To Me – it was used in the movie, Cabaret.'

'Yes, a wonderful scene when the Hitler youth starts to sing and everyone joins in.'

'I thought the song was written by a couple of New York Jews.'

The man glares at him and slams his hand on the bar.

'*Nein! Dem ist nicht so.* They stole the song and translated the lyrics. That is typical of the Jew – they are all thieves!'

'Perhaps I'm mistaken,' says Ignacio, now determined to change the subject. 'I wonder if I could have another beer and is it possible to get something to eat?'

'Of course,' says Klaus and his good humour returns and his eyes twinkle. He takes another bottle from the fridge, opens it and fills his guest's glass. 'I have bratwurst and potatoes and freshly made sauerkraut – would that be alright?'

'Yes, that would be good.'

The man disappears and busies himself in the kitchen. Returning with supper, he sets the plates on the bar and they begin to eat. The dish is simple and wholesome. When they have finished, Klaus takes the empty plates away. He comes back and they continue to chat. He is curious about his guest and asks him what he does. Ignacio talks about his work but does not mention he is on his way to Iguaçu. He says only that he is on holiday and just passing through. He feels his host eyeing him intently as he speaks and wonders if the man can sense he is not telling the truth, at least about his origins. It is almost as if Klaus knows he is German or certainly of German descent.

This is not the case. The proprietor cannot take his eyes off his visitor because he has fallen in love. If it were not for the Indian boys he fucked, he would die of loneliness. All Klaus has ever wanted is a nice Aryan lover, like the man sitting before him. He puts out a hand and touches Ignacio's forearm. The doctor thinks he is just being friendly and carries on talking.

'*Ja, ja, ja*,' says Klaus, although his guest can tell he is not really listening. 'You know, you should stay here for a few days. There is wonderful swimming in the lakes. You can go naked. No one is about. It's like being at one with nature. You're a free spirit. When I was young we always swam in the nude. All my friends did. I do, even now ...'

'Another time, maybe. But I have to leave early tomorrow.

In fact, I should go to bed,' says Ignacio, stifling a yawn.

The host looks disappointed as his guest bids him goodnight. Klaus returns to the kitchen and clears up. When he has finished he locks the front door and puts out the lamps and the fairy lights winking above the bar. In the gloom he places a hand upon the banister and feels his way upstairs. He enters his bedroom, closes the door and undresses. He stands naked in front of a long mirror admiring his physique. He has kept himself fit and looks young for his age. The swimming and regular weight sessions have served him well.

Klaus turns out the light and gets under the covers. He lies there thinking about the first boy he had sex with. They were fifteen and in the Hitler Youth. Reiner became a pilot in the Luftwaffe and had been shot down over England, his body immolated along with his aircraft. He was dark-haired and blue-eyed and looked just like the doctor. They had been inseparable and on weekends they went hiking in the hills. They would pitch a tent in the woods and cook their food over an open fire. Then they would kiss and make love under the stars. He remembers his boyfriend's strong limbs, the fine hair on his chest and his pale skin. He misses him deeply.

Klaus cannot stop thinking about his former love. Nor can he take his mind off his visitor. The man had not pulled away when he stroked his arm. Maybe he was just shy. He was probably thinking the same thought right now and was waiting for him. Of course he was. He gets out of bed and walks down the passage. He pauses outside Ignacio's room and turns the door handle.

Klaus enters and is surprised to find nobody there. The bed has not even been slept in. He hears an engine start and goes to the window. In the forecourt a man sits astride a motorbike. He revs the throttle before riding off into the night, the sound diminishing in the distance until only silence remains. The proprietor looks down the empty street. So, his bird had flown. He cannot help but feel sad. Well, there were always the local boys. They would have to do. Klaus stands to attention with his arms by his sides and begins to sing. As he does so, a tear rolls down his cheek.

Der Morgen kommt wenn der Welt ist mein
Der morgige Tag ist mein.

BUENOS AIRES

Wednesday 24–Wednesday 31 March 1976

It is midnight in the Argentinean capital. A crescent moon glows and the planets and constellations scatter the heavens in a cold dust. While people slumber squads of soldiers and armoured vehicles take up positions at key junctions across the city and establish checkpoints and roadblocks. There has been a coup and the military are now in control. Ariel had worked late and has just gone to bed when he is alerted by a phone call from La Nación's duty editor.

'It's happened – the armed forces have rebelled.'

The news is hardly unexpected since there has been talk of an uprising for weeks. Even so, the timing comes as a surprise to the journalist.

'Our nation's favourite pastime. Any resistance?'

'Not much ... some sporadic gunfire. The army has taken command of all facilities including the TV and radio stations.'

'What's the latest?'

'Isabellita is under arrest at the military base in Neuquén.'

'At least she's safely out of the way.'

Isabellita is the nickname of Juan Peron's recent widow,

Maria Estella Martinez, who assumed the presidency on his death two years previously. But she has never had the same level of support as the *caudillo*, let alone Evita, and opposition to her government soon increased. Her political defenestration was only ever a matter of time.

'Who's in charge?'

'A junta headed by General Videla.'

'Who'd have thought it – have you called Mario?'

'Yes, he's on his way here now.'

'Tell him I'm going to the Plaza de Mayo to see what else is happening.'

'Will do. Drive fast, take risks.'

'Thanks.'

The journalist gets out of bed and dresses quickly. He puts on his jacket and leaves the apartment. There is a taxi on the corner. The driver is listening to the radio and Ariel knocks on the window. The man winds it down and a sound of martial music floats over the airwaves.

'The answer is no. The place is crawling with soldiers.'

'I've got to get to the Plaza de Mayo! Look, you can have all my cash.' Ariel opens his wallet and pulls out his reserve of US dollars. 'That's a hundred bucks!'

The driver eyes the money with disinterest.

'You must be out of your mind and the answer's still no.'

Ariel pushes the wad into his hand.

'Go on, take it.'

The man raises a reluctant shoulder and accepts the cash as though this sort of thing happened to him every day. He fingers the notes and stuffs them into a money belt.

'All right. But if we get stopped, you're on your own, and I'm not going anywhere near the square so you'll have to walk the last couple of blocks.'

'Deal!' and the journalist gets in. The driver starts the engine and sets off down Avenida Independencia. The streets are deserted until they arrive at Plazoleta Olazábal where they encounter an armoured car and a troop of soldiers.

'Let me do the talking,' says Ariel.

A conscript motions with his assault rifle for the passenger to get out and tells him to keep his arms up. The journalist obeys and waves the press pass in his hand.

'Ariel Guzman – La Nación. I have to be at the Casa Rosada. General Videla's holding a press conference.'

The soldier takes the pass and checks it and calls out to his platoon commander. The lieutenant comes over and has a look at the credentials. He is satisfied and hands it back.

'You can come through. But you won't be able to enter the Plaza de Mayo, there's a cordon.'

Ariel returns to the car and they travel along Avenida Paseo Colón. As they approach the main square, the military hardware and personnel increase and the driver becomes agitated.

'Shit – this looks really bad. We're going to have to stop.'

'Take me as far as you can. I gave you a hundred bucks, remember.'

'It's no use to me if I get arrested!'

'Don't worry, no one's going to arrest you ...' because you are far more likely to be shot, Ariel mutters under his breath.

They continue to Calle Moreno where the taxi is flagged

down again. This time there are tanks as well as half-tracks and armoured cars. A row of empty lorries block a boulevard. Their occupants have formed a line, three-men deep, along Avenida de la Rábida, which surrounds the central plaza. Their faces are blackened with camouflage paint and bayonets glint in the moonlight.

Ariel leaves the car once more and approaches the nearest group of soldiers. Outwardly he appears calm but his heart is in his throat as he shows them his press card.

'Can I speak with your commanding officer?'

A soldier fetches a captain who is accompanied by his platoon sergeant. Ariel introduces himself and asks if he can interview the officer who agrees. He brings out his notebook and as the captain talks he writes. All is going well until Ariel starts to probe the junta's motive for the uprising.

'The country's screwed. Everyone is on the take. We need martial law.'

'But you've broken the military covenant.'

'No, we haven't.'

'You took an oath to protect the constitution.'

'We are the constitution.'

'Which election did you just win?'

The man pats his holster. 'This one.'

'Really? Some would say you're guilty of high treason …'

There is a blow and a blinding flash, as if a lightning bolt has struck Ariel in the face. He staggers, dropping his pen and pad as he puts a hand to his eye.

'No one speaks to the captain like that!' says the sergeant brandishing his pistol.

The officer picks up the notebook and biro and hands them back with a smile.

'I make the jokes around here. Your problem is, you ask too many questions,' and he sends the journalist on his way.

Ariel departs to the mocking sound of laughter. He walks towards the thoroughfare on San Martín, nursing his injured face. His head throbs and his ears are ringing. He pauses now and again to rest until his mind clears, although his head still hurts.

When he arrives at La Nación Ariel cleans up in the bathroom. He rinses the blood from the porcelain and checks himself in the mirror. His eye is swollen and sealed shut but the bleeding has stopped. His jacket and shirt are spattered with gore and he dabs the worst of it away. He tugs at the towel dispenser, dries his hands and climbs the stairs to the newsroom. Most of the staff are already there.

'*Compadre*, what the hell happened?' asks a colleague.

'A carabinero blew me a kiss.'

'Did you get his number?'

'No, he was too shy.'

Ariel sits at his desk and types up his report. His eye is painful and his head throbs but at least he has quotes. He will use the captain's final comment as the payoff in his article. It alone is worth the beating. As he pounds away at the keys, he senses someone at his shoulder.

'You okay?' asks Ovalle.

'Almost done. Ten more minutes.'

'I meant you, not the story. Your face is a mess. Go home. Leave your notes and I'll finish it for you.'

'I'm fine. But thanks for the offer.'

'If you say so.' The editor walks away then pauses. 'You do realise it's going to get much worse?'

'My face or the regime?'

Ovalle shakes his head and goes back to his office.

On Wednesday General Jorge Videla is sworn in as the new president at a ceremony in the Casa Rosada. The archbishop of Buenos Aires Cardinal Antonio Caggiano is there to give the occasion spurious legitimacy. No one is surprised since he is a former head of the Military Ordinariate and deeply involved with Odessa. The junta have decided each leader of the three services will rotate the office but, as the most senior, Videla will be first. It is a clever ploy by the army chief since he has no intention of relinquishing the presidency.

The press have been invited to record the ceremony. Among them is Ariel, wearing a patch over his injured eye. With his other eye he surveys the generals, their uniforms adorned with lanyard and gold braid, none of whom has ever fired a shot in anger, and wonders what sort of person would choose such an occupation. Men who possess not a shred of honour. Men who are prepared to kidnap, rape and torture. Men who would do anything to achieve power. They are not soldiers but thugs and cowards who sold their souls long ago. They are Latin America's own homegrown fascists. Adolf Hitler would have been proud. And he realises that Mario is right. Everything is about to get a whole lot worse.

BUENOS AIRES–MISIONES–BUENOS AIRES

Saturday 21–Monday 23 August 1976

Tiago Hecht gazes across the chlorinated blue of his swimming pool at the manicured gardens beyond. The grass glimmers amid the spray of water sprinklers and an iridescent mist drifts across the lawn. An Indian in a straw hat hoes a herbaceous border while another scoops insects from the pool with a net. Hecht wears a white towelling robe and is drying off after his early morning dip. He sits at a table on the sunlit terrace drinking coffee, the remains of his breakfast before him. Next to it is a packet of Kent and the Saturday edition of La Nación with its front page displayed. The headline declares in bold: The Wolf's Lair! Hitler's Secret Jungle Hideout. There is a photograph of the compound and another of the mess hall's interior with its portrait of the *Führer* and faded swastika drapes. Below is a picture of a priest. The caption reads: Fr Javier Ibarra. Misiones Survivor's Shocking Confession. There are five further pages about the story and several more photographs. The exclusive is by the newspaper's leading reporter.

Hecht hears a voice behind him.

'Sir, a call for you. It's your nephew.' The butler holds a silver salver. On it is a cordless phone which his employer takes.

'Hello ...'

'*Tio,* it's me, Hermann.'

'Dear boy. How are you?'

'Not so good. Have you seen today's La Nación?'

'I know. Tiresome. I thought the place had been destroyed – apparently not. But I'm surprised someone actually found it.'

'That's why I'm calling.'

'What do you mean?'

'The journalist who wrote the article stayed with us. I gave him horses for the trip and provided the guide.'

'You did what?' Hecht leaps to his feet, knocking over the table and sending the coffee pot and crockery crashing onto the terrace. 'You imbecile! What on earth did you do that for?'

The voice on the other end quakes with fear. Tiago Hecht may be Mattei's uncle but he is not a man to be trifled with. Not only is he head of the clan, he is also a billionaire and one of Argentina's most powerful men. Since Juan Peron's death, perhaps the most powerful. Among his many accolades, he is rumoured to have cuckolded the former president and been Evita's lover. He had also traced Che Guevara to his mountain hideout in Bolivia and was involved in the ambush where the revolutionary met his death. Hitler had been right when he thought that his protégé would one day become a leader of men. Governments have risen and fallen on Hecht's word alone. The junta seek his advice on everything, from economics to foreign affairs. He is president of the country in all but name.

Hecht stands and shakes with anger as he yells down the phone. He is so angry that he swears in his mother tongue.

'*Dumbkopf*! *Arschloch*! *Flachwichser*! You are an imbecile! A complete and utter imbecile! *Schwanzlutscher*! How can you not know who Ariel Guzman is?'

'He gave a false name and said he was doing a piece about the Guaraní for National Geographic.'

'*Gottverdamich*! And you believed him? Why didn't you tell me?'

'*Tio,* I'm sorry. I'm so sorry. I didn't know. I'll do anything I can to help.'

Mattei sounds as if he is close to tears. Hecht strides up and down the terrace shouting into the receiver. His voice carries across the garden to the man weeding the flowerbeds. He walks back to his chair, lights a cigarette and draws in a lungful of smoke before exhaling. Cursing, he rubs his brow, the cigarette between his fingers.

'Okay. There's nothing we can do about the story. It's out there. What you must do is erase all traces of the camp. Everything. And you must do it as soon as possible. I want all witnesses dealt with as well. Do you understand?'

'Yes, *Tio.* Anything you say.'

'And one more thing, bring me the priest.'

Hecht terminates the conversation and motions at his butler to take the phone away. He has another drag of his cigarette and looks at the view. The pool boy and the gardener carry on working as if nothing has happened and, apart from the broken crockery that litters the terrace and the overturned table, there is no evidence of the angry scene. Hecht sits and smokes. The secret of the Wolf's Lair has at last been revealed. But with it comes a solution to a problem they have been trying to resolve for years. And that is the whereabouts of Edelweiss: the future of the Fourth Reich. Ever since his disappearance, all leads have gone cold. Now they have one. A priest no less.

Hermann Mattei realised his uncle would be angry but he had calmed down in the end. He also knows it was not entirely his fault. The journalist could easily have asked someone else and got another guide. But he has been given his orders and must carry them out. It is his duty and the only way he can make amends.

He gets to his feet and tells one of the houseboys to find the guide as a matter of urgency. The youth rushes off and within a few minutes returns with the Indian. The man enters Mattei's study with his eyes downcast and holding a *campero*. He has seen the newspaper and knows he is in trouble. He does not yet realise how much.

'You wanted to see me, boss?'

'Did you know the man you took to the jungle works for La Nación?'

'I do now boss. But I didn't at the time.'

'Why did you volunteer to be his guide?'

'Father Javier told me to, boss.'

Mattei clenches his fists when he hears the priest's name, his knuckles turning white.

'What exactly did he say?'

'He said I was to take this person to his village, the one that burnt down, and ... to the camp in the jungle.'

'Why didn't you mention it?'

'Father Javier told me to say nothing. He made me swear on the holy cross. He's a priest, boss. If a priest asks you to do that, that's what you do.'

'How did you know about the camp?'

'All us Guaraní know, boss. But our elders have said we must never talk about it. The place is full of demons. It spooks us, so we avoid it.'

'Show me where it is,' and Mattei points to a large map spread across his desk.

In a faltering voice, the Indian describes its location and indicates a place not far from the Iguaçu Falls. He adds that it is about a day's ride from the abandoned village. His employer nods. He folds the map and puts it in his pocket.

'I have to leave now. I want you to go to the stables and rub my horse down. Make sure you do a good job of it.'

'Yes, boss. Sorry, boss.'

Mattei does not reply. The Indian follows him into the yard. The morning sun is hot and he puts on his hat and makes his way across the quadrangle to the stables. He walks through the main arch. It is dark and eerily quiet inside. Usually you can hear horses munching hay or moving around in their stalls. But there is only silence. The guide approaches the far end of the block where Mattei keeps his mount. The light is granular and the place full of shadows. There is a fusty smell of wood shavings and manure. Above each door a name is painted in gold script. One of them, Athos, is Mattei's horse. The gelding is a criollo, a native breed descended from the wild horses of the Pampas which have remarkable stamina. Every gaucho wants one.

The guide opens the stable door and closes it. He reaches for the light switch and turns it on. But nothing happens and he assumes the bulb is broken. It does not matter. His eyes will soon adjust to the darkness. He calls out the horse's name and clicks his tongue. There is no response. Not even a snort or a stamp. Instead, there is a low menacing growl followed by another then a third. The Indian turns and tries to open the door and realises it is locked from the outside. He grabs the handle, bangs on the wooden panels and shouts. It is pointless. No one can hear him. And no one hears his terrified screams, mingled with the furious barks and snarls of the hounds as they rip him limb from limb and grind his bones in their powerful jaws. At last there is no more screaming. The only sound is the dogs' rough panting as they stand grinning over the Indian's torn body and lick blood from their chops.

Mattei flicks the reins of his horse and calls on his companions to ride out. He takes the lead followed by his younger brothers and their male cousins. The group makes the same journey as the unfortunate guide had with Ariel only a few days before. At noon they pass the ruins of San

Ignacio Miní but do not stop and venture deeper into the jungle. Nor do they pause at the charred remains of the village church as they journey on towards the camp. After another day's riding they reach the Wolf's Lair and set about gathering fuel for its destruction.

It takes them the rest of the afternoon to assemble enough dry wood and stack it against the huts in the compound and along the palisade. When they have finished Mattei dips their torches in kerosene and lights them. They move from building to building and set fire to the place. In a short while the entire compound is ablaze and flames ignite the trees, scattering parakeets and monkeys. This time there are no tropical storms to dampen the fires and the camp burns fiercely. The conflagration consumes everything and by sunset the whole place has been reduced to a smouldering heap of ashes. The posse mount their horses once more and return home knowing that, before long, the jungle will complete their work and there will be no evidence the Wolf's Lair ever existed.

In a private room at a gentlemen's club in Buenos Aires' business district, a group of middle-aged men are gathered. They are dressed in blazers and silk ties and wear expensive watches that match their swimming-pool tans. The men are unremarkable and indistinguishable from the other club members except they are speaking German. The oak-panelled room is filled with cigar smoke and tales told by old comrades who have not seen each other for some time.

The ruling committee have come from far and wide. Walter Rauff now lives in Chile and has established a Nazi community, Colonia Dignidad, just a few hours south of Santiago. It has a cult status and its residents follow his orders without question. The country's military leader, General Augusto Pinochet, has used Rauff's knowledge of incarceration and torture to terrorise dissidents of his own regime, some of whom have been taken to the colony. When every ounce of information has been extracted, a process that can take weeks and sometimes months, the victims are murdered and their bodies butchered and fed to the farm pigs.

Erich Priebke is a frequent visitor to the colony. He resides across the border in Bariloche, a resort town in the Andes with a large German population. Rauff's former partner in crime lives modestly but has all the material comforts that he needs. His passion is fly-fishing and he can often be seen casting for trout in the clear waters of the lakes and rivers. Afterwards he would make a fire and grill his catch on a bank, accompanying his meal with a local Chardonnay kept chilled in a pool.

Apart from the committee's president, the most senior member of the group is Martin Bormann. He lives the furthest away, in the Paraguayan capital, Asunción. Among the various officials he has bribed is the chief of police. With this immunity, Bormann is able to indulge his favourite pastime of rape, abusing boys as well as girls, often underage. Such is his appetite and sexual deviancy that he is regularly treated for syphilis.

'All right, gentlemen,' says the president, tapping a gavel on the table. 'Time to get down to business. As you know, the secret of the Wolf's Lair is out. I suppose it had to happen sometime but we can no longer pretend the place never existed. It is inevitable that people will start asking questions and come looking for us. Before they do, we have to act. Those who were involved and are not part of the committee must be dealt with. Is that understood?'

The men seated at the table murmur assent.

'I have their names and addresses,' and the president hands a sheaf of papers to a minion who passes a copy to each person. 'Let's start with the man at the top. He's the most important. If he talks, our cover will certainly be blown. Who wants to take care of him?'

Bormann speaks up.

'I'll do it.'

The president looks at Hitler's former aide. Always the first man to volunteer and get his hands dirty.

'Fine. He actually lives in Buenos Aires. So it should be straightforward,' and Tiago Hecht crosses the name off the list.

BUENOS AIRES–POSADAS

Sunday 22 August–Wednesday 1 September 1976

Ariel is listening to the radio in his kitchen as he prepares breakfast. The news about the Wolf's Lair continues to dominate the airwaves. He spent the previous day touring television studios and talking about the trip to Misiones and his remarkable discovery. Everyone is amazed Adolf Hitler escaped the bunker and ended up in Argentina. The imp is out of the bottle and can never be returned. But already the news is history to the journalist. He knows Eva Braun is dead and he is certain Hitler is as well. All that remains of the *Führer*'s entourage are a few diehards hidden away in the continent's forgotten outposts. It is for the Nazi hunters to seek them out and deliver them up to justice. What interests him is the person called Edelweiss. Who are they and, more importantly, where are they? Only the priest knows and he refused to talk. At least, that was, until his death.

Ariel watches his omelette cook in the frying pan and hears the phone ring. He turns off the gas to answer it and hears a woman's voice.

'Hi, it's Carmen. We met on the plane to Posadas. Sorry for calling out of the blue. I just wanted to congratulate you.'

Carmen, the pretty flight attendant. He had forgotten about her.

'Hang on – how did you get my home number?'

A gentle laugh comes from the other end.

'I called the newsdesk.'

'They're not meant to give out personal numbers.'

'I know but I told them I'd missed my period and I really had to speak to you.'

'That's a good one. Pity I can't use it. Anyway, how are you?'

'I'm fine, thanks. Look, I know this might sound forward but do you fancy meeting up?'

'You're right, it does sound forward and, yes, I do. When?'

'How about tomorrow?'

'Tomorrow's okay. Do you like tango?'

'I love tango!'

'Great. Let's meet at the Confitería Ideal.'

'That's easy. I live in San Nicolás.'

'See you there at nine. We'll grab a bite to eat and dance the night away.'

'Dinner's on me.'

'Look forward to it ...'

Ariel replaces the receiver and flips his omelette before putting it on a plate. At the table he adds a twist of pepper from the grinder, chopped parsley and starts to eat. I missed my period. That was priceless. The woman certainly had balls.

The following day Ariel goes to work. When he arrives at La Nación, the porter steps out from behind a desk and congratulates him. So does the receptionist. Even the cleaner puts his mop aside to shake his hand. Everyone wants to share in his success. Ariel chats for a while then heads to the newsroom. As soon as he appears his colleagues quit their desks and slap him on the back and call him all sorts of names, not one of which could be printed in their paper.

Ovalle hears the commotion. He looks up and sees his friend being mobbed. The editor leaves his office. Amid cheers and whoops he raises his hands and hushes the gathering.

'Okay, okay, everyone. I just want to say a few words – thanks ...'

There are further cheers and, finally, the place falls silent.

'I've never known an edition sell out within an hour of hitting the newsstands. Our presses ran constantly to keep up with the demand. I'm surprised they didn't break down. This has got to be the biggest story since we landed on the moon. Actually, I think it's even bigger because no one could imagine something as incredible as this. Adolf Hitler escaped from the bunker and ended up here. The implications are vast. How did he get to Argentina and who helped him? And how many Nazis who were with him are still alive? I'm sure we'll find out in the next few days and weeks. Meanwhile, La Nación has doubled its circulation and we've sold the rights many times over. And it's all because of one man. Our good friend, Ariel ...'

The room erupts in applause and the journalist modestly accepts his friends' accolades and further backslaps. Voices call out for him to speak and the gathering quietens again.

'As you know, it was a team effort. It wouldn't have happened if I hadn't been given the green light by Mario, nor would it have been possible without the help of everyone here: the picture desk, editorial and the subs, not forgetting the printers who worked themselves to the bone so that the paper's later editions would make the streets. This, as always, was a collective effort. Thanks everyone ...'

There are more cheers followed by the sound of corks popping as bottles of sparkling wine appear and glasses are filled. Toasts are drunk to a free press, democracy and absent friends. The drinks are soon finished and, when the phones start to ring again, they go back to work.

Later, Ariel returns home to get ready for the evening. He has a shower and afterwards shaves with an electric razor. He switches off the appliance and feels his chin. Satisfied, he splashes on his best cologne, looks in the mirror and makes a movie-star face. He then puts on flared denims, a dress shirt and a velveteen smoking jacket. Ariel brings out the Cuban-heeled boots he bought in Havana and gives them a shine. He slips them on and leaves the apartment. In the lobby he checks his pigeonhole for post but there is none. At the taxi rank, he orders a driver to take him to the Confitería Ideal.

'Nice evening for it,' the man says as they set off for the venue. 'You on a date?'

'I am.'

'She must be hot.'

'How can you tell?'

'You're grinning like an idiot.'

'You're damned right.'

Ariel is still smiling when he arrives at the hotel. He is always early for any assignation, a habit he has never been able break. Besides, he is looking forward to meeting Carmen and it is a courtesy to be there first. He is a regular at the Confitería Ideal and not just to dance. He enjoys the old-world atmosphere and watching tangoists move across the floor. It was where Carlos Gardel and Mona Maris performed. The French-born maestro was the illegitimate son of a laundress and lived in poverty as a child. But he took the tango away from the immigrant dives and brothels and brought it into the golden light of cosmopolitan Buenos Aires. Yet he never forgot his roots or his underworld connections. It was rumoured he had a bullet lodged in a lung. He danced sublimely and sang like a bird, and was affectionately known as El Zorzal after the native song thrush. Gardel was killed at the height of his fame in a plane crash in 1935 but his spirit lived on in the dancehalls and bars of his beloved city.

The house band is playing jazz and Ariel orders a margarita at the bar.

'How do you like it?

'Straight up with salt on the rim. Make sure it's cold.'

The barman mixes the cocktail and Ariel observes the clientele as they parade around the ballroom. Some do a version of the tango but most waltz. The real dancing will come later. The place is illuminated by the wash of globe lights and has a high ceiling with gilded borders supported by Ionic columns. In the centre is a large atrium. The musicians are good, especially the trumpeter, a black man who jives and puffs out his cheeks as he plays. At the end of each song the audience clap and the air is filled with laughter and applause and the smoke of a hundred cigarettes.

The barman unscrews the shaker and pours the cocktail into a conical glass lined with sea salt and places it on the counter.

'Your margarita, sir. Would you like to run a tab?'

'Okay.'

Ariel raises the glass and has a taste. The cocktail is zesty and perfectly chilled. He takes another sip and picks an olive from a bowl. He places an elbow on the zinc counter and sees a woman in a figure-hugging dress approach. Carmen's dark hair flows freely and her mouth is wreathed in red lipstick.

'Right on time.' He kisses her cheek. 'What would you like to drink?'

'What's yours?'

'A margarita.'

'I'll have one, too.'

'Another,' Ariel tells the barman. 'And make sure it's as good as the first.'

Carmen seems even prettier than when they first met. Perhaps it is because she is relaxed and does not have to fake a smile. Her sloe-black eyes are almond-shaped and she has prominent cheekbones. Ariel wonders if she has Indian ancestry and realises that like most Argentineans she is probably a mix of Native American and Latin. Whatever her antecedents, she is beautiful.

Carmen chats about her work but not too much, and

Ariel does about his, again, not too much. They are content to be in each other's company and sip their cocktails while people come and go on the dance floor. Carmen is wearing a gold chain.

'That's a pretty necklace.'

'My parents gave it to me for my twenty-first.'

She holds it out and a six-pointed star glimmers.

'You're Jewish.'

'I am.'

'Likewise.'

'Really? I didn't know.'

'You mean, because I've a name like Guzman?' Ariel says and she nods. 'My father changed it. Guess he wanted to leave his past behind.'

'Many people have. My name's Borges, formerly Bergdorff.'

'Carmen's not that Jewish either.'

She laughs and sweeps back her hair.

'You're right! My parents are opera buffs. They adore Bizet. How about you?'

'Shakespeare.'

'Of course – *The Tempest*. One of my favourite plays.'

'My father's, too. He liked to think of himself as Prospero – you know, exiled aristocrat washed up in a strange new country with nothing left of his former life but a child and his magic.'

'My library was dukedom large enough ...'

'It certainly was for my dad. All he ever did was read – and write.'

'He sounds civilised. What did he write?'

'Apart from endless papers on literary criticism, he wrote poetry. He wrote a lot.'

'Did he publish anything?'

'I don't think so.'

'Why not?'

'He didn't care to. It was personal. He was working things out for himself in the same way some artists paint whatever's in front of them. Often it's the same thing, again and again.'

'Like Monet and his water lilies or Cézanne and his mountain.'

'You're cultured.'

'For an air hostess?'

'For anybody.'

'I studied modern languages at university. I work for an airline because I love travel. Also, I hate sitting behind a desk.'

'Sure. I'd rather be pounding the streets.'

'And knocking on doors?'

'If you don't knock, no one's going to open it.'

'Sorry, only joking.'

'You don't have to apologise. I've gone through people's rubbish bins.'

'Ugh!'

'I agree. It's rarely worth it, unless you're an alley cat.'

Carmen flashes a smile and they finish their drinks.

'Fancy another?'

'I do. I'd also love something to eat.'

'Let's get a table before they all go.'

Ariel orders more margaritas and they head to one of the last remaining tables. A waiter follows with the cocktails. After placing the glasses he asks for their order.

'What do you want? I usually have the steak.'

'Fine by me.'

'How would you like it done, madam?'

'Medium rare.'

'The same.'

The man departs and they drink their margaritas and talk. Their conversation ceases when the sirloin arrives, sizzling on a cast-iron skillet. The steak is plump and juicy, accompanied by a bowl of fries and a watercress salad. A bottle of mineral water is produced and they begin their meal with relish. When the cocktails and food are gone, the waiter returns to clear the table. Ariel pours them each a glass of water and they chat some more.

The band ceases playing and the musicians take a break before the main event. The hubbub increases and the floor starts to fill as people leave the tables and prepare to tango.

'Shall we dance?' says Carmen.

'It's why we're here,' and Ariel leads her onto the floor.

They find a space among the crowd. He places a hand on his partner's waist and she puts hers on his shoulder. When the band strikes up they move around the room, hips and thighs touching in time with the music. At the end of each song, Carmen arches her back and wraps a leg sinuously around his. Ariel is good but his partner is better. She knows precisely when to twist and turn and how to draw the best from him as they snake up and down the floor. The music ends with a flourish and the dancing stops. Carmen lies supine in Ariel's arms, her face beaming, her neck pulsating like a bird's, the barest sheen on her skin. And in her eyes, that unmistakable look.

They carry on into the early hours and are among the last to leave. Wandering out into the night air, they pass beneath a streetlight. Ariel draws his date close and kisses her. They embrace for some time before they break apart.

'Want to come back to my place?'

Carmen hesitates.

'Next time. I promise.'

'You've got my number.'

'And you've got mine. Call me.'

They kiss goodbye and Ariel signals a passing taxi. The vehicle flashes its lights and stops at the kerb and Carmen gets in. He watches the vehicle go down the road until it vanishes around a corner. It is the hour before dawn and the sky is dark and still as a pond. Ariel decides to walk home and as he wanders through the empty streets, he sings to himself. The night is tender and so is his heart.

José is the proudest man in Posadas. He has been telling his friends at the hotel taxi rank that he was Ariel Guzman's driver. He had met him at the airport and was pleased when the journalist said he might be needed again. The driver suspected he was onto something when they went up to San Ignacio Miní and, just before he left, the journalist had told him to get the Saturday edition of La Nación. Sure enough, the next day there was the story splashed across the front and over the following pages.

'Look, here it is,' he says, producing a well-thumbed copy of the newspaper. 'See for yourselves.'

José tells his fellow drivers how they went to the estancia and these mad dogs had attacked his car and tried to kill them.

'*Loco*, I tell you! I was terrified. We both were.'

It is a good yarn and during the next few days his mates ask him to repeat it several times.

The following week the newspapers are filled with other stories but José keeps his copy of La Nación and even takes it with him on his journeys. Early one morning he gets into his Chevrolet for another day's work. He turns the key in the ignition but the engine refuses to start. There is just a low hiss. José places one foot on the clutch and pumps the accelerator with the other. He turns the key again and realises something is wrong. It is too late. Before he can open the door there is a brilliant light and the car explodes in a ball of flame. The heat is so intense nobody can get near the Chevrolet and its driver burns to death. When the fire brigade arrive they hose down the vehicle and, finally, extricate his body. It is so badly carbonised José can only be identified from his dental records, which includes his gold-capped tooth.

BUENOS AIRES–POSADAS

Friday 24 September 1976

Although the revelation about the Wolf's Lair has been overtaken by more recent events, the tremors continue to be felt like the aftershocks of an earthquake. One man in particular has been affected by the news. Oberleutnant zur See Hans Schiller lives on Calle Juncal, near the capital's botanical gardens, which he often visited. In winter he would sit in the glasshouses and admire the tree ferns and other exotics that flourished there. After the sea, horticulture is the commander's abiding love and his house has a neatly tended garden filled with roses. He spends his days with a pair of secateurs, pruning here and snipping there, among the shark-infested stems. The roses give him joy in an otherwise prosaic and solitary existence. His neighbours know only that he is German and had been a submarine commander in the war. They do not know about *U-977* and its voyage across the oceans or who was on board. And this is just the way Schiller likes it.

Since the revelation, the commander has been buffeted like a stricken vessel between the jagged rocks of agony and despair. He had always thought he was an honourable man.

Someone who did his duty. He considered himself a loyal German who obeyed orders. To have served the fatherland in the war was the right thing to have done. Or so he had thought. Now he is less than sure. In recent years he has questioned the validity of the cause and feels that it was wrong. The Nuremberg trials had proved that. Many former Nazis condemned the verdicts as victors' justice. Schiller did not. The defendants got what they deserved.

He also knows that Hitler's escape is ultimately his fault. No one else could have piloted the submarine under such conditions and survived without a mutiny. Yet the commander's torment goes deeper, even, than this. What the crew of *U-977* never knew and he had kept hidden throughout the war, is that he has Jewish blood. His father's mother was a Liebermann, making him, in the eyes of the Nazi regime, a *mischling*. In itself, that would not have stopped him serving in the *kriegsmarine* or following the *Führer*. In those early days he had been a dedicated Nazi and turned a blind eye to pogroms such as Kristallnacht because he had never considered himself Jewish. To him, they were an alien race. But the discovery of Auschwitz and the other concentration camps had changed everything.

'It is a crime against God,' he had told himself. Schiller rationalises that, since he had never been involved in the Holocaust, he could not be held responsible for it. And yet he knows in his heart that he is. To be silent is to be complicit. It is time to clear his conscience. To tell the truth. He turns that day's edition of La Nación over and sees the newspaper's address and contact number on the back. He will speak to the journalist and tell him the story of how Hitler fled to Argentina aboard *U-977* and that he was the commander of the submarine. It is the right thing to do.

As his hand reaches for the phone on his desk he hears the doorbell ring. How unusual. He almost never has visitors. Perhaps it is a delivery. He has ordered bedding plants recently. Schiller rises and goes into the hall. On the other side of the glass panel he can see a vague outline. He flicks the bolt and opens the door but keeps the chain attached.

'You ... ?' he says.

'Yes,' answers the visitor. 'Me.'

'What do you want?'

'Let me inside and I'll tell you.'

'Very well,' says the commander, releasing the chain.

And Martin Bormann enters the house.

All is quiet at the mission in Posadas. The children and most of the community have left with the superior for their annual camp. Javier is one of the few who remain. He approaches the superior's office and, taking out a bunch of keys, lets himself in. At the safe in the wall he turns the dial. As the mission's accountant, Javier has the combination. Only he and the superior know it. Normally others would know too, but there is something in the safe that is so precious, it is beyond material value. It is not the Spanish gold and silver ducats or other treasures which lie within, including a fragment of the True Cross. It is a key kept in a plain brown envelope. A key that will reveal the world's greatest secret.

Javier removes the envelope and locks the dial and the office. In his room he sits at his desk, takes out a sheaf of paper and composes a letter. When he has finished he places the key with the letter in an envelope and seals it. He writes a name and an address and affixes stamps. Javier tucks the envelope in a pocket and dons his biretta. He leaves the building. In the street he stands for a moment and looks around. Everything is the same: the shop fronts, the road signs, the traffic passing by. Yet everything is different. His heart aches like an open wound. He knows he must be brave but the burden of his cross seems overwhelming.

'Dear Lord,' he says as he walks along the avenue to Plaza 9 de Julio. 'If this cup can pass me by ...'

BUENOS AIRES

Saturday 25–Sunday 26 September 1976

An armed guard checks the guest's invitation and the electronic gate opens. A Cyclopean security camera watches as the taxi passes a paramilitary with a machine gun and drives up a steep incline to a mansion. The house is modern with plate-glass windows that overlook a sweep of lawn and the sprawl of the city beyond. Palms and agaves stand in spiny groves and beetle-leaved camellias gleam in the sunshine. Barely a leaf or twig disturbs the sward of newly mown grass. The vehicle comes to a halt and a servant opens the door.

'Good afternoon, sir. Please make your way to the reception.'

Ariel walks past the mansion and, glancing through the windows, sees the sort of art more often found in a gallery or a museum. There are enough old masters, impressionists and modern abstracts to make a curator choke. He goes through a stone archway and enters a walled garden where a band is playing beneath a marquee. A waiter offers him a choice of Champagne or a fruit cocktail. He chooses the former, which is the colour of burnished gold. Ariel raises the glass and has a drink. The wine is certainly imported and possibly vintage. He takes another sip and looks at the rich and influential of Buenos Aires gathered on the lawn and cannot understand why he is there. But the invitation to Tiago Hecht's summer party had arrived at the office and he was not one to turn it down.

President Videla is standing by the swimming pool, resplendent in uniform and medals, with a beautiful woman who is not his wife hanging on his arm. He is laughing and joking with the American ambassador, Robert Hill. The journalist thought they were meant to loathe each other but apparently not. Laughing with them is Hecht. He notices the new arrival and raises an arm in salute. Ariel is surprised. Does the man actually know what he looks like or is he just playing the host? He soon has his answer as the billionaire leaves the president and diplomat to their japes and comes towards him.

'Ariel Guzman! At last we meet.'

Hecht puts out a hand and Ariel notices the softness of his skin. It is smooth and supple like a masseur's and the nails are manicured. Although in his mid-fifties, the host is leading-man handsome. His iron-grey hair is oiled and his face barely lined. He looks as though he eats carefully and exercises often. There is no excess fat or slackness anywhere. His physique is impressive as are his dark, intelligent eyes. He might nod and smile at his interlocutor but the eyes always questioned and scrutinised. Above all, they search for weakness.

'Thanks. I don't often get these sort of invitations.'

'You don't?' Hecht affects mock horror. 'Well, you should because the country needs people like you. Individuals. Those who don't follow the herd. There are too many yes-men – and women,' he adds as an afterthought.

Ariel sees the other guests by the swimming-pool, who are all laughing and saying 'yes' to just about everything. Whatever it is, it seems to be hilarious.

Hecht produces a packet of Kent and takes one before offering it to his guest.

'No thanks, I don't smoke.'

'Quite right. Filthy habit but I can't seem to get rid of it,' he says and lights up. He takes a drag and wafts the match back and forth then flicks it onto the path. 'Congratulations on your scoop, by the way. Some story.'

'I was lucky. It was just a hunch.'

Hecht draws deeply on his cigarette.

'So often the case. A man needs to trust his instinct, don't you think?'

'Works for me.'

'Indeed. Tell me, how did you know about Father Javier?'

'I knew of him but didn't know him as such.'

'I see. Strange, don't you think, that he decided to talk now, having kept his silence all these years. I wonder why that was?'

Hecht peers into Ariel's eyes and looks deep into the waters of his soul, searching for truths and elisions even he is unaware of.

'I don't know. I guess you'll have to ask him.'

The older man throws back his head and guffaws.

'Wonderful! Wonderful! Yes, I shall certainly have to do that,' he says, clasping his guest by the arm. 'Now, let me introduce you to some of my friends,' and he leads Ariel to the pool.

A tall, attractive woman with ash-blonde hair is surrounded by male admirers, most sporting crewcuts. She is dressed in an ivory silk jacket and matching skirt which hugs her fulsome behind.

'Linda, I want you to meet Ariel Guzman, our country's finest journalist.'

The blonde bares perfect teeth. She knows they are perfect, which is why she keeps smiling her smile.

'Pleased to meet you. Linda Hollis – US Embassy.'

'Which section?'

There is a beat before she speaks.

'Political.'

Ariel knows that Political means the CIA. Just as Legal Affairs is the FBI.

'Really? I thought you were with the press office.'

'I do that as well.'

'A lady of many talents,' and Hecht slips a proprietary arm around her waist. Ariel assumes they must be lovers or, if not yet, they soon will be.

'Sounds like a lot of work.'

'Certainly is. But I always have time for friends,' and she gives their host a squeeze.

'I'll let you both get on with it. You'll have plenty to talk about. Linda's a fine woman. And useful, too.'

Hecht pats her backside and goes off to chat with other

guests. They have been speaking in English and Hollis switches to Spanish.

'What do you think of your new president?' she asks, without the trace of an accent.

'I've got no opinion.'

'Of course you do. Another Latin American strongman?'

'Your Spanish is good.'

'My mother's Colombian and my father was a diplomat who specialised in Latin America.'

'Where was he posted?'

'Pretty much all over the place. He liked Argentina best.'

'Why?'

'Look around ... And, by the way, your English is good, too.'

'Mom was a New Yorker – that's how she met my dad. He lectured at Syracuse where she was studying. They fell in love and he took her back to Buenos Aires.'

'So you're a Yank as well.'

'Part of me is, I guess.'

'Which part?'

'It's not visible right now.'

Hollis laughs flirtatiously and sucks at the straw in her drink.

'Are your folks still around?'

'Sadly, not. Mom passed away some time ago. My father last year.'

'I'm sorry to hear that.'

'It happens. How about yours?'

'They're both fine. They live in California.'

'Whereabouts?'

'La Jolla, near San Diego.'

'That's where Raymond Chandler lived.'

'Really? I didn't know.'

'I'm a Chandler fan.'

'*The Long Goodbye* and all that. You know, you remind me a little of Marlowe.'

'In what way?'

'You're laconic.'

'And you're trouble.'

The American looks coy.

'You should visit someday.'

'Maybe I will.'

'I'd be happy to show you the sights.'

'I look forward to seeing them.'

They drink their drinks as they size each other up and consider the usual questions people of the opposite sex have when they meet for the first time.

'By the way, you didn't answer my question.'

'I'm sorry, what was it?'

'As if you can't remember. What do you think of Videla?'

'He's certainly another strongman.'

'Do you approve?'

'Do you?'

'He's been a good ally of the administration.'

'So I understand. I guess he's what your people would call an asset.'

'That doesn't mean you like him.'

'I don't get paid to have opinions.'

'Oh, but I thought you did.'

Ariel demurs. 'Not really. I look under stones and shine a torch.'

'Wouldn't you rather write about something else, something nice, like this?' Hollis gestures at the guests assembled in the sunny garden.

'Frankly, no.'

'Why not?'

'It would bore me to death.'

'So you crave excitement?'

'I certainly don't crave tedium.'

'Aren't you worried that one day you might turn over the wrong stone and find something that someone didn't want you to see?'

'I already have.'

'Doesn't it scare you?'

'Should it?'

'It would scare me.'

A waiter pauses to offer his tray. Ariel places his empty glass upon it and takes another.

'Would you like one?'

'No thanks. I never drink when I'm working.'

'This is work?'

'Government policy, I'm afraid.'

'Speaking of which – tell me about Ambassador Hill.'

'What do you want to know?'

'I thought he was keen on human rights.'

'He is. Why do you ask?'

Ariel observes the president and diplomat who continue

to laugh and chat by the pool.

'Only that your ambassador and the general appear to be having a fine old time.'

Hollis narrows her eyes and rattles the ice in her glass.

'The State Department supports human rights, everywhere, particularly in Latin America. But there are those who seek to deny others these same rights.'

'You mean Communists.'

'Name me one democratic nation that is Communist.'

'Name me one democratic nation that is not dominated by a wealthy elite.' Ariel smiles but his smile is not returned.

He hears a familiar voice call his name and is surprised to see Carmen walking towards them. She is wearing a tailored jacket with a navy-blue cocktail dress split at the thigh. Her hair is up and a straw hat is tilted rakishly.

'Hey, stranger, fancy seeing you here.' She gives him a kiss.

'The same. Have you met Linda Hollis? We were just expressing our love of freedom and democracy.'

'Yes,' they answer and both seem embarrassed.

'Oh, how come?'

'Social events, that sort of thing,' says Hollis.

'We must move in different circles.'

There is an awkward silence.

Carmen leans forward. 'Time to move on,' she whispers in the journalist's ear, then announces: 'If you don't mind, Linda, I'd like to introduce Ariel to some other friends.'

The American purses her lips.

'Sure. Enjoy the party,' and she walks away.

'What was that about?'

'Put her in a sack with a snake and I'd fear for the snake.'

'I know a lot of snakes who'd like to get in the sack with her.'

Carmen arches an eyebrow.

'Not me, naturally.'

'Naturally.'

'She works for the US Embassy.'

'Probably has chlamydia as well.'

Ariel laughs.

They stroll across the lawn and approach a group of tough-looking men in suits and shades who stand in a circle, chain-smoking. They are talking quietly in a guttural language, which the journalist recognises as Hebrew. Carmen introduces him and they switch to Spanish, although they have thick Israeli accents. They seem friendly enough and congratulate Ariel on his story. It is another sad chapter in the history of the world but, fortunately, one that is now closed.

'Thank God,' someone says.

Ariel asks them what they do and they grin and say, 'Business.'

'What sort of business?'

'Monkey business,' one of them answers and they chuckle.

The afternoon draws on and after further introductions and pleasantries they decide it is time to leave. A servant escorts the couple to the front gates where a line of taxis wait. The man ushers them into the leading car and it departs. As they travel to San Telmo Carmen rests her head on Ariel's shoulder as he strokes her hair. He can scarcely believe his luck. In a short while they are back at his apartment and the front door has barely closed before they tear off their clothes and tumble into bed.

The party is over and the last guests have gone. The band has left long ago. Waiters fold chairs and clear tables and place half-empty glasses on trays. The remains of the buffet are packed up and the freshly cut flowers, which were so carefully arranged that morning, are thrown away.

Tiago Hecht is relaxing in his study with a whisky and soda when he hears a car's wheels screech up the driveway. A door slams and is followed by the hall bell's chimes. He can hear someone padding along the passage. The sound is followed by a mumble of voices. He listens as footsteps approach and there is a knock on the door.

'Yes,' he says, and the butler enters.

'Señor Hecht, your nephew is here to see you.'

'Thank you, please show him in.'

The servant stands aside and Hermann Mattei comes striding into the room.

'We got him, *Tio* ...' he starts to say.

'You may go,' Hecht tells the butler and waits until he has closed the door. 'Can't you be a bit more discreet?'

'Sorry, *Tio*.'

'Fix yourself a drink.'

Mattei pours himself a dram of malt whisky from a row of decanters arranged on a rosewood cabinet. He adds ice cubes from a silver bucket and slumps in an armchair with his drink.

'Salud,' he says, raising his glass. 'It was easier than we thought. We picked him up in the central plaza. He didn't put up a fight or make so much as a squeak. It was almost as if he was expecting us.'

'Where is he now?'

'In the back of the car. Trussed up like a chicken.'

Javier hears voices but can see nothing since he is blindfolded. He realises he is naked and manacled to a metal bed frame. He feels groggy and wonders how long he has been there. He was abducted shortly after he had posted the letter. He remembers being chloroformed as he was bundled into the boot of a car, his mind a blank until now. The priest hears several men speaking German. He moves to a more comfortable position because the springs hurt his back and the frame creaks. The conversation ceases.

'Can you hear me, Father?' the voice is gentle, kind even.

'Yes.'

'Good, good. That is very good. Would you like a drink of water?'

'Yes, I would.'

A hand is placed under Javier's head and lifts it up and a glass is put to his lips. He swallows thirstily and gasps as the vessel is removed. His head is lowered again.

'Thank you.'

'I'm sorry we have to talk like this but I need information.'

'Yes.'

'You know what it's about?'

'I think so ...'

'Then, where is Edelweiss?'

'I have no idea.'

'But you know who Edelweiss is?'

'Yes, I do.'

'Where is he?'

'I'm sorry but I really don't know.'

Javier hears a muttered disappointment and something else in German that sounds like an order before the same voice resumes.

'Please, don't be like this. Tell us where we can find Edelweiss. We have no desire to keep you here. Wouldn't you prefer to be back at your mission?'

'Yes, I would. I would like that very much.'

'Tell us where Edelweiss is and we will let you go.'

'I promise you, I've no idea.'

'What name does he use?'

'I'm sorry, I can't tell you.'

'Why can't you tell me?'

'Because the Holy Father and the superior general of the Society have said no one must know.'

'I need to know. I have to know.'

The man on the bedframe tosses his head from side to side.

'I'm sorry but I can't say.'

'Can't or won't?'

'No ... I can't.'

'You must tell me. You have to tell me.'

Javier gives another shake of his head. There is more

talking in German and he can feel crocodile clips being placed on his fingers and toes.

'I don't want to hurt you. Truly, I don't. Tell me what name Edelweiss uses and I'll let you go.'

'No. I can't.'

'That is a pity. A great pity.'

Javier hears someone walking away followed by a hum as a generator is switched on.

'Two-hundred-and-forty volts is a lot. It can kill a man, and I don't want to do that. Just tell me what you know about Edelweiss.'

There is silence. The person standing by the generator is given a signal and pulls a lever. Javier's body tenses and begins to shake. He cries out in pain and his screams resound off the concrete walls. After a while the current is turned off and the victim becomes slack and starts to shiver uncontrollably as he chokes and struggles for air.

'What name does Edelweiss use?'

'His name ... His name ... I can't ...'

'You must! You must tell me his name!' The voice is insistent, almost angry.

'No ... No, I can't.'

There is a pause before the generator whines again. This time the voltage is increased and the bed starts to rattle. Javier arches his spine and a strangled cry comes from his throat. The shocks continue and he blacks out.

He regains consciousness as he is doused with a fire hose. The crocodile clips are removed from his fingers and toes and attached to his nipples and genitals. Javier moans as the teeth bite into his flesh and bruise the soft tissue.

'This can only get worse. And I won't stop until you tell me.'

'I know. I know that – and I forgive you.'

'I don't want your forgiveness. Save your forgiveness for believers. All I want is information about Edelweiss.'

Javier starts to pray and the words of the Hail Mary come tumbling out. He has not finished when the current surges again and the prayer dies in his throat. Electricity crackles like lightning through his veins and his blood simmers. The pain is intense and he can scarcely breathe. His whole body seems to be on fire. It feels as though he is being burnt at the stake.

'His name! Tell me his name!'

Javier hears the shouts but cannot talk even if he wanted to. At last the current is stopped and the agony recedes to a dull throbbing. His limbs ache and his testicles are numb.

'That was much worse, wasn't it?'

The priest tries to speak but no words come.

'I know you will talk eventually. No one can withstand this. No one.'

Javier moans and utters a single word.

'Yes,' the voice is encouraging. 'Edelweiss. Tell me about Edelweiss.'

He speaks, his voice a hoarse whisper.

'Edelweiss is beautiful, a beautiful white flower.'

The interrogator barks in anger and his victim shudders then thrashes violently as the generator hums once more.

'His name! I must have his name!'

The pain is no longer physical to Javier. It has become spiritual. The feeling of agony is almost exquisite. He knows he is close to death and that each step he takes along the way brings him nearer to his beloved Thomas More. The saint is standing with a bright host of angels, beckoning him.

'Come, my brother,' he says. 'Come to the Lord.'

There is shouting and other voices around him but they are not the voice of the English martyr.

'*Tio*, for God's sake stop! You'll kill him.'

'*Das ist mir egal*! *Es verdient zu sterben*! *Es verdient zu sterben*!' and Hecht demands the voltage is raised even higher.

The men surrounding the priest shout and curse and yet all Javier can hear is the sweet voice of Thomas, imploring him: 'Come my brother, come to the Lord.'

BUENOS AIRES

Monday 27 September 1976

A police car parks in the street and an officer gets out. It is a routine call but has to be investigated. He opens the wrought-iron gate and walks up the sunny path to the front door. The garden is planted with a variety of rose bushes and the policeman stops to admire them. He likes roses and relishes the scent as bees buzz from flower to flower. His wife likes them, too. Perhaps he ought to pick her a bunch. But he would have to ask first.

The officer rings the bell. There is no answer and he rings again. He is hardly surprised. The neighbour said they had not seen the owner for a couple of days and were concerned, hence the call-out. The policeman cups his hands and peers through the glass. He cannot see any movement and considers breaking the panel to let himself in but decides to check the back door. He walks down the path and turns a corner. The entrance is ajar. He pushes the door open and calls out.

'Señor Schiller, are you here?'

There is no response. He passes through the kitchen and into the hall. The place is empty and he enters the living-room and realises why the caller has not seen his neighbour recently. The man is hanging lifeless from a cord. There is no sign of struggle. Everything looks to be in place. The officer checks the pockets of the deceased and finds a note. It is as he suspected. Suicide.

On the opposite side of the street Martin Bormann watches the policeman return to his car and use the short-wave radio. He can hear static and disembodied voices and assumes the man is relaying information to headquarters. From his tone he does not appear to suspect foul play. The commander had resisted at first but he was no match for the likes of Bormann. Halfway through their struggle he seemed to give up and it had been easy to throttle him. When Schiller was unconscious, he disconnected the phone and wound the cord around his victim's neck. Standing on a chair, he hanged him from the light bracket. Then he wrote the suicide note and stuck it in a pocket. His work done, Bormann kicked over the chair and left by the back door.

The officer replaces his radio and waits for the pathology unit to come and remove the body. Unseen, the killer walks away. He has wrung the cockerel's neck. It is time for him to disappear again.

Ariel wakes and sees the woman beside him is asleep. In her dream state, she looks lovely and serene. He watches her breasts rise and gently fall with her breathing. After Tiago Hecht's party the lovers had spent the weekend together. They went dancing again at the Confitería Ideal and this time Carmen asked him to stay at her place. Ariel checks his watch. It is time to get up. He slips out of bed and goes to the bathroom. In the shower, he opens the faucet and water cascades over his head and shoulders. He scrubs himself, enjoying the sensation as jets pummel his body amid clouds of steam.

Carmen is not asleep. She heard her lover to go to the bathroom and waited for the sound of running water. She rises, takes Ariel's jacket and removes his wallet. She opens it and riffles through. Apart from the usual credit cards, ID and press pass, there is nothing of any note. Carmen returns the wallet then removes his keys from a pocket and places them on a piece of paper. She lays another page over them and with a pencil, rubs the graphite back and forth until an image appears.

The sound of showering ceases and a plughole gurgles. Carmen replaces the keys and puts the papers away and hops back into bed. Ariel emerges naked from the bathroom rubbing his damp hair with a towel and sees his lover is awake.

'Nice shower?'

'Certainly was,' and he reaches for his clothes. 'I wish I could stay,' he says, buttoning his shirt, 'but I've got to work.'

'When will I see you?'

'Tomorrow? I'll give you a call.' He turns and faces a mirror.

Ariel knots his tie and puts his jacket on. Carmen wraps a sheet around her body and gets out of bed to say goodbye. They embrace and he leaves. As soon as Ariel has gone she goes to her bureau, removes the paper and looks at the mark the keys have made. The tracing is clear and there should be no problem making another set.

Ariel is at his desk in the newsroom when the phone rings and he answers.

'Come to my office,' says Ovalle.

The door is open and he can see from his friend's face that something is amiss.

'Bad news, Father Javier has disappeared.'

'What happened?'

'He was last seen three days ago in Posadas when he left the mission to go for a walk. Eyewitnesses say he was abducted by a group of men in the central plaza.'

'Uniformed?'

'Plainclothes.'

'Probably cops.'

'Probably. Make some calls and see if you can shed any light on this.'

Ariel returns to the newsroom, opens his contacts book and phones the few senior police officers who will talk to him. As the morning wears on each comes back with a negative. Sorry, they would like to help but they cannot. Nobody seems to know where the priest is. Ariel calls the main hospitals, including the provincial ones. Perhaps Javier had been assaulted rather than abducted. Again, there is a blank. Ariel ponders, turning a biro in his hand. The priest would not vanish without saying something to somebody.

He wonders who else he can contact then remembers the blonde he met at Hecht's party. He flicks through his Rolodex and dials the embassy's number.

After a couple of rings a voice answers. 'United States Embassy, how may I help you?'

'I'd like to speak to Linda Hollis.'

'Whom shall I say is calling?'

'Ariel Guzman, from La Nación.'

'Just a moment, please.'

There is a pause before the American comes on the line.

'Hey there! Didn't expect to hear from you so soon.'

Hollis sounds friendly, which he takes as a good sign.

'Listen, I wonder if you could do me a favour?'

'I'm head of press, it's my job.'

'This is a tough one.'

'So, try me.'

Ariel explains about Javier's disappearance and that he appears to have been kidnapped. But none of the police seem to know anything or they refuse to say. He asks whether she can make enquiries on his behalf.

'I'll see what I can do and get back to you.'

'I'd appreciate it.'

Ariel waits for the call. A few minutes later the phone peals and he answers. It is Hollis. She sounds shocked.

'I really don't know how to say this ... but ... Father Javier's body is at the morgue. A person matching his description was found in the city centre early this morning. A hit-and-run, apparently.'

Ariel places the receiver under his chin and jots down the

information.

'Okay, I'll go there now.'

'I'll meet you at the morgue.'

'There's no need.'

'I want to. I'll see you there.'

'All right.'

He terminates the call and presses the editor's line to tell him what has happened.

'What! They found him here, in Buenos Aires?'

'According to the US Embassy.'

'Then it must have been the cops.'

'Or else they turned a blind eye. Anyhow, I'm off to the morgue – catch you later.'

Ariel picks up his notebook and leaves the building. He flags down a taxi and tells the driver to take him to the city morgue on Calle Junín. It is just a few blocks away and, when they arrive, he flashes his press card at the guard and enters. The American is already there looking as cool and tempting as a mint julep.

'I'm so sorry about Father Javier.'

'Likewise.'

'I've got permission to see the body but they need it to be positively identified. Can you do that?'

'No problem.'

They wait in reception and a pathologist appears. He is balding and bearded and has a calm, professorial air. He wears a white coat, with a pair of spectacles suspended from his neck – a stethoscope being superfluous in his line of work. He takes them down a sterile corridor, empty apart from a trolley pushed by an orderly. On it is a corpse.

The pathologist opens a swing-door and they enter the morgue. Beneath a sheet, a body lies on a porcelain slab. He flips the cover to reveal a man's face. Ariel steps forward. The victim is about the same age as the priest and plainly Indian. His eyes are closed and he seems at peace. It is, without doubt, Javier.

'That's him,' he says.

The pathologist is about to replace the sheet when Ariel puts out a hand.

'I want to see the body.'

'I don't think it wise. His injuries are severe.'

'That's why the Society has given me permission, as next of kin. They've asked me to view the whole body.'

The other man has no idea whether this is true or not and reluctantly takes hold of the shroud again.

'If you insist.' He draws it back so the corpse is completely exposed. Javier's body, particularly his nipples and genitals, is scored with livid bruises. In some places the flesh has been scorched. The injuries are unlike that of any road-traffic victim.

'How did he die?'

'I can't say. You'll have to wait for my report,' and the pathologist pulls the sheet back over the victim.

'When will that be?'

'Two days. Three at the most.'

He leads the visitors out of the morgue back to the lobby. They thank him and the pathologist says goodbye with a sad smile and returns to his work.

Out in the street Hollis stops Ariel.

'I wonder how Father Javier died?'

'It certainly wasn't a hit-and-run – he was tortured.'

'What makes you so sure?'

'I used to be a crime reporter. I've seen dozens of traffic victims and none of them ever looked like that.'

'I'm sorry, it's just so horrific ... I mean, who would do such a thing?'

Ariel turns on her, his eyes blazing in anger.

'You know what? I have no idea but I sure as hell am going to find out!'

Hollis is shocked by the outburst and he realises he has lost his temper. He apologises and starts to explain.

'Before I left the mission, Javier told me he would be dead soon. I didn't believe him. I thought he was being melodramatic, possibly traumatised by the awful memories he must have had of the fire. Now I know differently. He knew speaking out would cost him his life. I owe it to him to find out who did this, and why.'

'I'll help you in any way I can. I wasn't kidding when I said the ambassador is keen on human rights. The State Department takes these matters very seriously.'

Ariel is relieved. Hollis appears to be an ally and, right now, he needs all the help he can get.

'Thanks – and thanks for everything you've done today. I'd never have been able to find him without you.'

'That's okay. Can I give you a lift?'

'No, the office isn't far. I'll walk. I need fresh air.'

'I understand. We'll be in touch,' and the American walks

towards a silver BMW. She waves before driving off into the mid-town traffic.

Hollis arrives at the embassy, enters her office and closes the door. At her desk, she dials a number on a secure line. The call is swiftly answered.

'How'd it go?' says a voice.

'Perfect. Now we just have to watch and wait.'

'Nice work. Keep me informed.'

'Of course. Anything you say.'

In a mansion overlooking the city a well-dressed man with slicked-back hair replaces the receiver and reaches for a packet of Kent on his desk. He takes a cigarette, strikes a match and lights it. He has a drag and exhales. It seems as though it is the best cigarette he has ever smoked.

Ariel returns to La Nación and tells his editor what happened at the morgue. Ovalle appears resigned. Bad things always seem to happen in triplicate: first it was the discovery Hitler had escaped the Führerbunker then found sanctuary in Argentina and now this. What next?

'Hardly surprising given the circumstances. Go ahead. I'll make it the lead.'

'How much do you want?'

'Eight hundred, and box it as well.'

'You got it.'

At his desk Ariel slips a carbon between two sheets of A4 and inserts them into his typewriter. He taps out a headline: 'Wolf's Lair Priest Dead!' He turns the carriage wheel then types away as he relates that Javier was abducted in Posadas although his body was discovered several hundred miles away in the capital. He also describes the priest's injuries which were consistent with torture. He does not speculate about the cause of death; that would have to wait for the pathologist's report. In the box he gives some background on a life prematurely curtailed and concludes Javier was murdered. Someone, somewhere wanted him dead but who and, more importantly, why? When Ariel has finished he reads his story through and corrects some punctuation before pulling the paper from the typewriter. He files the original and gives the copy to the subeditors, suggesting they use one of his unpublished photos from the interview. He informs Ovalle the article is finished and leaves the office.

Ariel enters his apartment and raises the lid of a pine chest. Beneath a handwoven poncho a tallit is wrapped around a prayer book and kippah. They belonged to his father and smell of mothballs. He has never used them but kept them after the old man died. He tucks the shawl under his arm, places the kippah and prayer book in a pocket and departs.

Ariel makes his way to the Libertad Synagogue on Plaza Lavalle. He takes the metro to Tribunales and ascends the subway steps. He crosses the road and passes through the square and heads to the temple. The evening sun bathes the plaza in a warm light and the jacarandas are in bloom, their lilac flowers swaying in the breeze. The synagogue is a handsome building of pale stone with carved Byzantine arches, its roof adorned by a pair of marble tablets depicting the Ten Commandments. Ariel puts on his kippah and enters the temple and is dwarfed by its size as pillars soar heavenwards. The place is almost empty. A cantor intones verses from the Torah and a scattering of the faithful occupy the wooden pews. Ariel stands alone in a corner and wraps his father's tallit around his shoulders. He bows and faces the ark and, opening the prayer book, starts to say Kaddish.

BUENOS AIRES

Tuesday 28 September 1976

The chauffeur opens the door of a Rolls-Royce Phantom and a beautiful blonde alights, followed by a man wearing a brass-buttoned blazer and dark glasses. Tiago Hecht takes his mistress by the arm and they walk up the steps of the Casa Rosada, the guards snapping to attention as they pass through the colonnaded entrance and enter the marble hallway. On the other side is a courtyard planted with palms and, in the centre, a bronze fountain tinkles. They sign a register and another guard arrives and escorts them up a grand staircase, to the principal offices on the first floor and the presidential suite.

The walls are hung with portraits of Argentina's presidents and statesmen, including Juan Peron and Evita. The *caudillo* is wearing white tie and a presidential sash, his wife in a full-length silver dress which flows around her body like water. Hecht pauses to admire the stately furnishings. It would make the perfect headquarters for the Fourth Reich, which is why he has requested an audience with President Videla. The general owes his position to Hecht's support and he is about to call in the debt.

The guard knocks on a double door and a footman ushers the visitors inside. Sitting behind a bureau, framed by floor-to-ceiling windows, is Videla. He is in dress uniform and gets up to greet them, the braid brushes of his tunic flashing in the sunlight.

'Tiago, what an honour, and you too, Miss Hollis.' He takes the American's hand and dabs it lightly with his lips. 'Please, tell me what I can do for you,' and the president leads his guests to a cluster of red-damasked chairs in front of an ornate fireplace. They sit on the silk-upholstered seats and Videla summons the footman to bring refreshments.

'What would you like?' he asks Hollis. 'Coffee, or something cool, with ice? It's getting hot, already.'

'Orange juice would be fine, thank you.'

'Perfect. Fresh orange juice. And how about you, Tiago?'

Hecht frowns, as if the very act of choosing is a bore, before announcing: 'coffee, strong, black, one sugar.'

'I'll have the same,' and he clicks his fingers at the footman.

Videla preens. With his long nose, thin face and glossy hair, he looks like a corvid. His gimlet eyes scarcely blink as he makes small talk.

'Our purge of the left is going well. They're on the run now. We've rounded up the worst and the rest are cowering like rats in a sewer but we'll soon flush them out!' He grins at Hollis.

'I'm very glad to hear it. The United States has always been a friend to nations which actively engage in the fight against Communism.'

'The intelligence the State Department has provided has

been first rate – please pass on my best wishes to Ambassador Hill,' he says, and Hollis dips her head.

The lackey returns and places their drinks on the table with a plate of honey-coloured biscuits. Once he has gone the president gets down to business.

'Tiago, what can I do for you?'

Hecht sprawls in his chair and languidly smokes a cigarette. His eyes are half-closed, like a panther dozing in the sun and he barely suppresses a yawn.

'It is not in the stars to hold our destiny but in ourselves ...'

Videla gives a little laugh.

'I'm not sure what you mean.'

'I can't say too much at this stage but there is someone important whom your government must accommodate. Ideally, he should be given an honorary rank in the army – general would do. He will need an appropriate salary and an office in the palace, complete with staff.'

The president remains expressionless but his face darkens. He can hardly believe what he has heard and pretends not to be affronted.

'I would like to meet this man, he sounds most ... impressive.'

'Oh he is, have no doubt about that. He will be your successor.'

Videla is taking a sip of coffee when he hears this and almost chokes but manages to swallow the scalding contents. He gasps and wipes his mouth with a napkin.

'My successor? But I've just assumed the presidency – with your help of course.'

'And you're doing a wonderful job. But it does no harm to look to the future.' Hecht draws on his cigarette, raises his chin and emits a trail of smoke.

Videla stiffens in his chair. Who on earth does Tiago Hecht think he is, ordering him about like this? The man is little more than a hick from the backwoods. A very wealthy hick but a hick, nonetheless. His family has been in Argentina for less than a century and has only settled in Misiones because, apart from Patagonia, it is the country's least populated region and land is cheap. Whereas the general could trace his ancestry back to the country's founding father, Juan Díaz de Solís, whose expedition had entered the River Plate in 1516. Videla's forebears had fought and shed blood for the nation for almost half a millennium. Now this upstart is telling him his presidency is coming to an end.

'What if I refuse to go? I am head of the army, after all.'

'In name only. I could have you replaced tomorrow.'

'Tiago, you should be careful what you say. You might be rich and have friends in high places but you don't run this country.'

'Actually, I do. And you know it, which is why you have several million dollars stashed away in various private bank accounts from New York to Geneva. As do your fellow members of the junta. I bankroll the lot of you. The country belongs to me and I shall do with it as I wish.'

Videla gives a mocking look. His billionaire backer has overreached himself this time. There is one thing he surely does not control and that is the military.

'If you try to oust me the armed forces will rebel.'

'I doubt it. I've already spoken to the heads of the other services. They know what's good for them. And so should you.'

'Go screw yourself!'

Hecht remains impassive. He has an ace up his sleeve and now he is going to use it. He reaches inside his jacket and brings out an envelope which he places on the table.

'Most appropriate, considering the circumstances. Although the epithet applies rather more to you than me.'

Videla wonders what his guest could mean. He picks up the envelope, rips it open and removes the contents. His mouth gapes in astonishment as he sifts through in abject horror and disbelief. It is a collection of colour Polaroids taken from every possible angle. The photos depict a Roman orgy in full flow and he is centre stage, naked except for a crown of laurels.

'Is that you playing Julius Caesar or is it Nero – or, perhaps, it's Caligula?' Hecht leans forward to take a closer look. 'Caligula, I would have thought; your penis is on the small side. Anyway, you do strike remarkably heroic poses, except, I see, when you're taking it up the butt. I never knew you were bisexual – quite a revelation, I think you'll agree.'

Videla is aghast.

'How ... How did you know?'

'Let's just say, it's proof that I run the country and not you. I have copies, so you can keep these, though I doubt you'll be showing them to your fellow generals or, indeed, your wife and children.'

The president's shoulders sag and he shrivels like a

punctured balloon. He looks old, as if the life has been sucked out of him. At a stroke, his rank, his uniform, his years of years of military service have been reduced to nothing. Videla realises he has been played for a fool. Tiago Hecht must have known all along and was simply waiting for the opportunity to strike. Despite living in a palace, he is not a king, or even a knight, he is merely a pawn on a chessboard. But he has his pride. The man opposite has not been able to take that from him.

'He who sups with the devil needs a very long spoon.'

'And he who rides the tiger can never get off. Don't be too surprised. You chose to put your hand in with me, therefore you must accept the consequences.'

Videla seethes in silence. There has been a palace coup. The armoured limousines, police escorts and bodyguard were mere baubles. His power and its trappings have vanished in a wisp of smoke. Yet he knows he must be careful. If he pushes back any harder he might find himself in prison or in front of a firing squad. Tiago Hecht has called his bluff and completely outmanoeuvred him. Checkmate.

The brushes on Videla's shoulders weigh heavily. He can almost hear the wheels of the tumbril as it takes him to the guillotine.

'And when will I meet this ... person?'

'Soon. Hopefully in a week or two.'

'I see. What you've asked shouldn't be too difficult. I'm sure it can be arranged.'

'Our new president must have access to state papers and will need round-the-clock security. And by that I mean special forces, not those chimpanzees in the carabineros.'

Videla nods as if it were perfectly natural that a complete stranger should be granted such things.

'Consider it done. Is there anything else?'

'Not at the moment. I just thought you should know – things are moving swiftly now. I want to make sure everything is in place,' and Hecht stubs out his cigarette.

He rises and Hollis follows. Neither has touched their drinks. Videla gets up.

'I'll call you later in the week.'

'Of course. I look forward to it.'

They say goodbye and Hecht escorts his mistress out of the room. They descend the marble staircase, cross the vestibule and go outside. The chauffeur sees them and opens the door of the Rolls-Royce and the couple enter. The driver starts the engine and the car glides away through the traffic. In the plush interior Hollis laughs.

'Oh my God! That was awesome. In my years of service, I've never seen anything like it. Who'd have thought that about Videla?'

Hecht smiles. A dramatic gesture, if ever there was one, the timing could not have been more perfect. A real *coup de theatre*. He takes her hand.

'You have a great future ahead of you, Linda Hollis, a great future.'

The American looks at him adoringly. She has no idea what plans he has for her but, whatever they are, she is a willing accomplice. In fact, Hecht sees her as the new Evita, a spouse for the future leader of the Fourth Reich. They will make a handsome couple and she is the perfect woman to bear a future generation of Hitlers. He knows this because, like all good subjects, he has already tested the product. It is a pity he cannot keep her for himself but the cause is far greater than his personal desires and diktats.

As the vehicle travels down the capital's boulevards, Hecht reminisces. He recalls the hurried escape from the Wolf's Lair as they forded the rain-swollen river to Paraguay. And he remembers the *Führer*'s last moments, when he held the dying leader in his arms as he succumbed to pneumonia. Hecht has spent more than half his life trying to fulfil his master's final exhortation. Now, he is very close. And, when the new Reich begins, it will start with his own country, Argentina. Hitler's son will be president and leader of the armed forces. Before long, Brazil, Chile, Colombia, Peru, Venezuela and the other countries will be united under a single banner. Once again, the swastika will fly proudly over the seat of government. South America will become one vast nation of incomparable wealth, with enough oil, gas and minerals to sustain it forever. There will be a grand alliance with the United States and first the Soviet Union, then China will be destroyed in a nuclear Armageddon. All that remained would be an Aryan, capitalist world, led by a new Hitler.

'*Ein Volk, ein Reich, ein Führer*.'

'I'm sorry?'

'Oh nothing, just daydreaming ...'

Hecht gazes out of the limousine's tinted windows. He is thinking about the massed rallies of Nuremberg and the torch-held processions at night, making a river of fire as thousands of soldiers goose-stepped through the streets, their jackboots resounding across the cobblestones. And it is about to happen again. Once more boulevards will be lined with stormtroopers holding Nazi banners aloft, their arms raised high, shouting at the tops of their voices.

'*Sieg heil*! *Sieg heil*! *Sieg heil*!'

On his way to La Nación, Ariel stops at a kiosk to buy a copy of the day's newspaper. He checks the front page, expecting Javier's death to be the headline. Instead there is an anodyne account of a junta meeting with a photo of President Videla and his fellow generals. There is nothing about the priest. He flicks through the following pages and, finally, sees a single paragraph in the News in Brief section. It mentions only that Javier's body has been discovered in the city morgue and the cause of his death is, as yet, unknown. It does not say he was abducted in Posadas, or that his injuries were consistent with torture and that he was murdered. Ariel is furious. He tosses the paper into a bin. When he arrives in the newsroom, he goes straight to the editor's office and throws open the door. Ovalle appears uneasy.

'I've just seen the paper! Why the hell isn't Father Javier on the front page?'

'Calm down ...'

'You spiked my story!'

'Have a seat and I'll explain.'

Ariel is fuming. 'This had better be good.' He closes the door and pulls up a chair.

Ovalle winces and warily rubs the nape of his neck.

'It was going to run as the lead, believe me. But shortly after you left I got a call from the Ministry of the Interior.'

'How on earth did they know I'd found him?'

'The pathologist?'

'No, he's not the type. It must have been someone else from the morgue.'

'Possibly.'

'What did the ministry say?'

'As you'd expect. Drop this story or else.'

'But we're going to run it as a front page right? As soon as the report comes out.'

'It won't be coming out.'

'I asked the pathologist myself. He said it would take a couple of days. Three at the most. Once we have confirmation, we can run it.'

'As I said – the report will not be released.'

'The ministry told you that?'

'They did.'

'So ... I'll get a quote from the pathologist. He'll go on the record.'

'I doubt it.'

'Why?'

'If they called me, I presume they called him as well.'

'Then you're not going to run the story at all?'

'I'm afraid not.'

Ariel is dumbfounded. He cannot understand why his friend would do such a thing. What has happened to the colleague he once admired? Was it fear or because of his recent promotion to the board? Perhaps a combination of both. Mario was not joking when, on the night of the coup, he said things were going to get a lot worse. They already have. But so has he. He is now one of them. Ariel takes a deep breath and tries to stay calm.

'Did I hear you correctly?'

'You did.'

'And you're not going to run it because someone from the ministry told you not to?'

'I'm not going to run it because, if I do, the paper will be shut down.'

'They wouldn't dare do that!'

'They would. It's not the first time they've called. Things have changed since Videla got in. We got away with the Wolf's Lair yarn because the government didn't know about it until the edition hit the streets. And, besides, it's history. But that's it. They don't want any more exclusives about Nazis and secret jungle camps. It's finished.'

'Are you serious – is La Nación now the junta's mouthpiece?'

'I've got a business to run. People depend on me for their livelihoods, including you. If the paper gets shut down, we're all out of a job!'

'I didn't become a journalist so I could work for the Ministry of the Interior!'

'You know what, Ariel, you can walk if you want to but I have a family to think about. In the past few weeks I've had dog shit put through my letterbox, silent phone calls in the middle of the night and yesterday, besides a call from the ministry, I got a bullet in the post. I can't live with a gun pointed at my head!'

Neither man speaks and they sit and brood in silence. A sound of traffic rises from the street and beyond the door comes the muted clatter of the newsroom. But that is all. Ariel takes out his wallet and opens it.

'In that case, you can have this,' and he throws his press card on the desk.

Ovalle raises his hands in apology and leans back in his chair.

'I'm sorry. I'm stressed and doubtless you are, too. Why don't you take some holiday and I'll see you in a few days?'

'Tell me, honestly, will you run the story about Father Javier or anything else related to him?'

'No, I won't. And I've explained why.'

'In that case, I quit.'

'Please, think about it.'

'I already have,' and Ariel gets up to leave. His hand is on the door handle when his friend speaks again.

'By the way, this arrived for you. It's got a Posadas postmark,' and Ovalle holds out a buff envelope.

Ariel takes it and departs without a word. At his desk he gathers his contacts book, camera and notepad. He leaves behind everything else, including the framed citations and award ceremony photographs. He has no need for them now. His colleagues are busy and no one notices him walk out of the room.

Ariel makes his way to Plaza San Martín and enters the park. A wind gets up and dust devils whirl along the path. He finds a bench and opens the envelope. Inside is a key, the sort used for safety deposit boxes. There is also a handwritten letter. He begins to read.

Dear Ariel,

By the time you receive this I shall be dead. Perhaps you already know. It does not matter. What matters is that since I no longer dwell in the realms of the living, I'm not bound by the rules of the temporal Church. In other words, I can finally tell you the truth as it was told to me by Sister Maria in her last confession.

I mentioned Edelweiss. It is the Nazi codename for a man called Ignacio Cruz. He is Adolf Hitler's natural son. He was born at the camp in the jungle. When Eva Braun died, Maria became his nurse. She was due to be killed but one of the men in the camp took pity on her and helped her escape. However, without his knowledge, she took the child. The Nazis destroyed our village as an act of vengeance. Maria hid in the forest and eventually made her way to the mission in Posadas. The baby was adopted by the orphanage and Maria became a nun. Ignacio and I grew up together although I never knew his true identity until Maria's confession. But we are as close as brothers.

Ignacio is now a doctor. All I know is that he works near the Iguaçu Falls. Go there and find him. Tell him I sent you and that he must leave the country. His life will be in grave danger. You must inform the Society's superior general in Rome. They have promised to protect Ignacio should his identity ever be discovered. Tell him that he

must go to the Vatican. It is the only place he will be safe. The key is for a safety deposit box at the Banco Provincia on Calle San Martín. Inside is Ignacio's original birth certificate, the one the Nazis issued. Maria took it when she fled to prove that she was no fantasist. Make sure you destroy it.
Your brother in Christ,
Javier Ibarra SJ

PS The security code is 06-11-45. It's Ignacio's date of birth. The box is in the Society's name.

Ariel reads the letter again then replaces it in the envelope. A young woman with a stroller walks past and he remembers the cradle in the cabin. It had been slept in, after all. And not just by anybody but Hitler's own son. He understands now why the priest had refused to tell him. He inspects the key in his hand. It seems so small and insignificant and yet there are people who would commit murder, or worse, to have it.

He gets up from the bench and heads to the Banco Provincia a couple of blocks away. The air is sultry and he drapes his jacket over a shoulder. Opposite the art deco edifice he waits for the lights to change then crosses the street and enters the building. Inside, the temperature is frigid and he puts on his jacket. He approaches a counter and rings a bell. A clerk rises from his desk.

'Yes, sir?'

'I'd like to see the manager.'

'Can I ask what it's about?'

'A safety deposit box.'

'Do you have the key and the security code?'

'Yes.'

'Just a minute, I'll call him. Please take a seat.'

Ariel sits in a leather armchair. The bank is hushed, like a mausoleum, a place where the money god, Mammon, slept. Hidden deep within the bowels of the building is some of the Nazi gold brought to Argentina by *U-977* and now in the custody of a certain billionaire.

The manager arrives. He wears a dark suit and tie and has the solemn air of an undertaker. He asks the visitor for ID before escorting him to a door where he taps in a code. There is a solid click of bolts and they descend a flight of steps into a well-lit vault. A gate blocks the way and there is a buzz as the barrier unlocks. They pass through to another gate. The manager punches in more numbers. It opens and they enter a room where a uniformed guard is seated behind a table.

'Please sign the register and print the box owner's name.'

Ariel obeys.

'And repeat the security code.'

He does so and the manager consults a list.

'That's correct. Now, can you show me your key?'

Ariel hands over his key. The guard takes a duplicate from a row on the wall, which he gives to the manager who compares them. He is satisfied and hands the visitor his key and the copy and together they walk to the safety-deposit room. They enter and face a wall of shiny steel boxes.

'There it is,' the manager says, pointing at one. 'The keys must be inserted at the same time and turned together. There's an annexe so you can view the contents undisturbed. If you need anything, just ask for me, I'll be upstairs.'

Ariel waits until he has gone before he approaches the box. He inserts the keys and opens the drawer. Inside is a document, nothing else. He removes it. In the annexe he sits at a green baize table. A camera in the ceiling winks.

Ariel unfolds the document. The paper is printed in Gothic script and has a Reich stamp in one corner. Beneath the heading, *Geburtsurkunde*, is the name: *Josef Braun Hitler*. There is a date and a place of birth – *Deutschland* and he realises the Nazis must have considered the camp German territory. He wonders if the boy was named after Josef Goebbels – possible, since Hitler had been godfather to the Minister of Propaganda's children. The parents are identified as *Adolf Hitler* and *Eva Anna Paula Hitler, geborenen Braun*. The boy's birth is confirmed by their signatures and witnessed by two others: *Martin Bormann, Reichsleiter* and *Dr Ludwig Stumpfegger, Obersturmbannführer*. Ariel recognises Bormann's name but not the doctor's and assumes he must be another senior Nazi.

He stares at the birth certificate. Here, in front of his eyes, is incontrovertible proof that Hitler had a son. If this piece of paper fell into the wrong hands, the man would almost certainly perish. But, as Javier said, he is innocent and Ariel has promised to help. The priest has paid with his life. Now it is up to Ariel to ensure that nobody else does.

He folds the document and puts it inside his jacket. As he

leaves the annexe, he returns the duplicate key to the guard, who replaces it on the rack. The man releases the gate and Ariel walks down the corridor and passes through the next barrier before ascending the stairs to the security door. He presses a button, hears the locks spring, and enters reception. The clerk at the desk does not look up as he departs.

Out in the street Ariel stops a taxi and tells the driver to take him to the Church of the Inmaculada Concepción in San Telmo. He does not give his home address in case he is being tailed. As the car pulls away Ariel settles into the back seat, the birth certificate of Hitler's son in his pocket.

As soon as the journalist leaves the vault, the guard makes a phone call. He had watched him examine the document on a monitor beneath his desk. The images were grainy and he had been unable to ascertain precisely what it was but he could see it was written in German and stamped with an eagle and swastika. The guard is Jewish and has been a Zionist informer since he arrived in Argentina as a child refugee before the war. He has been waiting thirty years for someone to open the security box. His codename is Patience.

A woman is waiting in a car outside the bank. There is a buzz and her earpiece crackles into life.

'It's a Nazi document,' says a voice. 'He's got it with him.'

'*Tov toda ...*' she says.

A young man appears on the pavement and hails a taxi. Carmen watches the vehicle pull away. She is about to follow when she notices a tall, dapper gent emerge from a Rolls-Royce with tinted windows. Tiago Hecht is accompanied by a fashionably dressed blonde in high heels, her face obscured by her hair. Together, they go into the bank. After a few minutes they emerge with a mole-like individual who looks like the manager. He smiles and rubs his hands and does everything apart from actually bow. Hecht walks back to his limousine with the blonde. As she enters she turns her head and Carmen sees her face. It is Linda Hollis.

The taxi deposits Ariel outside the Inmaculada Concepción. The interior is cavernous and tiers of guttering candles flicker in the gloom. The light filtering through the high windows is murky, like dishwater. He cannot remember the last time he was in a church. It must have been for a funeral but whose? All around him is the iconography of an alien religion. A nonbeliever condemned to his own *auto-da-fé*. Ariel waits in the sepulchral silence but no one appears. He is safe, at least for now. He emerges into the glare of the street, puts on his sunglasses, and walks to his home on Calle Chacabuco. A group of children are playing hopscotch on the pavement in front of his building. They stop as he approaches.

'You're Ariel Guzman,' says a boy.

'I am.'

'My dad says you're a dirty Communist.'

'He's not the only one.'

Ariel goes inside and takes the lift. He unlocks his apartment door. He knows he does not have much time. In the kitchen he fills a glass with water, gulps it down and pours another. Feeling calmer he returns to the living-room and places the glass on the coffee table. He sits on the sofa and produces the document from his jacket. He has another drink of water before examining the birth certificate. In his hands is the Nazi Holy Grail. And because of this, Javier has told him to destroy it.

Ariel picks up a box of matches and strikes one. He holds the wavering flame close and is about to set the paper alight when he pauses. He extinguishes the match and drops it into an ashtray. Despite the priest's entreaty, he realises the evidence might be useful. The problem is where to hide it. He surveys the room. Behind a picture or a mirror would be too obvious.

He looks at the rows of books that line the walls.

Ariel removes a dark-green, leatherbound volume – the Oxford edition of *The Complete Works of William Shakespeare*. He flicks through the pages and slips the birth certificate and letter inside and puts the book back. He stands there surrounded by hundreds of volumes and admires his own conceit: paper hidden among paper.

Ariel goes to his desk, opens a telephone directory and finds the person he is searching for: the Jesuit Principal of Argentina, Father Maximilian Ruiz. He dials the number and asks for the cleric, telling the receptionist it is of the utmost importance and that he is prepared to hold for as long as it takes but he must speak with the principal. He is politely told to wait. Nevertheless he is surprised when, a few moments later, Father Maximilian comes on the line.

'Señor Guzman, how may I help?'

'I can't tell you over the phone. I have to see you.'

'Can you give me an indication of what it's about?'

Ariel hesitates. He does not want to mention the word Edelweiss, or even Javier, in case the line has been tapped.

'It's about a friend.'

'I think I know whom you mean. Come to the college at Manzana de las Luces and ask for me.'

'I'll be there as soon as I can.'

A vehicle pulls into Calle Chacabuco and parks opposite an apartment block. Moments later, a young man leaves the building and hurries to the metro station before he disappears from view. The driver checks the mirror and over both shoulders. She steps onto the pavement and approaches the block. At the entrance she produces a set of keys and lets herself in.

Carmen crosses the hall and takes the lift. There is a clank and whirl of machinery. When it comes to a halt, she opens the gate and waits. Silence. She walks down the passage her shoes tip-tapping across the parquet floor. She stands outside a door and listens. Nothing. She turns a key and enters.

The place is just the same. In a corner is a yucca plant and the windowsills are lined with cacti and geraniums. On a wall, a pair of Picasso prints hang beside a handwoven Indian tapestry. Carmen looks at her watch and allows herself ten minutes. She uses her years of training and tries to think tangentially. She opens the filing cabinet drawers. The top ones have diaries and notebooks and she searches through them but there are only reams of pages filled with shorthand. The others contain bank statements and utility bills. Carmen sifts through each drawer and finds nothing of interest. She returns everything to its place and surveys the room. Ariel must have been in the flat for no more than a few minutes. Not a lot of time to think of a place to hide something important. He could have the document with him but it is unlikely. If it were her, she would have hidden it.

Carmen's gaze falls upon the bookshelves.

The volumes are arranged by subject and listed alphabetically. She walks along the stacks and scans the spines for the letter S. She stops in front of a dark-green volume and opens it. Carmen flicks through and there, on the title page of *The Tempest*, is the document she is looking for with a handwritten note. She takes the book and lays it on the low table. Taking a mini camera from her handbag, Carmen photographs the birth certificate and Javier's letter. She puts her camera away, returns the pieces of paper and slips the volume back into place. With a final glance around the apartment, she leaves.

Father Maximilian Ruiz bows his head in sorrow and disbelief. The principal has learnt not only about his fellow

Jesuit's disappearance and death by torture but also the existence of Hitler's son. It really is incredible – indeed, he wishes it were not so. But he knows what Ariel has told him is the truth. At last he raises his eyes and speaks.

'I must do as Javier says and contact our superior general. He will inform the Holy Father.'

'Will the Church be able to help?'

'I believe so.'

The principal is in his late thirties but seems older, with the calm air of the contemplative. He has spent most of his life working in the slums and shanty towns of the city. His appointment to such a senior position in the clergy surprised many but not those who knew him. No one doubts the cleric's holiness or his intelligence, and many have tipped him to become a cardinal, even pope. He refuses to countenance such talk. His sole mission in life is to serve Christ.

And yet his years of spiritual exercises have left him unprepared for this. Maybe nothing could have. He raises a hand and smooths his balding pate.

'You must go to Iguaçu and bring our brother here. I will think of a way to get him out of the country. I'm afraid the Society cannot assist you on your trip north. It would be fatal to do so. The military watches our every step now.'

'What if Ignacio refuses to come?'

'I don't think he will. Javier's death should be enough to convince him.'

'Okay. But once I've got him here, he's your responsibility.'

Father Maximilian looks at the journalist and smiles wanly.

'Yes,' he says. 'Yes, he is.'

Carmen is waiting in a bar in downtown Recoleta. It is unusual for her lover to be late. She sees a familiar figure enter with a canvas holdall looking flustered and waves at him. He returns the greeting and makes his way to her. They kiss tenderly and she notices he is unshaven.

'Sorry I took so long. Had to go home and pack my bag.'

'Where are you off to?'

'I can't say and it's best you don't know. I'll be gone for a couple of days.'

'What's up?'

'It's a long story. But I've quit my job.'

'Are you serious ... why?'

'The editor refused to run my piece about Javier. He had a call from the ministry and got spooked.'

'Jerk.'

'Videla's government is getting heavy and wants to shut us down. 'No more Nazis,' I was told. So I resigned.'

'You did the right thing.'

'We'll see ...' and Ariel casts around for service. 'I need a drink.'

'No problem, they know me here.'

Carmen gets the attention of one of the waiters who almost knocks over a table in his haste to serve her.

'*Si, guapa*, how can I help?'

'*Dos Quilmes, por favor*. Nice and cold.'

'Right away.'

He soon reappears with the drinks, the beers frothing in chilled glasses. 'There you are, gorgeous. Anything else?'

'No thanks,' says Ariel and the waiter gives him a surly look and slopes off. '*Conchasumadre*,' he spits at the man's back and turns to his girlfriend. 'Does everyone fall in love with you?'

Carmen laughs.

'Not everyone. *Salud*!'

'*Salud*!'

They touch glasses and taste their beers. Ariel smacks his lips and places his drink on the table.

'Just what I needed. Now, where was I?'

'You quit your job.'

'That's right but I can't understand how the ministry knew I'd been to the morgue.'

'Maybe it was someone from there?'

'That's what Mario said but I don't think so ... unless ... oh, shit ... I don't believe it!'

'What?'

'Why didn't I think of it?'

'Think of what?'

'Linda Hollis!'

'What about her?'

'I contacted Hollis because I was getting nowhere with the story. None of my sources came up with anything. There was a complete blank. Then I had the bright idea to phone her – I asked if she could make enquiries on my behalf. Sure enough, she got straight back and told me Javier's body was at the morgue. She insisted on meeting me there.'

'Hollis was with you?'

'Yes. I thought it a bit odd but what could I say? I wouldn't have found him without her. She must have called the ministry!'

Ariel curses quietly and Carmen takes his hand in hers. She realises that she is about to break all intelligence protocols but the agency now has the information it needs.

'There's something you ought to know about Linda Hollis.'

'I'm listening.'

'Hollis might be CIA but she also works for Tiago Hecht.'

'How do you know?'

'Let's just say I know.'

Ariel removes his hand and scrutinises his lover. The look is not kind.

'Your embassy friends?'

'Maybe.'

Ariel grabs his bag and leaps to his feet.

'Who the hell are you? No, don't tell me I can guess.'

'Please ...'

Ariel gasps with the sudden realisation of an unhappy epiphany.

'You've been following me right from the start. That's why you were on the flight to Posadas – and that's how you had my phone number. The newsdesk would never have given it out!'

'Sit down and I'll tell you.'

'You don't need to tell me anything.'

Carmen's eyes vainly search her lover's.

'You've no idea what you're up against.'

'Whatever it is, I certainly don't need your help.'

'You're way out of your depth – you're drowning.'

'Then take your foot off my head!'

People on nearby tables turn their heads and whisper but Ariel does not notice. He is already walking out the door. As soon as he is in the street he starts to run. He dashes across the road and vehicles slam on their brakes and there is a sound of squealing tyres and blaring horns as he dodges between the rush-hour traffic. Ariel keeps running until he sees a taxi and flags it down. He makes sure nobody is following before he jumps in and orders the driver to take him to Jorge Newbery airport.

'Quick as you can.'

TEL AVIV–JERUSALEM

Tuesday 28 September 1976

A pair of fans whirr on Yitzhak Hofi's desk but do nothing to alleviate the late-summer heat. As they turn, their draught ruffles a stack of papers in a flurry of wingbeats. The only reason they do not take off and fly about the room is because a standard-issue service pistol holds them down. A propeller in the ceiling struggles to create any sort of breeze. Hofi has opened the office windows, which is strictly against regulations, but right now he would rather die from a sniper's bullet than the enervating temperature. The windows look out across the city of Tel Aviv and the Mediterranean winks and flashes like a silver shekel.

A balding, stocky man, Hofi has a high forehead and boyish good looks. He is head of Israel's security agency, the Mossad, an organisation still basking in the glory of the successful raid on Entebbe in June, which freed over 200 civilian hostages with the loss of just one man, the operation's leader, Yonatan Netanyahu. It was, all things considered, a price worth paying. Yet Hofi knows that complacency has no part in an intelligence organisation. It can often be lethal, as they discovered to their cost at the Munich

Olympics, when Palestinian gunmen slaughtered eleven Israeli athletes. It was assumed that sporting events were off-limits to such groups. The Mossad chief is no stranger to conflict, having served in the Haganah as a young officer in the 1948 war and, later, as head of Northern Command in the Yom Kippur conflict of 1973. He has seen comrades fight and he has seen comrades die. But they have done so in the service of Israel. And Hofi is no different.

He is waiting for an officer from Sayeret Matkal, the special forces unit. Yuri Kantor is a man he trusts implicitly and whom he has known since the creation of the Zionist state. Hofi was his platoon commander in the Haganah and served with him in the Six Day War and again during Yom Kippur. He has watched his progress through the ranks with pride and recommended him for his recent promotion to lieutenant colonel. Kantor could have risen higher but he preferred field operations and had consistently refused a staff job. Hofi now needs Kantor for a particular assignment and believes only he can carry it out.

The chief's office is open and a thickset man appears at the entrance.

'Come in, shut the door.'

The visitor does so. His hair is dark and curly and he has a heavy brow and powerful shoulders. He looks like a former boxer or wrestler, without the cauliflower ears. He advances with a quick, light step that belies his bulk. His nose has been broken and reset more than once and his hazel eyes are richly fringed with lashes.

'What's this about?'

'Have a seat and I'll tell you.'

The agent takes a chair which creaks as he sits.

'I've got a job for you. This assignment is, without doubt, the most difficult you'll ever undertake. But you alone must do it. I have chosen you above anyone else because I know you won't fail.'

Hofi explains what the Mossad has learnt through its operatives in South America. It is well known a number of Nazis evaded justice after the war, using the Odessa escape route, and that many operate freely on the continent. But, mostly, they are of lesser importance. Adolf Eichmann was the big prize and only the Auschwitz butcher, Josef Mengele, continues to elude them. In time they can be tracked down by other organisations and brought to justice. All this, Kantor knows.

'There was a story recently about Hitler and Braun escaping the Führerbunker and fleeing to Argentina.'

'Yes, I heard about it.'

'We believe the information to be credible.'

'You think he's alive?'

'No, I don't. Braun perished in the camp and we're sure Hitler died of fever a few months later, most probably in Paraguay. Physically, he was in poor shape and it would be impossible to keep his identity secret for so long. But there is something else.'

'What?'

'Hitler had a son ...'

Hofi tries to gauge the agent's reaction but he can discern none.

'His codename is Edelweiss. He is alive and living, we

think, in the north of Argentina at Iguaçu, near the Brazilian border. He may even be in Brazil.'

'Why should this involve the agency?'

'I thought you'd ask that.'

'We don't concern ourselves with the offspring of any other Nazi.'

'This is different.'

'In what way?'

Hofi realises the man is playing devil's advocate. He also knows that, since Kantor will be risking his life, he must understand the rationale behind the mission.

'Nazism was a cult which relied exclusively upon the personality of Hitler. Even with his death, it lives on. But it's insignificant, supported by a minority who lack political influence. However, all cults need a leader and now, potentially, they have one.'

'You mean the remaining Nazis intend to anoint the son as the new *Führer*?'

'According to intelligence.'

'Surely it depends on whether he accepts the role.'

'We cannot take that risk.'

'So you consider this a pre-emptive strike?'

'If you want to put it that way, yes.'

Kantor faces his chief as the desk fans turn back and forth. Through the open windows, the sea shines tantalisingly and the horizon curves away forever. Apart from the fans, the room is quiet.

'Does the agency consider this person to be an existential threat?'

'It does.'

'Because he's Hitler's son?'

'Yes. And for that reason alone. Let me put it another way. In the 1920s nobody could imagine Hitler's potential for destruction. Back then he and the Nazi Party were a joke. A bad joke but a joke nonetheless. A few years later he was in power and a few years after that, Europe was at war. The result was the Holocaust.'

'And you think this can happen again?'

'Listen, imagine you're assigned to eliminate a minor radical figure, a fringe politician, but you refuse because of – whatever reason, whatever scruple; that this man was Adolf Hitler. You had the opportunity to kill him and you did nothing.'

'I don't see any correlation between father and son. If the son were a Nazi, you might have a case.'

'This isn't a court of law, Yuri. We don't have that luxury. If there's an existential threat to Israel, our constitution obliges us to act.'

'Has the prime minister sanctioned this?'

'Not only him but also President Katzir and the entire cabinet.'

'Why me?'

'Because you're the only person who can do this.'

'I wasn't considered for Entebbe. You said I was too old.'

'You were. And, besides, Yoni was the best man for the job.'

'He was – until he got whacked.'

'I know he was a friend of yours. And I'm sorry.'

'But why me?'

'Do I have to spell it out to you?'

'Yes. You do.'

'Show me your left arm.'

Reluctantly Kantor places it on the desk. There is a scar on the inner forearm.

'Six numbers. Six numbers that represent six million Jews. You got the tattoo in Treblinka and you burnt it off in 1948. You stuck your bayonet in the fire and seared your own flesh. I saw you do it!'

'And because of this, I have to do the job?'

'Yes, Yuri. For the six million. You survived. But they did not. You must do this for them.'

The agent listens to the whirring fans. He supposes his chief is right, he just wishes someone else could do this. It is the only mission he has ever wanted to refuse. Perhaps, if he were younger, he would not be so reticent. He used to burn with zeal. Now the fires within are dying. He feels his age – he is almost fifty and close to retirement. He does not want to have to kill ever again. Instead, it seems that it is to be his fate.

'All right. I'll do it.'

'I was sure you'd understand.'

'What's the plan?'

'You'll go to Buenos Aires, one of our operatives there will brief you.'

'What's his name?'

For the first time in their interview, Hofi smiles.

'She. Her name is Carmen.'

'Really?'

'I know what you're thinking but she's good. She put the tail on our source and has plenty of frontline experience. She was in the Golan in '73.'

'Infantry?'

'That's right. Intelligence.'

Hofi produces a facsimile of the birth certificate and a copy of Javier's letter, which Kantor reads. He is also shown a pair of photographs of the target. One is a high-school graduation picture, the other of him matriculating as a doctor, wearing a gown and mortarboard. He looks like any other earnest young man about to take the path of his chosen career. Apart from his eyes, which are exceptional. They are the palest blue.

Hofi gathers the documents and photos in a manila envelope and gives them to the agent. He sees him to the door.

'*Shalom*,' he says.

'*Shalom*,' the agent replies.

Kantor has his orders and knows he must fulfil them. But before he departs for the airport there is something he must do and that he does before every mission. This time will be his last. He leaves headquarters and takes the highway to Jerusalem. The traffic is light and he motors along in the nearside lane only pulling out to overtake a slow-moving lorry or bus. As he approaches the Dome of the Rock shines like an orb in the morning sun bestowing benediction upon the city: a place where Muslim, Jew and Christian all lived under the same heaven. They resided in an uneasy truce, often leavened with antipathy and violence. Yet, he believes one day there will be peace.

Kantor parks his car at the foot of the Mount and walks to the Old City. He passes the Garden of Gethsemane with its gnarled olive trees, silent witnesses of Christ's agony. He remembers fighting along the same street with his platoon in '67 as they battled their way towards East Jerusalem and had to use the olive grove for cover. He had never fought so hard in his life and yet he knew they would succeed. After all, it was written.

The agent walks up the hill and enters the Old City through a stone doorway which, as someone once said, you could barely fit a camel. The streets are narrow and filled with people, mostly hawkers and tourists. The shops sell everything from religious ornaments and antiques to spices and silks. Kantor makes his way along the crowded streets, passing the blue tiled Al-Aqsa mosque and walks on to Temple Mount. He stops at a security gate and a soldier scans his ID before he is allowed through. On the other side he pauses and puts on a kippah before he approaches the Western Wall. In a corner a group of Haredim wearing sackcloth sway back and forth, blowing horns as they urge the Messiah to come and save the faithful.

Kantor stops in front of the wall. He reaches into a pocket and produces a slip of paper. On it is written a single sentence. He folds the paper and puts it in a crack. Placing his hand upon the ancient stones, he closes his eyes and recites the same prayer over and over.

'Lord, thy will be done.'

IGUAÇU

Tuesday 28 September 1976

A man walks through the forest, the thunderous sound of water a constant presence. The falls dominate the landscape and the earth seems to shake with their voice. In his hand he carries a leather bag that contains the various medicines and accessories he needs to treat his patients. The most common ailment is malaria although other illnesses, such as typhus and scarlet fever, are prevalent.

As he walks the jungle steams and a mist drifts through the trees and drips off leaves and branches. The boughs are covered with lichen and moss and hung with pale orchids. In gullies and along riverbanks giant ferns grow in the mild air. He listens to the falls' incessant roar which drowns out every living thing. In spite of their conversion by the Jesuits, local tribes continue to make sacrifices to appease the water god. According to legend, the deity, M'Boi, wanted to marry a beautiful girl called Naipi, who took fright and fled with her mortal lover, Taroba, in a canoe. In a rage, the god gouged out the river creating the falls and cataracts, condemning the lovers to eternal death.

Ignacio enters the village and the inhabitants rush out

and greet him. He is making his usual visit and, apart from the local priest, he is the only outsider they ever meet. They gather in a circle and the children hug his legs. He strokes their heads and asks if they have been good.

'*Sí, sí*,' they say. '*Como un ángel*!'

To Ignacio they are, indeed, angels. Untainted by contact with the outside world and, therefore, in his eyes, pure. The children grab him by the hand and each tries to pull him in a different direction. They want him to see their home first, regardless of whether anyone is sick or not. But the doctor has an itinerary from which he will not be swayed and insists on seeing those who need him. The first is an elderly woman with sciatica. She is barely able to move, let alone get out of bed. As a result, she has sores that are even more painful than her inflamed joints. He has asked her family to make sure the wounds are washed and kept clean and to massage her body daily. He bows his head and enters the dwelling and greets his patient.

'Good morning, Isabel, how are you today?'

'*Ay*, Dr Ignacio, not so bad thank you,' and the woman manages to raise herself on an elbow.

He sits beside her and opens his bag.

'Have you been able to sleep?'

'What do I want to sleep for? I can sleep when I'm dead. If I sleep all day, I can't watch my grandchildren play. Sleep is for sloths and there are plenty of those out there in the forest.'

Ignacio brings out a thermometer, shakes it and puts it in her mouth. He takes her pulse, looking at his watch as he does so. After thirty seconds he lets go of her wrist, removes the thermometer and checks it.

'Your blood pressure is fine and you don't have a temperature.'

'What did you expect? I'm a model patient.'

'Yes, Isabel, you are. Now, let me look at these sores.' He helps her roll over onto her side and she raises her nightshirt.

He removes the bandages and swabs and dresses each wound then covers them with fresh liniment. At last they are beginning to heal.

'And, have you been taking the painkillers I gave you?'

'Yes, Dr Ignacio,' she makes an innocent face. In fact, she has been feeding them to the chickens, which wander in and out of the hut searching for scraps, because they make her drowsy. Her son cannot understand why his hens are laying so few eggs and seem to spend the entire day asleep in the shade. He has scolded his youngest child for hypnotising them but the boy swears it has nothing to do with him. If he had asked her, his mother could have told him. But he has not and so remains ignorant. When the pain gets really bad, Isabel asks her son to make her *mate* with crushed coca leaves. It is much more effective than those bitter white tablets the doctor prescribes, although she would never tell him this.

Next, Ignacio visits a middle-aged man with haemorrhoids. Unlike the first patient, Rodrigo does nothing but whine and complain that he is close to death. His wife tells the doctor he is driving the family mad with his constant griping. Ignacio assures her he is doing his best to cure the patient but Rodrigo must play his part. He has to change his diet which, at the moment, consists of nothing except pork fat and potato.

'You need more roughage and omega oils. You must only eat fish, rice and raw vegetables.'

'But I hate fish! They're too bony. And as for rice and raw vegetables, yuk!'

'Then you will continue to bleed copiously from your ass.'

Ignacio gives his patient a packet of suppositories and tells him to take one morning and night.

'I'll see you in a fortnight.'

'I might be dead by then!'

'In that case, we can all rest in peace.'

'Amen to that!' says Rodrigo's wife.

Ignacio thanks the woman and leaves her to her complaining spouse. His last patient in the hamlet is a girl with typhus. He is fortunate he caught the disease early since it was often fatal. The girl is taking a course of antibiotics, which he tops up with a daily injection of doxycycline. He finds her sitting up in bed playing with her dolls. After an examination Ignacio gives the girl a jab in her arm and is soon on his way again. There are several other villages in the parish and he must visit each one before his day's work is finished. When he returns home the sun is setting over the falls, turning the waters the colour of blood.

Ignacio's cabin is perched on a cliff and has clear views across Iguaçu. He chose the location himself and the natives built it for him as a gift, refusing to take a cent in payment. He receives a modest salary from the government and does not allow the indigenous people to pay for their consultations. His home, therefore, is a manifestation of their gratitude. It is well-built, with solid timber walls and a thatched roof which, in spite of the rains, has never leaked. Overlooking the falls is a veranda with a drop of more than a hundred feet to the boiling cauldron beneath.

The house is divided into two sections: on one side is a surgery that is open every morning, except Sundays; the other contains his own quarters, which are no more than a bedroom with a separate bathroom and an open-plan kitchen and living room. In a corner is a wood-burning stove that Ignacio cooks on and which heats the water. A diesel generator provided the electricity. The home is sparsely furnished and modest but he has never wanted for anything. He even has a record player.

Ignacio puts his bag on the table and selects Bach's *Cello Suites* from the rack of LPs. He removes the vinyl from the sleeve and places it on the turntable. Then he switches on the player and lowers the steel arm and hears an amplified scratch as the needle touches the record. There is a brief silence before the air swells with the low thrum of music. The cello's notes soar above the noise of water, the falls a kettledrum booming in the distance.

BUENOS AIRES–IGUAÇU–BUENOS AIRES

Tuesday 28–Wednesday 29 September 1976

Ariel gazes out of the aeroplane window at the city lights which glimmer like phosphorescence far below. How could he have been so naïve as to trust Carmen? The signs were there: her work as a flight attendant despite her education, her fluent Hebrew and her Israeli friends at Hecht's party. All these things shouted spook, but he had been oblivious. He doubts even that Carmen is her real name. What makes it worse is that he has fallen for her. Schmuck, as his father would have said.

Ariel takes a swig of gin and tonic and begins to rationalise. Although he has no job and Javier is dead, things could be worse. Ignacio Cruz is alive and he has promised to help. Once he has found the doctor and persuaded him to come to Buenos Aires, his part is over. The rest is up to the Church. The man is their problem, not his. Perhaps he could ask for his job back. With hindsight, he understood why Mario had pulled the story. A call from the ministry was one thing but a death threat was another matter entirely. His friend is right. He has a wife and children to think about. The path of least resistance is best.

Ariel takes another sip and shakes his head. Who does he think he is kidding? Would he really work for a newspaper which was at the beck and call of a military junta? No. But there is something else that puzzles him: Hecht, and why he, of all people, had been invited to his summer party. His host had even congratulated him on the Wolf's Lair story. Yet the man is in cahoots with the government. In fact, he is the government.

It all becomes clear as Ariel makes the connection between the billionaire and Linda Hollis. She would have told Hecht about his visit to the morgue and he would have informed the ministry. And yet one piece of the jigsaw was still missing. Unless, of course, again Hecht. It has always been Tiago Hecht. It was he or his henchmen who abducted and murdered the priest. Only Javier could have told them about Edelweiss.

Ariel searches in his pockets for the holy medal. Our Lady of Guadeloupe. He admires the coin and puts it back. He looks out of the window once more, but the view is obscured by cloud. He finishes his drink, reclines his seat and closes his eyes.

The flight is delayed by headwinds and the sky occluded when the Fairchild touches down at Posadas Airport. The only illumination comes from the runway lights and the control tower. In the terminal Ariel approaches the desk and enquires about the next flight to Iguaçu. There is an airstrip near the falls which is mostly used by commercial traffic.

'Let's see ...' and the booking clerk checks a manifest. 'There's one at 6:30 in the morning. Would you like to reserve a seat?'

'Yes. I'd also like two return tickets.'

'Two, you say?'

'That's right. I'm picking up a friend.'

The man quotes a price and Ariel pays with a credit card. A machine on the desk hums and prints out the tickets.

'That's one single and two returns for Puerto Iguaçu. I've booked you seats on both flights and the tickets are valid for a month.'

Ariel picks up the tickets and goes out to the taxi rank. 'Take me to the Continental,' he tells a driver. He has not had time to call the hotel or to ask for José. He does not know his friend is dead; it was never reported in the newspapers. The police investigation found that the car explosion was the result of a faulty fuel line.

The phone on Hermann Mattei's desk rings.

'Hello.'

'Señor Mattei?'

'Yes.'

'A passenger answering your description just bought a ticket to Iguaçu. The flight departs 06:30 tomorrow, arriving Iguaçu shortly after 07:00. He asked for two returns – said he was picking up a friend.'

'Did he mention anything else?'

'No, sir. Just that.'

'Thanks for the information.' Mattei ends the call.

A suave-looking man is sitting in an armchair smoking a Cohiba and drinking brandy from a balloon glass which he swirls nonchalantly.

'We've got him, *Tio*. He leaves for Iguaçu first thing in the morning. He's also bought two return tickets.'

Tiago Hecht makes no reply and puffs on his cigar. He has just arrived at his nephew's estancia by helicopter. The aircraft has been refuelled and is parked outside in a field. Everything is going according to plan. He has been waiting thirty years for this moment and now, at last, he is going meet Edelweiss. The Fourth Reich is about to begin.

Yuri Kantor leaves passport control and waits on the concourse of Buenos Aires International Airport. He is travelling light and only has a carry-on bag. He does not think his stay in the city will be long. He searches faces in the crowd and sees an attractive brunette approach. She is young and svelte and moves with feline grace. The agency has chosen well. The woman is a perfect honeytrap.

'Carmen,' she says.

'Yuri,' he responds.

The woman leads the way to her car, which is parked in the diplomatic section. Neither of them speak. Carmen starts the engine and heads to the city centre and the Israeli Embassy. When they reach the highway she starts talking, keeping her eyes on the road.

'We're tracking our source – he's on his way to Iguaçu

now. Once he's found Edelweiss he intends to bring him back here. We've been told the Vatican is prepared to help him escape. If they succeed it will be hard, if not impossible, to find him again. So, the agency wants you to eliminate the target before he leaves Buenos Aires. Intelligence indicates he will stay at the Jesuit mission, Manzana de las Luces, which is located close to the embassy. There is a constant watch on the building. Estimated time of the target's arrival is within the next twenty-four hours. Any questions?'

'None so far,' says Kantor and he looks at his colleague. But Carmen does not notice, her eyes are fixed on the highway.

The taxi turns into the plaza and draws up at the Hotel Continental. A bell strikes midnight, its toll echoing across the empty square. The clouds have vanished and the sky is clear. The moon glows as pale as a peeled fruit and the heavens pulse with tiny constellations. Ariel goes inside. The place is familiar and yet seems different from his last visit. He is unsure whether he or it has changed but somehow there has been a transformation. The man at reception recognises him.

'Nice to see you again, sir.'

'You, too. I haven't made a reservation but I wonder if my previous room is available?'

'That one is occupied. There's another on the top floor which also overlooks the park.'

'Okay, I'll take that.'

Ariel signs the register and the concierge gives him a key. He crosses to the lift, presses a button and watches the display change as he ascends. The lift arrives and he walks along the corridor and enters his room. It is almost identical to the last one, except the pictures and bed face the opposite way. The place is humid and he switches on the air-conditioning and soon there is a cooling draught.

Ariel opens the fridge, fills a tumbler with ice and empties a Johnnie Walker miniature. He adds a dash of Coke and has a slug. Hungry, he opens a jar of peanuts and pops a handful in his mouth. The journalist sits on the bed with his drink. Why did Ignacio Cruz have to be his problem? The entire world would be after him now, with Hecht and his goons being the least of his concerns. Presumably Carmen's mob would have their tabs on him as well, to say nothing of the CIA. He has a sip of whisky and considers what it means to be a Jew. Here he is, the child of a refugee from Nazi Germany, trying to save Adolf Hitler's son. The irony is bitter.

Ariel knocks back his drink and returns to the fridge. He takes another miniature and adds the rest of the Coke. He needs something to calm his nerves and raises the glass once more. The bubbles fizz beneath his nose. He gulps it down, giving himself a headache, but he is glad to have eased the pain. He reaches for the phone and dials reception, asking to be woken at 5 am. Then he strips off. In the bathroom he peers in the mirror and instantly regrets it. He looks like a ghoul. His cheeks are hollow and his eyes haunted.

Standing over the bowl, Ariel empties his bladder and

flushes the toilet. He has a wash and returns to the room. In bed, he extinguishes the lamp then draws the sheet around his shoulders and closes his eyes.

Ariel sleeps fitfully and his dreams shape-shift into a nightmare. The lights in the morgue burn brightly and people loom in and out of focus, their voices muffled and distorted. The body of a young man lies naked on a slab, his wrists and ankles lacerated by chains, his torso scored with burns.

To Ariel's horror the corpse sits up and looks straight at him.

'You promised,' Javier says. 'You promised to help.'

It is not yet dawn when the phone on the bedside table rings. Ariel wakes and fumbles for the receiver.

'Yes?'

'Good morning, sir. This is your wake-up call. It's five o'clock.'

'Thanks,' he says, relieved the night is over at last.

Ariel lies in the dark, feeling wretched. His mouth is parched from the air conditioning and it seems as though he has not slept at all. He raises an arm to shield his eyes, switches on the lamp and throws the covers aside. He has a shower and dresses then packs his bag, making sure he has left nothing behind, and goes down to reception. The same concierge is on duty. The man is grey and cadaverous and Ariel realises he must look as bad.

'Sleep well, sir?'

'I've had worse,' he says as he settles his bill.

Ariel leaves the hotel. A taxi is waiting to take him to the airport. The vehicle drives down deserted streets, just a police car or garbage truck rattling by. As they travel through the city night drains away and a cold dawn washes over the suburbs. The taxi joins the highway and traffic increases. In the opposite lane cars flicker past. Ahead, tail lights beckon like devils' eyes.

They arrive at the terminal and Ariel crosses the asphalt to a Cessna. Raindrops splash the ground and he turns up his collar and increases his pace. He ascends the aluminium steps and boards, stowing his bag in a locker. He does not have long to wait before the pilot's voice announces they are ready for take-off, asking everyone to fasten their seatbelts. Ariel obeys and listens to the engines whine as the propellers spin. The pitch rises in a crescendo and the aeroplane accelerates down the runway and lifts into the sky. As it climbs a watery sun rises above the steaming mass of jungle.

Ariel leans out of his seat and looks along the aisle. There are a handful of people on board, all male. Most are broad-chested and hard-faced and he assumes they are either military personnel or employees working for the logging industry. He turns away and checks his watch. They will be there soon.

Half-an-hour later the aeroplane lands at Puerto Iguaçu, the country's most northerly airport. The runway is short and bumpy but adequate for a small craft like the Cessna. It is pouring and the cabin windows are streaked with tears as the aeroplane comes to a halt.

The engines are cut and the fuselage door opened. Ariel puts his jacket over his head as he runs across the apron and enters the terminal. A sleepy official waves him through. Out in the forecourt is a line of taxis. A driver lowers his window and Ariel asks if he has heard of a Dr Cruz.

'Dr Ignacio Cruz? Of course, *jefe* – everyone knows him around here.' Ariel can scarcely believe it. The Virgin, or some heavenly body, must be watching over him. The man even looked like José with his beer belly, pencil moustache and tobacco-stained teeth.

'Can you take me there?'

'Sure I can. Climb aboard before you drown.'

And the car moves off, the windscreen wipers swishing back and forth in the deluge.

Ignacio stands on the veranda and surveys the view. It is raining and mist obscures the falls. This usually happened in the early morning, until the sun rose sufficiently to warm the air and burn away the clouds. Often, a rainbow traversed the gorge in a prism of light. He hears the sound of an engine and is surprised to see a taxi pull up. A young man emerges and runs to the house carrying a holdall, his shoulders hunched against the downpour. The car departs as the stranger approaches. Before he has reached the door, Ignacio is waiting on the threshold.

'You're early, the surgery isn't open yet.'

'I don't need a doctor.'

'Then what do you want?'

The person is anxious, as though someone might be following him.

'I'd rather talk inside.'

'All right, come in.'

He enters and Ignacio closes the door. The visitor is bedraggled but smartly dressed in a linen jacket and soft leather shoes and looks the city type. He also has a Buenos Aires accent.

'Would you like coffee?'

Ariel sees the pot warming on the stove, which fills the cabin with a rich aroma.

'Yes, please.'

Ignacio pours coffee into a pair of mugs. He hands one to Ariel who gratefully accepts the drink. He has had no sustenance at all that morning. The coffee is black and strong and warms the pit of his stomach.

'Tastes good.'

'It's made locally. I rarely drink anything else, apart from *mate*. Anyhow, let's talk.'

They take their coffees to the kitchen table and sit. Ariel wraps his hands around the mug and has another sip. Ignacio waits for him to speak but his companion seems reluctant.

'If you don't need a doctor, how can I help?'

Ariel is momentarily is lost for words. The man before him looks just like Adolf Hitler. Although he is tanned and bearded, he has the same dark hair and penetrating blue eyes. Certainly, he is the *Führer*'s son.

'It's about Javier.'

At the mention of the priest's name, the doctor's face lights up.

'My heavenly twin! I haven't seen him in ages. How is he?'

'I'm afraid, he's dead.'

Ignacio's joy is replaced by a look of shock.

'I'm sorry, I didn't know. What happened?'

'He was abducted and murdered.'

'Why?'

'Because of me.'

'What do you mean?'

'It's a little complicated ...'

Ariel explains he was the journalist who interviewed the priest and discovered Hitler and Eva Braun had escaped from Berlin, and that he had found their camp in the jungle. The story made the front pages of his newspaper and had gone around the world.

'I know. I read all about it. So, Javier was killed because of that?'

'Not only that. They wanted to make sure he never spoke about anything else.'

'Who are 'they'?'

'Nazis.'

Ignacio looks uncomfortable and shifts in his chair. Beyond the house the cataract roars. He wonders if his visitor is some dread harbinger from the underworld.

'What – Nazis, do you mean?'

Ariel chooses his words carefully.

'Javier wanted everyone to know what happened to his village despite the risk to his own life. But there was a much bigger secret which he refused to reveal because he knew it would be fatal. He promised I'd know the truth in the event of his death. After speaking out he must have realised he didn't have long to live and so he sent me a letter. He wrote that Hitler had a son who was taken by his nurse and brought to the Jesuit mission in Posadas, where he was adopted. He asked me to find the son because the man's life would now be in grave danger.'

Ignacio stares into his cup of coffee.

'What do I have to do with all of this?'

There is a thunderous roar and Ariel is unsure whether it comes from the cataract beyond or his own inner ear. But it sounds like the end of the world.

'You are that son.'

Ignacio is silent. He sits without moving, his features as cold and hard as granite. He bangs his fist upon the table, making the mugs jump, and leaps to his feet. He points a finger and trembles with fury.

'You're wrong! You're completely mistaken! This is a terrible hoax!'

Ariel remains seated and speaks calmly.

'No, it's not. I have your birth certificate and Javier's letter with me. Here, see for yourself,' and he produces the evidence.

Ignacio glares at the papers lying on the table as though he wished he could vaporise them.

'Go on, take a look.'

He picks up the birth certificate and holds it at arm's length as if it were something deadly.

'Where did you get this?'

'From a safety-deposit box at the Banco Provincia on Calle San Martín. Javier included the key in the letter he sent. The security code was your date of birth.'

Ignacio tosses the document aside.

'It's a fake.'

'No, it's not. It's genuine. Look at the stamp and the signatures.'

'Even if it is real, you've got the wrong person.'

'Your birthday's the same. You were born on the 6 November 1945. That's more than a coincidence, surely? But don't take my word for it, read the letter.'

Ignacio reluctantly takes up the note. He recognises the handwriting and gentle tone. It can only have been written by the priest. It is his brother's last confession.

'Javier asked me to find you. You must come with me to Buenos Aires. I've already spoken to the Society's principal. The Church will give you sanctuary. It's your only hope.'

The doctor puts the letter back on the table, resolutely shaking his head. He has made up his mind.

'I refuse to leave. My place is here with my people. They need me. I'm not going anywhere.'

'If you stay, you will die.'

'What does my death matter to you?'

'It doesn't matter to me at all. But it mattered to Javier. It mattered a great deal. He was killed because of you. He gave up his life for his best friend.'

'I'm sorry Javier died. But he didn't die because of me ... Because of who I am ...'

'Yes, he did! He was murdered by Nazis. They tortured

him to get your name and find out where you live. His silence cost him his life. I saw his body in the morgue. Whether you like it or not, you're Hitler's son, the man they call Edelweiss. You are the next *Führer*!'

Ignacio cries out in agony and buries his face in his hands. He does not care if someone wants to kill him but he cannot live with the knowledge that the most evil organisation the world has ever known wish him to be their leader and would stop at nothing to achieve it. Hundreds, perhaps thousands, of people could perish. It would be a catastrophe. He realises there is only one thing he can do. He must disappear.

The doctor groans and draws a hand across his face as though wiping away tears.

'I'll come with you. But first I need to pack some things.'

'There's no time. Just bring your wallet and passport.'

'What about these?' He gestures at the papers on the table.

'Destroy them.'

Ignacio takes the letter and his birth certificate to the stove and opens the door. There is a blast of heat and a glow of embers. He shoves the papers inside and they burst into flame. He watches them incinerate, stokes the fire with a poker and closes the door.

'That's done.'

'Let's go.'

They are about to depart when they hear an unusual sound. An incessant drone grows steadily louder as though a swarm of locusts were approaching. They look out of the window and see a helicopter descend, its blades slicing the air. The pair watch transfixed as the aircraft hovers above the ground, the draught of the rotors scattering sodden leaves and grass. The engine is cut and, before the blades have stopped, three men jump out and rush towards the property.

Ariel cries out in panic.

'We've got to get out of here!'

It is too late. The door swings open and the intruders stand at the entrance blocking the light. Ariel makes a dash for it and a shot is fired. He screams and falls to the floor clutching his side.

'We're unarmed!' shouts Ignacio, his hands raised.

The man who fired the weapon does not answer. He puts his gun back in its holster and, taking a step forward, raises an arm in salute.

'*Heil* Hitler! It is an honour to meet you, sir. Truly an honour. You look like your father. A strong resemblance. He would be proud.'

'My father?'

'Yes, sir, your father. The greatest person who ever lived and whom I once had the honour to serve. Reichsführer Adolf Hitler!'

Ariel lies on the floor groaning and clasping his side. Blood drips from his fingers onto the boards. Ignacio lowers his hands.

'Why did you shoot him?'

'This vermin? He's no use to us anymore.'

The doctor understands. Finally, the Nazis have come for him as he always knew they would. He knows what he has to do. It is fate.

'Identify yourself.'

The man who spoke straightens and clicks his heels.

'My name is Tiago Hecht or to be precise, Oberleutnant Tiago Hecht. During the war, I served in the Waffen-SS and fought on the Eastern Front. At your service!'

'And him?' he asks of Hecht's burly companion – the only one not to have put away his weapon.

'He's my bodyguard.'

'And you?'

The younger man comes to attention.

'Hermann Mattei. At your service!'

Ignacio gives a small smile of satisfaction.

'*Willkommen, Kameraden*. I'm delighted you're here. I've been waiting a long time, although I never doubted you would find me. I congratulate you on your perseverance.'

'Sir, we are ready. Everything is in place. An entire army is waiting at your command. You only have to say the word and the glorious new Reich shall begin!'

Ignacio's eyes gleam coldly.

'The time has come for the world to know its true destiny.'

Hecht, the acolyte, is overwhelmed. After all these years it has happened. The son, whom he has not seen since he was an infant, stands before him a man. The *Führer*'s own flesh and blood. Hecht's chin trembles and he begins to shake before his god. There is a quaver in his voice and his eyes brim with tears.

'*Mein Führer … Mein Führer …* We await your orders!'

'Of course. But first we must get rid of this vermin, as you rightly call him.' He puts out a hand. 'The gun.'

'Sir, it would be an honour. Go on, give him your piece,' Hecht tells the bodyguard.

Mattei barks a warning.

'*Tio*, be careful!'

His uncle ignores him.

'*Halt die Klappe! Der Führer hat gesprochen!*'

The bodyguard hands over his weapon. It is a Walther PPK and, when fully loaded, has eight rounds. Ignacio takes the pistol and levels it at the journalist. It feels good to have a gun in his hand again. He has taken the path less travelled and this is where it has led. The fate of the whole world resided in a single bullet. All he has to do is pull the trigger. His finger tightens and the hammer draws back.

'Goodbye, Jew.'

'What are doing?' says Ariel, his eyes pleading for mercy.

'Say your prayers, Jew.'

'Ignacio ... Please ... No ...'

'*Ja, toten die Jude.*' Hecht laughs. The others join in and the room is filled with a guttural mirth.

'Look at the kike, begging for his life!' says Mattei.

'One less cockroach ...' and Hecht urges Ignacio to shoot. '*Mein Führer*, do it!'

Ariel shuts his eyes and the world goes dark. He holds his breath as he waits for the inevitable bullet. It seems as if he has fallen into a pit, an endless void where everything has been reduced to this moment. Ariel hears several loud bangs in rapid succession and shudders involuntarily. Nothing happens. There is silence. He blinks and opens his eyes. Three men are sprawled upon the floor. The bodyguard and the younger man lie face down and do not move, the other is on his back. Hecht stares up in disbelief. There is a stain on his shirt and blood trickles from the corner of his mouth. He attempts to rise but does not have the strength and collapses.

'*Mein Führer*,' he says. '*Liebe Führer, nein*.'

Ignacio raises the pistol once more and pumps the remaining rounds into Hecht's chest as bloody holes erupt. He puts the gun on the table. There is a trail of smoke and the air reeks of cordite.

'You okay?' he asks.

'I guess ...' and Ariel gets unsteadily to his feet.

'Let me have a look.'

Ariel takes a chair and raises his shirt and the doctor inspects the injury. There is a gash on the lower right side.

'You'll be fine, it's just a graze.'

'Just a graze?'

'Another inch and you'd have lost a kidney and bled out. The nearest hospital is in Posadas.' Ignacio takes a syringe and bandages from his bag. 'I'll plug the wound and strap you up for now. We can deal with it later.'

He gives Ariel a jab and his flesh goes cold. Then he swabs the injury and places a dressing around the patient's middle.

'How's that?'

'Not too bad.'

'See if you can stand.'

Ariel rises keeping a hand on his abdomen.

'All right?'

'I think so,' he says. His side feels tender but otherwise he seems fine.

'Now, help me get rid of these assholes.'

Ignacio drags Hecht's corpse to the veranda. He returns and lifts up Mattei's shoulders while Ariel takes his feet. They bring him onto the balcony and put him beside his uncle then go back for the bodyguard. They place his corpse next to the others and Ignacio stoops and raises them onto the wooden rail. They are big and heavy and it requires considerable effort. He pauses before grabbing each man by the legs and pitching him over the edge. They tumble, one after the other, into the ravine. Their bodies strike the water with a resounding splash and sink. After a while, they surface and are carried downstream. The men watch as the corpses are swept away by the rapids, until they disappear from sight. Ignacio goes back to the house for the gun and returns and hurls it into the abyss. The pistol spins through the air, drops into the water and is gone.

They stand at the rail and watch the swirling river.

'I really thought you were going to shoot me.'

'Sorry, it was the only way I could think of getting the gun.'

'How did you know I'm Jewish?'

'I didn't. I just thought it sounded plausible.'

They go inside and Ignacio picks up his medical bag. He takes his passport and wallet from a drawer.

'Okay,' he says and they leave the house.

A jeep is parked beneath a tarpaulin which drips steadily in the rain. Ignacio used it for his weekly visits to town to buy groceries and medical supplies. Alongside the jeep is a battered Norton Triumph. Ariel walks to the vehicles but his companion stops and points at the helicopter.

'We'll take that.'

'You know how to fly one of those things?'

'I took a pilot's course during military service.'

'How did you do?'

'I passed.'

They walk across the glade and clamber aboard. Ignacio puts on a set of headphones and hands another pair to Ariel. He flicks switches in the control panel and checks the instruments.

'She's fully fuelled. We should be able to make it to BA in one hop.'

'The sooner, the better.'

'Hold on. This might be a bit hairy. I haven't flown in a while.'

Ignacio turns a key and presses the starter button and the rotor blades begin to churn. Soon the aircraft is revving at maximum. He clasps the control stick and eases the helicopter into the air. It makes a single revolution before rising up over the forest. When they reach cruising height Ignacio points the nose and the chopper heads away from the falls and races across the treetops, the morning sun burning through the clouds. He adjusts the gyrocompass and sets a course due south and the helicopter clatters above the jungle, the Parana an ochre ribbon meandering below.

The estuary gleams like a snail's belly in the morning light as the aircraft makes its final approach to Buenos Aires. The pilot contacts the control tower at Jorge Newbery, giving the helicopter's call sign, and asks to be allowed to land. Permission is granted and the tower directs them to a specified zone. In a few minutes the chopper touches down and the men alight and enter the terminal. They sign a form and pay the landing fee and go straight to the taxi rank. Palms idle in the breeze and there is an oily scent of oleander and aviation fuel.

Ariel tells the driver to head for the Jesuit college in the city centre. The car leaves the airport and, as they make their way through the traffic, Ignacio addresses his companion.

'How are you feeling?'

'The anaesthetic's worn off and my side's sore. But I don't think I'm bleeding.'

'I'll have a look when we get there and give you another shot. Then I'll stitch and dress it for you.'

The vehicle drives on through the busy traffic and they stop at a junction.

'By the way,' says Ariel. 'I owe you for saving my life.'

'You risked yours to come and find me.'

'You can thank Javier for that.'

'Yes. I have a lot to thank Javier for.'

The lights change and they set off once more through the teeming streets. They arrive at Manzana de las Luces and ascend the steps. Ariel rings a bell. A shutter opens and an old man with a childlike face peeks through the grille.

'Yes?'

'We've come to see the principal.'

'Come in.' The porter closes the shutter and the door opens. 'If you ask at reception, Sister will call him for you.'

They enter the hall and he locks the door behind them. The place is as silent as a tomb and an odour of dust and incense lingers. A grey-haired nun is seated behind a desk. Ariel asks if she can contact Father Maximilian. She puts down her breviary and peers over steel-framed glasses.

'And who are you?'

'Ariel Guzman. Tell him I've brought a friend.'

'I'll let him know right away.'

She makes the call then hangs up.

'He'll be with you shortly.'

The nun returns to her devotions and the visitors wait in the hall. It is not long before they hear footsteps and the principal appears.

'Ariel, good to see you,' he says and they shake hands.

'I'm Maximilian,' he says to the doctor.

'Ignacio.'

'You'd better come to my apartment.' Without another word the priest turns and walks away and the others follow.

They climb a narrow staircase, go down a passage and pause at a stout oak door. Father Maximilian brings out a bunch of keys and ushers them inside. The room is austere, the walls bare except for portraits of the Society's principals. They are pale-faced and dressed in black, most holding a prayer book or a religious ornament. Their expressions are grave and pious, a look of sorrow, or possibly disappointment, in their eyes. On the desk is a crucifix, the wounded figure carved from ivory.

The principal asks if there is anything they need and Ignacio informs him that his companion is injured and he must treat the wound.

'We had uninvited guests,' and he explains what happened.

Father Maximilian is unperturbed.

'The world is a better place without them.'

'Are there others?' asks Ariel.

'Unfortunately, yes. The government is full of neo-Nazis and their sympathisers. Fortunately, they don't know you're here. Now, come and lie down on the divan. It's where I have my siesta and also where I do my best thinking.'

Ignacio opens his bag and takes out what he needs. He removes the soiled dressing and gives his patient another injection then swabs the wound and sutures it. He cuts the thread, ties a knot and puts on a fresh bandage.

'There we go. If it hurts or starts to bleed you must go to hospital and get it dressed again. Otherwise, you should be fine and the stitches can be taken out in a week or so.'

'The people at Iguaçu are going to miss you.'

'And I'm going to miss them.' Ignacio gets to his feet, puts the bloody bandage in a bin and pulls up a chair. 'What now?' he asks Father Maximilian.

'I've spoken with our superior general and he has informed the Holy Father. Pope Paul insists you come to the Vatican. According to him, you were brought up in the care of the Church and therefore you're our responsibility. You'll be given a new identity and become a lay brother of our Society.'

'A lay brother? But I'm a doctor.'

'It's the only way the Church can protect you.'

'Will I ever be allowed to leave?'

'That's entirely up to you, although I don't think it wise. You'll be safe there.'

Ignacio realises his life is no longer his own. His past or, at least, its antecedents, has caught up with him. He must accept this fact, with all its limitations, if he wishes to live.

'When do I leave?'

'Tonight. I've booked you on the next flight to Rome. My name on the passenger list shouldn't arouse suspicion. I often visit the Vatican. I usually travel economy but this time I've reserved a seat in business class. It means fewer people will see you on the plane.'

'Are you coming with me?'

'I'm afraid not. People know who I am and your identity is no longer a secret – at least, not to the security services. I'll call the desk before you arrive at the airport and ask for my seat to be transferred into Ariel's name. You'll be using his passport.'

'We don't look alike,' says Ariel.

'Superficially, perhaps. But you're the same age and the same height. You both have dark hair and blue eyes, although they're different hues. Passport photos are only black-and-white and the description matches you both.'

'In my photo I have a beard. I only recently shaved it off.'

'Now you're growing one again.'

'Not really. I just haven't used a razor in a while,' and Ariel strokes his stubbled cheek.

'That's the ID sorted. But how do I get to the airport without being seen?'

'You'll go in my official car with my driver. If you keep your head down until you leave the city, those watching will assume I've sent my chauffeur on an errand. He's a retired policeman. He'll be able to shake off anybody who tries to tail you.'

'Is there anything else I can do?' asks Ariel.

'Yes, there is. Except it's not without risk.'

'Okay. What?'

'It would be useful to have a decoy. I'm sure we're being watched. If you leave here dressed as Ignacio, whoever's waiting is bound to follow. They cannot risk him escaping. Keep to the main streets and public places and you should be fine. By the time they discover who you really are, he'll be gone.'

'Why don't I take his passport and ID since he'll have mine?'

'That's a good idea.'

'Are you sure about this? I mean, whoever comes after you thinking you're me ...'

'As Father Maximilian says, there's a risk. But as soon as they get close they'll realise they have the wrong guy and it will give you valuable time.'

In the plaza opposite Manzana de las Luces, the killer waits. An unmarked van is parked nearby and he can hear voices in his earpiece. The Mossad team are monitoring every call and have a microphone directed at the building. But the signal is intermittent and they can hear only snatches of conversation from the principal's room. The man's nerves jangle, knowing that his target is so close.

He notices the birds which flit here and there and alight

on lamp posts and telephone wires. They have dark, crested heads and yellow beaks and sing lustily and he wonders what they are. He is sure the boy selling newspapers at the kiosk would know. He plainly liked them too as sometimes he threw crumbs and watched them fight over the scraps. They are zorzals although Yuri Kantor does not know this as he observes the birds while hidden in a doorway.

The principal and his visitors wait out the remaining hours in his room. Food and drinks are delivered and empty plates and glasses taken away. The light deepens as day turns into afternoon and evening becomes dusk. A clock strikes and Father Maximilian rises from his chair and switches on a lamp, filling the room with an amber glow.

The sun descends over the city and darkness falls. Zorzals make a final burst of song and settle down for the night, perching on eaves and in trees. After a last warble they cease and fluff out their feathers and close an eye. Only a car or motorbike disturbs the silence. And in the shadows, the killer waits.

It is time to go. Ignacio and Ariel swap clothes and exchange passports and IDs. The journalist now wears a weather-beaten safari jacket and hiking boots, the doctor looks like a fashionable city slicker in chinos and leather loafers. The principal is right. They look similar and the clothes fit them well.

Ignacio gives his companion a hug. 'Come and see me in Rome.'

'I will. Safe journey.'

'Thanks. And thank you for all you've done.'

'It's certainly been an experience.'

'One I'm sure you'd rather not have.'

They embrace each other once more and face the principal.

'Okay,' he says.

They leave the apartment and descend the stairs. The place is empty. The porter left some time ago and the nun has joined her brethren in the church for Compline.

'If you go now, we'll make our way to the garage. My driver's already there.'

'Take care,' says Ignacio.

'You, too,' says Ariel and he opens the door and lets himself out. When he has gone Father Maximilian locks up and escorts Ignacio to the basement.

Ariel stands alone on the pavement. He then proceeds along the main boulevard as the principal advised and makes his way to Plaza de Mayo, which is always busy, whatever the hour. He does not see a man slip out of a doorway, making sure he keeps his distance. He walks down Calle Bolívar to the park. It is full of people taking the air. He finds an empty bench. It is almost over. Soon Ignacio will be airborne and, once in the Vatican, he can disappear into the embrace of the Church. Ariel thinks about Javier and how the priest's revelation had set everything in motion. It seems so long ago. He puts a hand in a pocket and searches for the holy medal then remembers the doctor is wearing his jacket. At least, Ignacio has the Virgin's protection.

Ariel looks around. Nearby is the bronze statue of the nation's liberator, General Manuel José Belgrano, banner in hand, astride a prancing horse. Beyond the fountains is the Casa Rosada, its bastions draped with the colours of the national flag. In the centre of the square the May Pyramid rises palely into the sky. It was built in 1811 to commemorate the first anniversary of the revolution. The night is thick with the scent of jasmine as people wander to and fro. In the gardens cicadas sing and the air is filled with fireflies.

He gets up and is about to go towards the pyramid when a stranger approaches and asks him for the time. Ariel looks at his watch and feels a sharp blow to his chest. It is as though he has been punched: the air is knocked out of him and he collapses. The man places an arm around his victim's shoulders to stop him falling and sets him down on the bench. He puts a hand inside Ariel's jacket and removes his wallet and passport. His assailant checks the documents then puts the wallet back, takes the passport and walks away without a word.

The pain is intense and Ariel finds it hard to breathe. He clutches his chest. It is wet and sticky and his hand is covered in blood. He has not been punched but stabbed with a stiletto. He sits on the park bench bleeding to death. No one comes near. Everyone assumes nothing has happened. Ariel is in too much pain to speak or cry out. He closes his eyes then opens them and sees a myriad of lights swimming before him and thinks they must be stars. He wonders why there are so many and why they keep moving. The lights fly faster and faster until they become a dizzying blur. But they are not stars, they are fireflies.

BUENOS AIRES

Friday 1–Monday 4 October 1976

The pathologist who performed the autopsy on Javier also does the same for Ariel. He looks at the naked body on the slab and wonders why two men should perish so violently and at such a young age? He also tells himself it is unwise to ask questions. He does not want another phone call from the ministry. And so he puts on a visor, picks up an electric saw and begins to open the man's chest cavity. When he has cut through the sternum he switches off the machine and fixes a clamp and opens up the rib cage. As soon as he sees the punctured heart, he has his diagnosis.

'At least, it was quick,' he says, prodding the organ with a finger. 'Pity, it's a good one, too.'

The pathologist leaves a technician to stitch up the torso and, removing his surgical gloves, he goes to his office to write the report. In it he states: 'Caucasian male, early thirties, death caused by catastrophic blood loss, result of trauma to the heart from a sharp instrument.' He notes there is a flesh wound in the lower abdomen that has already been treated and is unrelated to the cause of death. The body is released and, because Ariel has no close relatives, it is collected by the local authority.

The journalist is buried three days later. The funeral is a joint a ceremony conducted by Father Maximilian and a rabbi from the Libertad Synagogue. Since Ariel has not been baptised, the interment takes place in the dissident section of the Municipal Cemetery in Chacarita. Attendance is sparse with just a few colleagues from La Nación turning up including Mario Ovalle.

After the rabbi has said Kaddish, the undertakers lower the coffin into the grave. Father Maximilian dips an aspergill in a vessel and splashes holy water across the earth and into the vault. When he has finished, Ovalle steps forward and places a floral wreath at the head of the grave. He has declined to give a eulogy, knowing it would be the last thing his friend and erstwhile colleague would have wanted. He stands for a moment, his head bowed, and makes the sign of the cross. He realises Ariel's death is not his fault but he feels guilty just the same. Perhaps it is because he allowed him to quit his job. He knows his guilt will not bring his friend back. Guilt always seemed such a pointless emotion but it was also what made you human.

The mourners thank the priest and rabbi and soon depart. There is no wake and they have work to do. The principal invites his fellow celebrant back to his rooms at Manzana de las Luces and the man accepts. The college has a famous library, with copies of the Dead Sea Scrolls and the Gnostic Gospels, which the rabbi is keen to study. As they walk away Father Maximilian notices a young woman in a veil, wearing black. She does not look at him and yet, from the way she holds herself, he can tell she is weeping. He pauses and wants to comfort her but the other man takes him by the arm.

'Let her be.'

The priest and rabbi move on leaving the woman to her sorrow. When they have gone she places a single red rose next to the wreath. Beneath the veil her cheeks are stained with tears. Carmen can find no words to say but she knows that her grief is prayer enough.

The solitary mourner says a last farewell to the man she loved, realising she will never meet his like again. With a final look at the open grave, Carmen turns and leaves. She walks through the cemetery to the car park and gets into a vehicle. She removes her veil and puts on a hat and a pair of dark glasses and drives away to the city centre. The traffic moves at a crawl but she does not mind. There is plenty of time in which to make her rendezvous.

Carmen arrives outside the US Embassy in Avenida Colombia and parks beneath a walnut tree. It is fully in leaf and shades the vehicle from the glare of the midday sun. She turns off the engine and waits. Armed marines guard the entrance but they will not be able to protect her intended victim.

The hours pass and shadows grow. At precisely 5:30 pm the embassy gates open and her target drives out in a silver BMW. Carmen starts her vehicle and tails the car as it passes through Plaza Italia and turns into the wide boulevard of Avenida Santa Fe. After several blocks the BMW approaches the business district. At the traffic lights on the main junction of Avenida 9 de Julio, Carmen draws up alongside.

The driver looks across and even though the other woman is wearing a hat and sunglasses, she is sure that she recognises her and so she smiles. The last thing Linda Hollis sees is the long black barrel of a silenced Glock raised through an open window. Before she can react, Carmen squeezes the trigger and fires three shots point-blank at her head. When the lights change, she takes off into the mid-town traffic.

Despite the light being green the BMW remains stationary. Drivers sound their horns and yell at the woman to get a move on. They can shout and honk all they want but she cannot hear. Lying slumped across the steering wheel, Linda Hollis is dead.

ROME

Friday 10–Wednesday 22 December 1976

Rain falls on the Eternal City. People hurry to and fro, holding umbrellas and dodging puddles that cover the streets and plazas. Dark clouds shroud the hills and the great dome of St Peter's glistens like a semi-precious stone. A young man in a café is having breakfast and listens to the rain drumming on the awning.

Moshe Levin drinks his cappuccino and takes a bite from his favourite snack: mascarpone and sliced Parma ham on crusty white bread. Observant in almost everything, Levin makes an exception for prosciutto. He cannot believe how something so sublime could not be kosher. It is the food of heaven. As a student of theology, he wonders what Moses or Abraham would have thought. Maybe he should ask his supervisor. Unfortunately, the rabbi is from Hebron and is not known either for his sense of humour or for his love of air-dried ham. Levin realises that he should probably let the matter rest.

After passing his civil service exams and spending four years at headquarters, the Israeli foreign ministry had sent him to Rome. Levin has been there for a year learning diplomacy and the fine arts of tradecraft. Ostensibly, he is studying for a doctorate on the Soteriology of the Judaeo-Christian Tradition. In reality, he works for the Mossad. Recently Levin has been given a simple task, the sort any spy should be able to do without breaking sweat and that is to find one man. The mission seems straightforward but it requires a degree of subtlety. He cannot make any enquiries because the man is not supposed to exist. All he has to go on is a face. And there are many faces in the Eternal City.

The café, at least, is a good place to eavesdrop since it is popular with the clergy. So far, Levin has learnt nothing useful. His reports to headquarters have been no more than travelogue. He raises his cup to take another sip, sees there are only dregs, and orders another. He also asks for another sandwich.

'Just the one.'

The waitress smiles and soon returns with his order. Levin loves Italian girls and those in Rome are the prettiest he has seen. Haughty of course and sometimes a temper too, but he admires that in a woman. It is hard to seduce one if they know you are Jewish so he pretends to be a seminarian. Italian women like defrocking a would-be priest, even a circumcised one.

The rain stops and a winter sun emerges from the clouds and rinses the plaza in light. Bernini's columns gleam and pigeons bob and dance then, with a sudden wing-clap, take off across the square. Levin finishes his breakfast and pays the bill. He walks to the basilica and climbs the long flight of steps. At the entrance he removes his fedora and shows his

ID to a Swiss Guard and passes the faithful who patiently wait in file. He is early for his tutorial and he wanders around the church admiring its stately domes and frescoes. There is so much agony and ecstasy in the faces of the saints and martyrs that he finds it impossible not be moved. As he once mentioned to his supervisor, it was enough to make you Catholic. He was unsure if the rabbi agreed since he had pretended not to hear.

The man Levin is looking for is no more than a couple of hundred metres away in another part of the Vatican. He is secluded in the Apostolic Palace where ordinary visitors, including those with diplomatic status, have no access. Ignacio Cruz is staying in the private apartments reserved exclusively for the Pope and his personal staff. His trip to the airport went without incident and he had safely boarded an Al Italia flight using Ariel's passport. It was only when he checked his pockets midway through the journey that he found the holy medal. He knew Javier must have given it to the journalist since Our Lady of Guadeloupe was his friend's favoured guardian. He kept the coin in his desk as a memento along with Ariel's passport.

When Ignacio arrived in Rome he was met at the aircraft steps by a papal escort and taken in an armoured limousine straight to the Vatican, where he was greeted by the Society's superior general, Pedro Arrupe, and debriefed. It was some days before they learnt of Ariel's death because he was carrying Ignacio's ID instead of his own. Nobody knew why and all subsequent enquiries had drawn a blank and the case was closed. Police also visited the doctor's house in Iguaçu but found it empty. Apart from a small bloodstain on the floorboards, there was no evidence of a struggle and they assumed he must be doing his rounds somewhere out in the forest. He had not been reported missing and they were sure he would turn up before long.

As for Tiago Hecht, his nephew and the bodyguard, their disappearances were noted and the authorities searched high and low but the piranhas and river crocodiles had done their work and their bodies were never found.

In the meantime, Ignacio has been given a new identity and a Vatican passport. He also has an important meeting. His Holiness Pope Paul has asked to see him. It is only with his approval that Ignacio has been able to stay in the palace. Shortly before the appointment he leaves his room and walks down the corridor to the papal apartments. A guard checks his pass and he enters the inner sanctum. A member of the Curia shows him into the pontiff's office and closes the door. An elderly man in a white cassock and pellegrina, with a matching zuchetto, rises and greets him. Ignacio genuflects, bows his head and kisses the ring on the outstretched hand and is brought to his feet.

'Welcome, dear brother in Christ.'

'Thank you, Holy Father.'

'I'm sorry I haven't been able to see you earlier, I've been so busy. The world seems to reside in a state of perpetual crisis. But enough of that – we have much to talk about.' The pontiff shows his visitor to a chair, high-backed and gilded, like a throne. 'I'm so glad you made it. Father Maximilian tells me that things are bad in Argentina.'

'I'm afraid so. Particularly since Videla seized power.'

'The devil has many servants.'

The pontiff is birdlike and precise in his movements and his eyes glister. He seems much older than his years and his face appears forlorn, as if the sins of the whole world are borne on his thin shoulders. Ignacio is struck by the Pope's humility. A man of God who understands he is merely fulfilling a role that has been ordained by fate. He has all the trappings of an emperor yet knows such riches are only temporal. He is a king without a country. In fact, his only kingdom are his people.

'The superior general tells me you've had an eventful journey.'

'You could put it that way, yes.'

'Please, tell me what happened.'

Ignacio recounts how Ariel found him at Iguaçu and the near fatal confrontation with Hecht and his henchmen followed by their escape in a helicopter. He is full of praise for the journalist and Father Maximilian, without whose help he would never have made it to Rome.

'I'm delighted you're here, believe me. But you must understand, while you may be under the tutelage of the Church, you're not out of danger. There is only so much the Vatican can do. Even the pontiff is at risk, which is why I have the Swiss Guard. However, the threat to my life is because of the office I hold, not because of who I am. The threat to yours is specific precisely because of who you are.

In other words, there are people who wish you harm.'

'You mean Mossad?'

'Yes. It was they who killed Ariel.'

'I thought as much.'

'Since the creation of Israel, which the Church now wholeheartedly supports, its government has a mandate to eliminate anyone or anything that threatens the state.'

'In that case, I should go elsewhere.'

'Unfortunately you can't. Your face is known. They will be searching for you. So, it's best that you hide. Where better than the Vatican?'

'Doesn't this compromise the Church?'

'Yes and no. We are in an invidious position. I believe my predecessor, Pius, made a grave error in not speaking out forthrightly against the Nazis and not doing more to protect the Jewish people. He had his reasons and he was human and frail, like the rest of us. But a pope should not bear false witness against another pope. There were notable exceptions among the clergy – some saved many lives at great risk to themselves and, indeed, some perished. But the Church's response to the Holocaust as a whole is a stain on our history which we cannot eradicate, we can only acknowledge.'

'Then why protect me?'

'Because you're a child of the Church. From the moment the girl handed you to the mission in Posadas, you became our responsibility. Regardless of who you are. All children are born innocent.'

Ignacio remembers the orphanage and the kindness of

the nuns who cared for him, particularly Maria, who was like a mother. And yet he wonders if some people's destiny is determined at birth.

'Do you believe there are those who should never have been born?'

'You mean Judas?'

'Among others.'

'All I can say is that the Iscariot fulfilled the scriptures. It's one of the great paradoxes of the Faith. Christ had to die in order for the world to be saved.'

'And what of my … ?' Ignacio lowers his gaze. He cannot bring himself to say the word.

'Alas, that is a question which can never be answered; at least not on this earth. Throughout the centuries philosophers have tried to divine the will of God. I would not say that it's a pointless exercise but it's certainly a hopeless one.'

It is an appropriate response for a man not noted as a theologian although it does nothing to assuage Ignacio's abiding sense of guilt.

'I can't help thinking it would be better if I were dead.'

'The Lord brought us into this world. Only He should take us from it.'

'Why did He take Ariel instead of me?'

'It was his time, that is all.'

Ignacio has never forgotten the day when Father Bartolomeo and Maria informed him who his natural parents were. His world had imploded. They might as well have told him he was the spawn of Satan. The pain still lingered like the pale scars on his wrists. It was a curse which he longed to escape and he wondered if he would ever be free.

The Pope can see his visitor is perturbed and gently prompts. 'Is there something in particular that bothers you?'

Ignacio appears at a loss. Perhaps His Holiness can enlighten him.

'Yes, there is. Again it's about my … It's about him or, more specifically, his sins. I feel tainted. As if the blood of his crimes were on my hands.'

'You are not responsible for Hitler's actions, grievous though they were. Or anyone else's for that matter.'

'Israel doesn't see it that way.'

'I know. But six million perished after all …'

A clock on the mantelpiece chimes and, for a moment, time stops. A wind stirs the muslin drapes and a vestal light enters the room and fills it like a presence.

'I've already cost the lives of two innocent men. One of whom I considered my twin and the other, even though we only knew each other briefly, was like a brother. Now they're gone.'

'I'm truly sorry about that. You must pray for them. That is the only thing you can do. We're all here for a reason.'

'Everyone?'

'Yes. Even you.'

'So, I must live?'

'The kingdom of God resides in us all. You have done much good work already and you've much good work yet to do, this is what the Lord asks of us. You're a doctor. You can use your gifts in the Vatican. There are many sick and elderly who require your care. I realise that living here may seem like being in a gilded cage but, in time, I hope you'll feel liberated by such constraints.'

'Like the religious?'

'Indeed. The Jesuits have accepted you as a lay brother and I believe that is what is best for you and for the Church.'

'In that case, I shall be happy to remain and administer to the sick.'

'I'm glad. Christmas is almost upon us and so we prepare for the birth of our Saviour. In spite of everything there is much to be joyful about.'

'Holy Father, you've set my mind at rest and I'm grateful for all that you've done. I shall endeavour to do my best and serve the Church.'

'That's wonderful. I'm happy to have met you at last and I hope I'll see you again soon,' and the pontiff rises from his chair.

Ignacio does the same and folds his arms across his chest.

'May I have a blessing?'

The Pope raises a hand and makes the sign of the cross.

'Lord, bless your faithful servant and all his work. *In nomine Patris et Filii et Spiritus Sancti*. Amen. Go in the peace of Christ.'

Ignacio bows once more and leaves. He is escorted back to his room, where he spends the rest of the day arranging books on his shelves and putting the clerical clothes and undershirts of his new wardrobe away. His meals are shared in a communal dining room with Catholic clergy from all over the world. Another from a faraway country elicits few questions, if any.

Bishop Giuseppe shuffles along the corridor to the clinic. His left foot or, more precisely, his big toe, is painful. He has no idea what is wrong and fears it might be rheumatoid arthritis. But the toe is swollen right up to the joint and he can barely walk. He wonders whether his foot, or even the entire limb, might be amputated. A tear comes to his eye and he stops and leans on his cane and dabs it away with a handkerchief. He blows his nose loudly and sniffs before folding the cloth and putting it back in a pocket. A one-legged bishop would be no good at all. After a few more steps he reaches the clinic and, having paused for breath, he opens the door. Giuseppe enters and sees a young nun seated behind a desk. She is pale and dark-eyed and pretty, with a downy moustache on her lip. There is a mole on her neck the size of a raisin and he has to resist the urge to pluck it.

'Hello, I'm Bishop Giuseppe. I have an appointment.'

'A sore foot, isn't it? Please take a seat. The doctor won't be long.'

He ambles to a wooden chair and sits heavily. He is the only person there but he can hear voices in the other room. There is an odour of surgical spirit and talcum powder. The smell gets up the bishop's nose and he sneezes.

'Bless you,' says the nun and Giuseppe chortles.

'And the same to you, Sister.'

After a few minutes the door is opened by a good looking,

clean-shaven young man as he sees out his charge.

'If there's any further problem, please don't hesitate to come and see me.'

The man's Italian has a strange accent but what is most notable are his eyes. The patient thanks the doctor and he turns his glacial gaze towards the bishop.

'Please, come through.'

Giuseppe lurches awkwardly into the surgery. Ignacio closes the door.

'How can I help you, Bishop?'

The prelate cannot help staring at the man's eyes. They are mesmerising and shine like quartz. He shakes his head and huffs and looks at his foot.

'It's my big toe, Doctor. Agony. It's as though the devil's prodding it with a fork, all day and all night. I can barely walk – or sleep.'

'Let me have a look.'

Giuseppe slips off his shoe and removes a white cotton sock. He raises his bare foot. The toe is raw and weeps like an overripe plum. Ignacio takes the foot tenderly in his hands and inspects it before putting it down.

'Gout.'

'What?'

'You have gout.'

'That's ridiculous! We're not living in the eighteenth century. I can't possibly have gout.'

'I'm afraid you do. It's quite common, even now, particularly in older men.'

'But I'm not old! I'm only fifty-three.'

'Well, it's gout anyway. I'll give you an injection of hydrocortisone and a course of antibiotics.' He notices the cleric's red pigskin slippers. 'You should change your footwear, your shoes are too tight. I suggest you wear sandals and no socks.'

The bishop looks appalled, as though a Protestant has asked him for Communion.

'I'm not some hairy-toed friar – people would be shocked!'

Giuseppe works for the Curia with a sinecure to administer papal knighthoods and orders to the great and the good, and even the not so great and the not so good. A fee was usually paid and he had no qualms about taking his cut. It's for administrative purposes, he would say, if anyone ever asked, which they rarely did. Besides, the practice of simony was harmless and had been going on for centuries. The recipient got the kudos of the award and the Church received much-needed income. What did it matter if a few liri went into his pocket? After all, a bishop was required to have certain standards.

'Friar or not, you need to change your shoes and you need to change your diet. No more red wine, cheese or cream.'

Giuseppe's bulbous eyes almost pop out of his head when he hears this. His favourite food is fettuccine carbonara washed down with a glass, or two, of good Chianti. Except for prosciutto and soft cheese, he rarely eats anything else. Perhaps an orange or a slice of melon in season but that is all. No red wine, cheese or cream? He might as well lay down and die.

'Impossible! Absolutely impossible. I'd rather starve.'

'Try. You can eat pasta but have it with pesto instead of cream. And, if you must eat cheese, just have a sprinkling of Parmesan. And only one glass of wine a day.'

Giuseppe feels a little better when he hears this.

'I suppose I can do that. By the way, if you don't mind me saying, your accent's strange. Where are you from?'

Ignacio's blue eyes flash in the morning light.

'Have a guess.'

'No idea – Brazil?'

'You're close. Argentina.'

'Whereabouts?'

'In the north. Iguaçu.'

'Ah, the missions. So, you're a Jesuit?'

'Yes, I'm a lay brother.'

Giuseppe bobs his head approvingly. He liked the Jesuits.

'Are you involved in the liturgy here?'

'No. I thought it was only for seminarians and the ordained.'

'It is, mostly, but we have lay people, too. Would you like to be?'

'Of course, if it's not too much trouble.'

'Apart from my work in the Curia, I'm also the assistant director of liturgy. We're short of servers over Christmas. How about bearing the cross at midnight Mass in the basilica? Pope Paul will be the celebrant.'

Ignacio remembers he has not been to confession for some time. It would be an appropriate penance.

'I'd like that – I'd like that very much.'

'Consider it done. I've a meeting with the pontiff this afternoon.'

'Give him my best wishes.'

Giuseppe's face brightens when he hears this.

'You've actually met him?'

'Last week. He's an impressive man.'

'He is indeed! Sadly the Holy Father's not well but we hope and pray.'

'I'm sorry to hear that.' Ignacio examines his patient's foot again before releasing it. 'Let me give you a jab and some antibiotics and you can be on your way.' He opens a glass-fronted cabinet and removes a syringe from its wrapper. He sees the bishop wince.

'Don't worry, it won't hurt. I promise.'

He fills the syringe from a bottle and places the needle above the joint and pierces the epidermis. The doctor is right. His skill is such that Giuseppe feels almost nothing at all. Ignacio produces a packet of pills and writes out a prescription which he gives to his patient.

'Take one of these before each meal. Do this for a week and come and see me again.'

Giuseppe puts his sock and shoe back on and Ignacio shows him out of the surgery.

'I'll be in touch about the Mass.'

'Thanks and remember avoid rich food, especially cheese.'

'*Si, Dottore* ...'

The bishop shuffles out of the surgery and makes his way down the marble corridor. All this talk of fasting and abstinence has made him peckish and he decides to have an early lunch. He turns a corner and walks down another long passage at the end of which stands a Swiss Guard wearing the traditional blue-and-yellow striped uniform and steel helmet. The man recognises him and opens a door and he goes outside. Tourists smile and take pictures and Giuseppe smiles back. He hurries across the square, as fast as his pigskin slippers will carry him, to his favourite café. Even at mid-morning the place is crowded and all the tables are taken. He looks about and sees one occupied by a monsignor who worked in a nearby office.

'*Ciao*, Antonio, can I join you?'

The man called Antonio looks up. He is the same size and shape as the bishop and also has the same appetite. He is tucking into an almond cream pastry with a fork, a double espresso at his elbow.

'*Ciao*, Giuseppe! Of course.'

The other cleric manoeuvres himself around the table and sits on a chair that is too small for his bulk.

'How are things?'

'Not so good. Just saw our new doctor about my foot. I've gout, apparently.'

'Gout? In this day and age!'

'I know. But he assured me it was true.'

'That's too bad. What did he say?'

'He said I must eat nothing but fettuccine carbonara and drink a bottle of Chianti a day.'

The monsignor giggles and has another forkful of pudding. Giuseppe beckons a waitress and as the girl approaches he airily waves away the menu she offers.

'The usual please,' he says and is about to ask for a carafe of red wine when he remembers Ignacio's edict. 'And a glass of Prosecco. Would you care for one?' he says to his companion.

'Why not? It's Christmas.'

'Make that two.'

Giuseppe mops his brow while he waits for his order. Even though it is winter, he is hot and the café airless with the door and windows closed because of the weather. The sound of cutlery on plates and noise from the kitchen makes people talk loudly and there is a hubbub of numerous conversations.

'What's the doctor like?'

His companion beams as he remembers their conversation.

'*Simpatico*! Wonderful hands, very gentle. He gave me an injection and I didn't feel a thing. That's the sign of a good doctor. I'll tell you what, though – he has the funniest accent. It's like he's chewing gum when he talks,' and Giuseppe works his jaw up and down.

'Where's he from?'

'Argentina. From the north – Iguaçu, he said. He's a Jesuit lay brother. But the most amazing thing are his eyes.'

'Really?'

'Yes. Pale blue, like a Siamese.'

He continues to describe the doctor and does not notice the studious young man at the next table with his head buried in a newspaper. Moshe Levin cannot believe what he is hearing. He leans closer and listens.

'The doctor only arrived recently but he's already met the Holy Father. He must know people. Anyway, I asked if he wanted to be involved in the liturgy at Christmas and he was happy to help. So, he's going to be the cross-bearer at midnight Mass, when the Pope's officiating.'

'That's wonderful!'

'Isn't it? And what's so nice is that I could tell it meant a lot to him. For some it's just a chore but for others it's an honour. As it should be.'

Levin does not miss a word. When the bishop and monsignor's talk turns to other matters, he pays his bill and leaves. The young man calmly walks away. Everything must seem natural. He stops by a gypsy playing an accordion and, when the man has finished his song, Levin throws some coins into a hat. He walks on swinging his umbrella and doffs his fedora to a group of old ladies as they pass.

Levin arrives at the embassy in Via Michele Mercati. He rushes upstairs to the communications centre and starts to type up his report. As soon as he has finished, he sends an encrypted message to headquarters marking the communiqué urgent.

TEL AVIV–ROME

Wednesday 22–Sunday 26 December 1976

Yuri Kantor is in the Mossad chief's office. This time, instead of bright sunshine, a storm is blowing out to sea. The sky is overcast and rain lashes the windows. He knows he killed the wrong man in Buenos Aires and, although he feels bad about it, there was little he could have done. Such collateral damage often happened on operations. It was just one of those things. But it did not make him feel any better.

Yitzhak Hofi is at his desk. In his hand he holds Levin's telex. His voice is resolute.

'We've just received important news from Rome. Confirmation Edelweiss is at the Vatican. We know where he works and what he does.'

'I see.'

'The target has nowhere else to go. He's ours.'

Hofi describes how the information was gathered and outlines the operation, which has already been planned. There will be five two-man teams but the most important will be the agent who procured the intelligence and Kantor. The others are there to act as back-up. Levin has procured VIP tickets so they can sit in the front row at Mass on Christmas

Eve, when Edelweiss will be carrying the ceremonial cross.

'On the stroke of midnight a figure of the infant Jesus will be presented to the Pope on a cushion. It is the highlight of the ceremony. At the same moment the church bells ring out. The noise, apparently, is quite deafening. Your partner will feign a seizure. Edelweiss will be standing nearby and you'll signal to him that a member of the congregation is in distress. Being a doctor, he won't fail to attend. You'll take the agent to a place where the target can safely be despatched.'

'What method should I use?'

'Whatever you like. But make sure it's clean. Since he's not meant to exist, there'll be no diplomatic incident. Not a public one anyway.'

'Are you sure we've got the right man this time?'

'Yes, I'm sure. After this, I'll let you go. I promise.'

'When do I leave?'

'There's an El Al flight departing at 16:30. Your ticket is at the desk. As in Buenos Aires, you'll be met at the airport and taken directly to the embassy. You'll see the rest of the crew there. Some of them you know already. There's forty-eight hours before operations commence. Plenty of time to scope the location and work out any probabilities.'

'Tell me about my partner.'

Hofi knows what the agent means. Can Levin be trusted with such an important assignment?

'He's new. Only been in Rome a year and he's never worked with an active service unit before. But his reports have been exemplary and he got the intelligence, after all.

Don't worry, you've got plenty of muscle.'

Kantor gets up to leave.

'Yuri ...'

'Yes?'

'This is our best chance. Maybe our only chance.'

'Don't worry. I shan't fail.'

Hofi looks at him. He knows the agent will be as good as his word.

The air is cold and clouds hang above the Eternal City, promising snow. They are waiting in Levin's apartment and the younger man paces the room and chain-smokes. Kantor is sitting on a sofa oiling and checking a Beretta automatic and its silencer. Several ammunition clips litter the cushions. Unlike his companion, he does not seem perturbed.

Levin stops pacing and faces him. 'Have you ever used one of those things before – I mean, on a job?'

Kantor cannot believe what he has just heard. Hofi has teamed him up with this guy? He puts the weapon down and wipes his hands on a rag.

'Do yourself a favour, go for a walk.'

Levin realises he has spoken out of turn and apologises. He extinguishes his cigarette and leaves the apartment. When he has gone Kantor drops the rag and gets up. He stretches and starts to exercise. It is important to keep his body supple.

After Kantor's arrival in Rome he and Levin had met up with the rest of the team at the embassy. They worked out the details of the assassination using a map of the basilica, looking for possible escape routes to be covered. The following day they visited St Peter's, posing as tourists, and made a note of the various angles so that someone would always have a clear view of the target. In the end, it will depend on his partner's ability to feign a seizure and get Edelweiss's attention before anyone realises what is happening. If the Swiss Guard become involved, they will have to be neutralised. But the team are sure the guards will be concentrating on the Pope's security rather than on a member of the congregation.

Kantor stops limbering up and looks around the apartment. It is pleasantly furnished with a fine view across the rooftops to the park beyond and the Villa Borghese. A kilometre to the south-west is the Vatican. On a desk he sees a collection of photographs. Most are family snaps but one in particular catches his eye. It is the picture of the Jewish boy in the Warsaw Ghetto. He is wearing a cloth cap and a raincoat is belted across his body. He looks frightened as he holds his hands in the air while Nazi storm troopers point their weapons at him. Kantor wonders why Levin has a copy. Were his family Polish, too? Perhaps he and the boy are related. The man is too young to have been in the war and he assumes Levin's parents escaped and fled to Palestine, either before the conflict or shortly after. What interests Kantor is that he had known the boy. He was called Mikhail and had been a good friend of his youngest sister. He always wondered if the child had survived.

His own family had been transported to Treblinka with

other prisoners from the ghetto after the failed uprising. The journey took three days, with no food or water. Several people in their wagon died, most of them elderly. On arrival he was separated from his mother and two little sisters, who were taken away to the gas chambers. Kantor, his father and elder brother were brought to the work camp. They laboured in the forest, felling trees and cutting logs to fuel the fires of the crematorium down the road.

The prisoners worked every day, from dawn till dusk. Kantor would listen to the clank of cattle cars and the trains' long whistle as they arrived at the station and disgorged their human cargo. He still heard the sound in his dreams. Even though the fires of the crematorium burned constantly, there was no fuel for the inmates and they had to scavenge what they could. At night, in winter, they hugged each other and beat themselves with their fists to stop themselves freezing to death. Each morning a work party went into the woods to bury the latest victims. Food was so scarce that men committed murder for a crust of bread.

In October 1944 the Nazis fled as the Soviet army advanced. Before they left the guards razed the extermination camp to the ground then raked over the ashes and sowed the earth with lupins. Nevertheless, bones and teeth and pieces of clothing would emerge from the soil. When the Russians came, father and sons escaped into the forest and joined the partisans. After the fall of Berlin, they made their way to Palestine along with hundreds of other Jews. The family travelled on foot through the Balkans to Greece and arrived on one of the first boats carrying refugees to the

Promised Land. Upon reaching the shores of Haifa, they fell to their knees and kissed the sand. Some of them still wore their concentration camp uniforms. Kantor stood on the beach with his father and brother and knew there would be no turning back. This land was their birthright and they had come to claim it. Less than three years later they were fighting again, this time for the survival of Israel. It seems as if he has been fighting all his life. Kantor always wondered why. Then he looks at the photograph of the boy called Mikhail and he understands.

Levin walks along the banks of the Tiber as the green river rolls on. The trees are naked and their bare branches point at the winter sky. He feels like an idiot. He knew he had said what he did because he was nervous. Yet he was meant to be a professional. Whatever it was it could not be unsaid and therefore he had even more reason to prove himself.

The truth is, he admires Kantor. The man is not a cold-blooded killer, unlike some. He seems morally incorruptible, as though he has a core like tempered steel which cannot be tarnished. Levin wishes he could be like him. Maybe one day he will.

He walks along the riverbank, his hands dug into his overcoat pockets. He thinks of Romulus and Remus, abandoned at the water's edge and rescued by the she-wolf, Lupa. She had suckled the boys and nurtured them and in time they found the city of Rome. It had been the cradle of civilisation for a thousand years until it sank into depravity and decay, its bones picked clean by the barbarian hordes. With the advent of Christianity, Rome had risen again and was now the rock of one of the world's great monotheist faiths.

Levin saw Judaism and Christianity as twin pillars of the Temple, which kept the roof of heaven from tumbling upon humanity. When the faiths were strong, the world was safe. But when the pillars rocked, the stones loosened and fell and crushed those below. He considered the religions to be complementary. He had tried to explain this to his supervisor who would look at him gnomically and tug his beard. The rabbi, he suspected, thought him heretical. It did not matter. The man was a zealot who believed only Jews would be saved when the Messiah came. Even so, Levin knows he must be careful – he wanted to achieve his doctorate, after all. Then he would lead the life he had always wanted, as a world-renowned theologian, albeit one who put mother Israel first.

Ignacio watches as snowflakes float from the sky and coalesce in icy drifts against the windowpanes. He sits at his desk and turns the holy medal over in his hand. Our Lady of Guadeloupe: first Ignacio's guardian, then Ariel's and now his. He says a prayer for them both and replaces the medal in a drawer.

He leaves his room and makes his way to the sacristy in the basilica. Scores of clergy mill about and St Peter's has the happy atmosphere of a festival. He finds himself amid various servers and members of the choir as they don their vestments, while the Pope and his fellow celebrants prepare in a separate room. There is an air of expectation and everyone talks in whispers. Ignacio sees Giuseppe speaking with another cleric whom he presumes is the director. Both men are robed. The bishop notices him and approaches.

'*Ciao, Dottore*. Nice to see you.'

'You, too. How's the foot?'

'Much better, thanks. Look, I can bend it now.' The bishop drops his slipper and raises his foot, moving it about.

'I see you haven't changed your shoes.'

'Ah, but I have. I bought a larger pair. You were right, though, the others were too tight,' and he puts his slipper back on. 'Now, go and get yourself dressed. The clothes are arranged by height, the tallest are on the left. You'll be wearing a cassock and surplice like everyone else. The cross is in the corner.' He points to a silver crucifix mounted on an ebony shaft. Ignacio estimates it must be at least seven feet tall. He thanks the bishop who returns to his conversation with the other cleric.

Ignacio takes a scarlet cassock from the mahogany cupboard and hangs his jacket on a hook. He buttons the cassock and puts on the white linen surplice and smooths the folds. He checks himself in a mirror then goes to the cross. It is heavier than he thought. He lines up with the other servers and they proceed out of the sacristy into the corridor. The choir is already in the balcony above the nave. Thurifers light their charcoals and blow on them and a priest spoons incense into each vessel. The servers close the lids and swing their thuribles, wafting perfumed clouds along the passage. Smoke billows and it smells as though a cypress grove is burning.

There is a hush and Pope Paul emerges from a door, followed by a rustle of garments as everyone genuflects for his blessing. They rise and Ignacio leads the way, bearing the cross before him. The thurifers are next, followed by the servers and, finally, the celebrants in reverse order. The last person in the procession is the pontiff wearing his mitre, the crosier in his hand. Over his vestments is a purple velvet cloak embroidered with gold thread, its hem borne by two boys. They enter the basilica and proceed along the north transept, the pontiff blessing the faithful who bow and cross themselves as he passes. Music plays and choristers' voices raise high the vaulted roof.

The Mossad team are in position. Kantor is standing next to Levin in the front row. Both men have their eyes fixed on the person holding the cross. He is tall and dark-haired but it is only when he turns and faces the congregation and they see his eyes that they know for sure it is Edelweiss. The other members of the hit squad cover the entrances to the palace and the door that leads to the Whispering Gallery and the roof. The only escape route is down the nave but their target will not get that far.

Ignacio puts the cross in its holder, then places his hands together and waits for the other servers to join him on the domain. The Pope arrives and, accompanied by his acolytes, he ascends the steps and stands before the altar to celebrate Mass.

After the gospel is read the pontiff delivers his Christmas homily. His voice is thin and frail but rings out clearly from the speakers placed along the columns. His message is one of joy at the Lord's birth on this most holy day of the Church's calendar. He also asks for every Christian to renew their baptismal vows and their faith in God. Usually Levin would listen with interest but all he can do is stare at the target. Kantor notices and murmurs in his ear. His turn will come soon enough.

The Pope finishes his sermon and returns to the celebrant's chair where he hangs his head in prayer. When he rises, the congregation follows and the pontiff begins the celebration of the Eucharist.

In the wings an altar boy holds the figure of the infant Christ on a crimson damask cushion. At the stroke of midnight the lights are extinguished and the basilica is plunged into darkness, only the burning candles provide illumination. The boy advances to the altar bearing the sacred figure. He kneels before the Pope who takes the cushion and raises it up high for all to see. At that moment the lights are switched on and the bells of St Peter's peal. They are joined by dozens of other bells held by servers and those in the choir. The whole church reverberates to the happy noise and people break into applause.

Levin falls forward onto the marble floor and starts to shudder and twitch, foaming at the mouth. Kantor steps out from the pew and takes him in his arms and gesticulates at the servers. At first they do not notice then one points in their direction and Ignacio hastens towards them. All around people are clapping and bells are ringing as the pontiff holds the Christ-child aloft.

'What's the matter?'

'My brother's an epileptic. He's having a seizure.'

'Let's get him away from here.'

Together, they carry the convulsing Levin from the domain to one of the transepts. Other members of the congregation appear to help, but they are members of the assassination team. They bring the stricken man to a side chapel and lay him on the ground, where he continues to gurn and shake, while the group gather around in a semi-circle. Ignacio kneels and takes Levin's tongue from between his teeth. He talks to him and holds his hand. He peers into the man's eyes to check the dilation of his pupils and is shocked. They are completely normal. There was nothing wrong with him at all. If a person were having a seizure, the pupils would be much larger, often covering the entire iris. He cannot believe it. Why would anyone pretend?

Ignacio looks at the man beside him who reaches into his jacket and he understands.

He leaps to his feet and pushes past the agent. A bullet whines by his head and he hears the crack of another as it ricochets off a stone pillar. He runs to the nearest door, leading to the palace but it is blocked by two burly men.

Ignacio is certain they are not Swiss Guards. He turns and rushes to the far side and finds the same. The only way out is the entrance to the Whispering Gallery, which is now unmanned. He twists the handle and races up the stairs. Close behind, he can hear a heavy tread. He enters the gallery and runs to the opposite end, to another door. This time it is locked. He turns and sees the man with the gun appear at the head of the stairs. His only escape is the roof.

Ignacio opens a window and climbs out. The air is freezing and the tiles are covered with a dusting of snow. A crystal moon glows and the stars shine wintry bright. He stumbles across the roof to the edge but there is no way down, just a vertiginous drop onto the flagstones below. With nowhere to go, Ignacio faces his adversary. The man is only a few yards away. For a moment they both stare at each other. Kantor raises the Beretta and takes aim. A single shot will do it but he does not pull the trigger. Instead, he lowers the weapon. Ignacio is amazed then realises his assassin is giving him a choice. Either he can take his own life or the gunman will take it for him.

The figure walks to the edge of the roof and spreads his arms wide, like a diver on a high board. Beneath him is the plaza, filled with the faithful who were unable to get into the church. Some shout and point but most are watching the spectacle inside the basilica. Light pours from the open doors and clouds of incense smoke as the great campanile tolls across the square. Ignacio jumps.

A cry goes up from the bystanders as they see someone tumble through the air and strike the pavement. A Swiss

Guard drops his halberd and runs over and takes hold of the broken body. He tries to comfort to him but the man appears beyond help. All Ignacio can hear as his life inexorably ebbs away, is the joyous sound of bells. The bells, the bells, the bells which are ringing out to heaven ...

JERUSALEM–ROME

Wednesday 12–Monday 17 January 1977

Yitzhak Hofi hurries down the corridors of the Knesset to the cabinet war room deep in the bowels of the building. It is smaller than the usual place they occupy and is both soundproof and bombproof. He is not late for his meeting, in fact, he is several minutes early, his haste the result of anxiety. And he is anxious because he has a lot explaining to do. The mission to eliminate Edelweiss has not been a success. Although seriously injured, the man did not die when he leapt from the roof of St Peter's. At first it was uncertain whether the target would survive but now he is out of danger. Edelweiss is currently under armed guard in a private room in the Vatican's Bambino Gesù hospital. As its name suggests, the hospital's primary purpose is the care of sick children rather than adults, but it is owned and run by the Vatican and the most secure place there is in which to treat their patient. More importantly, the target is isolated and cannot be reached by outsiders. Everyone who enters the ward must pass through a security screen manned by the papal bodyguard. The instruction comes from Pope Paul himself. Yet again, the Mossad has failed.

Hofi enters the war room perspiring and out of breath and closes the door.

'Sorry I'm late,' he says, even though he is not.

'Come and join us,' says Prime Minister Rabin in his gravelly voice.

A decorated former general, Yitzhak Rabin is the most dovish of those present. It had taken a lot to get him to authorise the Entebbe raid the previous year. He felt the cost of potential failure and casualties would be too high, not for the forces of Sayeret Matkal – who were risking their lives in the operation – but among the 200 hostages. There were bound to be civilian fatalities and what could be considered an acceptable number? Thirty, forty, perhaps even as many as fifty? That was a heavy toll for any military operation, let alone a rescue mission. Was it not wiser to negotiate with the terrorists and have a prisoner swap? After all, there were plenty of PLO gunmen languishing in Israeli prisons. Nobody would have to die. He had been persuaded otherwise by his Defence Minister, Shimon Peres, who is also present at this meeting and one of the government's notable hawks. Peres had convinced his friend and former political rival that it was unacceptable for Israel to be seen to negotiate with such people, it would set a precedent and forever be a thorn in the nation's side. There would not be just one Entebbe, but many. The cabinet concurred and Rabin reluctantly agreed to the operation.

The meeting is being held in camera and most of the cabinet have been excluded. Those present form the government's inner circle and include the Minister of Information,

Aharon Yariv, another decorated former soldier. Yariv had commanded a brigade on the Golan Heights during the Yom Kippur conflict and was previously chief of military intelligence. Considered a brilliant negotiator, he had led the Israeli delegation during the post-war Kilometre 101 talks with Egypt's General Mohamed Ghani el-Gamasy. The talks resulted in a prisoner swap in exchange for supplies to the Arab nation's beleaguered Third Army, which had been surrounded by the Israeli Defence Force. Yariv is also head of Operation Wrath of God, the mission to track down and eliminate the PLO terrorists responsible for the massacre of Israeli athletes in Munich. He has a dark sense of humour. Before each assassination the target's family would be sent flowers with a card reading: 'a reminder we do not forgive and we do not forget.'

The others around the table are the Minister of Internal Affairs, Shlomo Hillel, previously a Mossad agent and diplomat, and the Deputy Prime Minister, Yigal Allon, another ex-general and an old comrade of Rabin. With the current Mossad chief now present, the doves and hawks are equally split.

'Hofi, tell us what you have and start from the beginning as not everyone here knows the details,' says the prime minister.

The chief quietly explains about Operation Daniel, the quest to find and eliminate Edelweiss. He describes how they used the anniversary of the Misiones village fire to set a tail on a potential source. Unknown to Ariel, his father, Otto, had worked for the Mossad. It was he who had provided the intelligence that Adolf Hitler and Eva Braun had escaped the Führerbunker and she had given birth to a son.

On the pretence of wanting to convert to Catholicism, Otto had befriended the Jesuit principal in Argentina at that time, who he knew was conflicted by the Vatican's ambivalence towards Nazism and the establishment of Odessa and its ratline to South America. They met many times at Manzana de las Luces, where the unsuspecting principal instructed his charge in the tenets of the Catholic faith. Otto was a diligent pupil who seemed particularly concerned with the concept of redemption. Was it possible to do great evil and yet be forgiven? If so, what was the point of hell and damnation? It was an interesting conundrum and they spent many hours discussing and comparing their theologies. During these talks the principal let slip what he knew about Edelweiss. It was perhaps the single most important piece of intelligence the state of Israel had ever received. But further enquiries and operations had drawn a blank. As the years went by they were not entirely sure the target was actually alive or if he had ever existed. Nevertheless, they continued to search for Edelweiss until they had proof one way, or the other.

After the death of Otto Guzman, the agency knew Ariel would likely be sympathetic towards Israel because of his father's experiences in Nazi Germany before the war. He had never been approached but operatives had kept a close watch on him and bugged his apartment to make sure. Several false leads led nowhere. Then, an agent at Canal 7 notified headquarters that Javier, the sole witness and survivor of the Misiones tragedy, had agreed to be interviewed for the first time about the fire. Whatever he said or did not say, the Mossad were certain the journalist would pursue the story. As it happened, they struck gold when the priest confirmed the Nazi leader's flight and also the establishment of the camp near Iguaçu. The hare was up and running, all they had to do was follow the scent.

The next part of the operation was to tail Ariel and, for this, they used Carmen. From phone taps and covert observation, they knew the journalist was heterosexual and, like all red-blooded males, would be susceptible to the charms of the opposite sex. The agent had been used before as a honeytrap in London and Rome and on both occasions senior PLO operatives were eliminated. The head of the airline that Ariel used to fly to Posadas was also in their pay. Carmen was placed on board as part of the cabin crew.

'And that is the background to Operation Daniel,' says Hofi.

'How come the target wasn't taken out in Buenos Aires?' enquires Yariv.

'We tried. But time was against us. It was only a matter of hours before Edelweiss got on a plane to Rome. We had to act there and then. Unfortunately, the target swapped clothes and ID with our source and went walkabout. It was dark, they both looked similar and the wrong man got killed.'

'And you used the same agent again in Rome?' asks Peres.

'Yes, we did. I was sure he would complete the job and, to be honest, I'm at a loss as to why he didn't.'

'What happened?' It is Hillel speaking.

'You mean on the roof of the basilica?'

'Yes.'

'According to our agent, he pulled the trigger but the pistol jammed. By the time he cleared the blockage, Edelweiss had jumped.'

'What weapon did he use?' asks Rabin.

'A Beretta 70. The .22 LRS version with silencer.'

'They don't jam – ever!' says Allon.

'He insists this one did.'

'And you believe him?' It is Peres.

'The point is, the target survived,' says Rabin. 'Discussing the pros and cons of the weapon used changes nothing.'

'Who was the agent?' says Hillel.

'Yuri Kantor,' answers Hofi.

'I know him. An excellent choice. I'd call him the best,' says Yariv.

The chief is grateful for his colleague. He has taken the operation's lack of success personally and, what is more, he knows that his job is on the line.

'Where's the agent now?' asks Peres.

'Hopefully on a beach somewhere. He's been retired,' says Hofi.

The others nod. After a lifetime in the service of Israel the man has earned his rest.

'The question is, what do we do about Edelweiss?' Rabin surveys those around the table.

'We continue with Operation Daniel,' says Peres. 'And we don't stop until the target's dead. There are other methods.'

'Like what?' asks Allon, who is no fan of the defence minister – the man was a hawk but has never been in action despite joining the Haganah in 1947. An armchair warrior if ever there was one.

Peres raises a sceptical eyebrow. The former general is a capable soldier but he is also adept at making enemies and not only on the battlefield. If he wishes to have a career in politics, he would be wise to dial down his animus.

'Shimon is right. There are other ways and means,' says Hillel. 'But none of them are straightforward and the difficulty is being able to gain access.'

'I think we're looking at the problem through the wrong end of a telescope,' counters Yariv.

'What do you mean, Aharon?' asks Rabin.

'We're considering methods of execution but the window of opportunity to eliminate Edelweiss has closed. Everyone knows it was our lot involved in Rome and neither the United States, nor the Vatican will look kindly on a further attempt on his life. There's a Democrat in the White House and we need Washington far more than they need us. If we want a peace treaty with Egypt and handshakes in the Rose Garden with Jimmy Carter and Sadat, this is not the way to go about it.'

'What do you suggest?'

'We tell the Pope to give him up.'

'Really, just like that?' says Peres, unable to hide his incredulity.

'No, not just like that Shimon, but we have leverage. The Vatican is in a difficult position. Pope Pius turned a blind eye to Hitler and the rise of Nazism and several notable clerics aided and abetted war criminals. Many of whom, as we know, escaped to South America. In other words, they owe us.'

'I'm not certain the Pope will see it that way,' says Hillel.

'That's where you're wrong. We already have a substantial body of evidence on the Church's involvement with Odessa. They were certainly complicit. Not all the clergy, by any means, but enough. If we present that evidence together with the threat to expose Edelweiss and the fact the Vatican gave him sanctuary, we should be able to get our man.'

'Do you really think the leader of the world's one billion Catholics will appreciate our holding his feet to the fire?' asks Allon.

'No, Yigal, I don't. But it's worth a try, isn't it?'

Everyone around the table considers Yariv's proposal. It is admirable for its chutzpah, if nothing else.

'Aharon, you have a point,' says Rabin. 'If we cannot eliminate Edelweiss, at least we can make sure he's in our custody and isolated. But we will have to give guarantees. The Pope will not allow Edelweiss to be harmed in any way. There is also the problem of how to get him here.'

'The Vatican can fake his death. He gets a virus or pneumonia in hospital, whatever. In the morgue, his body can be switched and another person buried in his place. Meanwhile, Edelweiss is sedated and brought to Israel in a specially adapted coffin. We'll say one of our guys at the embassy died. The carabinieri won't open or X-ray it because of diplomatic immunity. When Edelweiss arrives we give him a choice: jail and solitary confinement for the rest of your life, or we perform plastic surgery and establish a new identity. Then we place him under house arrest and keep him far away from the public eye.'

'Where could he go?' says Rabin, who is intrigued by the prospect.

'I haven't thought that far ahead. Maybe an army base? Or the Golan. It's off-limits to non-military personnel.'

The men in the room are silent. All is quiet except for the hum of air conditioning.

'Okay,' says Rabin. 'Does anyone have any objections to the plan or, indeed, any other proposals?'

The others reply negatively, although only Peres is against it. The idea of Israel becoming a haven for Hitler's son is anathema to him. But he knows he must bide his time. One day he will surely be prime minister and Edelweiss's fate will be his decision and his alone.

'In that case, Aharon, since it's your idea, you can be in charge of the operation. The agency will no doubt want to brief you further. You'll have to go to Rome where you can put all your diplomatic skills to the test. The meeting is now adjourned.' The prime minister rises and leads the way to the door.

Rabin walks down the corridor accompanied by his security team. He is a brave man who is not afraid to make tough decisions. It is this bravery which will prove to be his downfall. Years later President Bill Clinton will preside over a historic handshake on the White House lawn between the Israeli premier and the PLO leader, Yasser Arafat, concluding a treaty between the two states that exchanges land for peace. A deal that is unacceptable both to right-wing Israelis and radical Palestinians. But it is not Fatah or Hamas who will pull the trigger, it is the Israeli internal security force, Shin Bet.

Pope Paul is in his office in the Apostolic Palace. Beside him is Pedro Arrupe, the only other man in the Vatican who knows the true identity of Edelweiss. Sitting with the pontiff and his adviser are Aharon Yariv and Moshe Levin, acting as a translator for the general, who does not speak Italian. On the table between them lie several dossiers. Each is stamped with the words Odessa and Top Secret, in English and Italian. The pontiff and the superior general have just leafed through them all. The evidence they contain will be made public if the Vatican refuses to comply with the Israeli government's demands to hand over Edelweiss in exchange for his wellbeing and their silence.

The Pope and Arrupe converse in hushed tones before the pontiff addresses his visitors.

'There is one question you must answer. Will Israel accept this as a final and lasting atonement for the Church's sin in relation to the Holocaust?'

Yariv is unsure how to answer the question in theological terms and he looks at Levin.

'Yes, I believe it would,' says the younger man. 'In Judaism we must also atone for the wrongs that we commit. Think of this as being the Church's Yom Kippur. According to the medieval Jewish scholar, Maimonides, the sinner must abandon his sin, remove it from his mind and resolve in his heart never to repeat it. As the prophet Isaiah said: 'let the wicked forsake his way and the man of iniquity his thoughts.' He should also regret his past, as is stated in the Book of Jeremiah: 'he must call Him who knows all secrets to witness that he will never turn to this sin again.'

'Holy Father, as you know, we cannot erase our past or our sins but God will grant us absolution if we seek forgiveness. Atonement in Judaism is not so different from the Church's Sacrament of Confession. If we genuinely seek the Lord's forgiveness, He will forgive because He is merciful and all-powerful. And, in both our faiths, we must atone for our sins with an act of penance. Therefore, handing over Edelweiss to Israel would be a physical manifestation of atonement.'

'And what guarantees can you give me that he will not be harmed in any way?'

'You have our word, sir. That is all we can offer,' says Yariv.

The Pope and Arrupe put their heads together again and whisper like a confessor and his confessant, although it is impossible to tell who is playing which part. After a while the pontiff speaks.

'In that case, I must accept,' he says. 'Pedro, please inform the doctor of my decision. Tell him the Church has no alternative and that I am truly sorry. I will pray for him every day.' The Pope faces his visitors once more. 'We will make the necessary arrangements and be in touch. Thank you, gentlemen.'

Yariv and Levin stand. The general is delighted and

relieved the negotiations have gone so well. It is an extraordinary diplomatic triumph for the state of Israel. But the spy is not so sure. He feels it is wrong to have coerced a religious leader in such a way, particularly a man of singular grace like Pope Paul.

As they are about to depart, Levin pauses.

'Holy Father,' he says.

'Yes?'

'May I have a blessing?'

'Certainly, my son.' The pontiff raises his hand and makes the sign of the cross, giving Levin his benediction.

The Israelis are escorted out of the palace by the Swiss Guard. They leave the environs of St Peter's and enter the broad acres of the plaza. Light breaks through the clouds above the basilica and pigeons turn and wheel in a winter sky. As they make their way to the embassy, Yariv laughs and claps his companion on the back.

'Well done, young man. Excellent tradecraft asking for the Pope's blessing as we left.'

Levin makes no response. It had nothing at all to do with tradecraft. He was being sincere.

Bishop Giuseppe is resting on a stone bench in the palace garden. It is a pleasant location where he often passed the time and where he liked to say the office. But today he cannot concentrate and so he closes his breviary. He is sad and not even the turtle doves calling to each other in the olive trees can raise his spirits. He heard that morning his friend, the doctor, had died. It happened in the early hours, a heart attack, according to the hospital. Giuseppe is surprised as he had thought the patient was making good progress. There was even talk he might be able to walk again. The fall had crushed his lower vertebrae and broken his pelvis and both legs but his spinal cord had not been severed. An amazing stroke of luck and miraculous in its way. The bishop never knew quite what possessed him to throw himself off the basilica roof, on Christmas morning of all occasions, but everyone had their furies.

Giuseppe observes his foot. His gout is cured and he feels much healthier after the doctor suggested he change his diet. Now he only eats fruit for breakfast and has cut down on red wine as well. He even has had to have his clerical clothes taken in at the waist. His brethren kept teasing him about it. He thinks of the pretty dark-haired nun who worked at the clinic. He had had to tell her himself. The poor thing was distraught. No doubt she had been in love with the doctor, he was a handsome man after all. And those blue eyes of his – quite exceptional.

Giuseppe hears mewing. One of the garden's feral cats approaches and entwines itself around his legs. He has names for them all and this one is Mischief. They are meant to keep down the rats but all they ever do is stalk sparrows and chase lizards.

'What do you want, you naughty cat – food, I suppose?' and he strokes the feline's arched back. 'Well, you'll have to wait, it's not teatime yet.'

When no titbit is forthcoming the cat slinks off. Giuseppe

watches it go. He has asked Pope Paul if he might be allowed to officiate at the doctor's funeral and this has been granted. Apparently, the doctor had asked to be cremated if anything happened to him. The bishop will scatter his ashes around the garden. He is sure his friend would have liked that.

TEL AVIV–GOLAN HEIGHTS

Thursday 20–Friday 21 October 1977

Yuri Kantor is in a café on the Tel Aviv waterfront and watches the waves purling up the beach. It is one of his favourite pastimes – he can spend hours doing nothing, just gazing out to sea. He is drinking an espresso and picking at a plate of baklava. He is fond of the pistachio pastries and always orders some with his coffee.

A pretty woman walks towards him and he gets up to greet her.

'*Shalom*,' he says, although he hesitates to kiss her on the cheek.

'*Shalom*,' she answers, and gives him a peck.

They take their seats and both seem happy to see each other.

'What would you like?'

'Mint tea, thanks.'

A waiter arrives and takes her order. When he has gone, Kantor appraises his colleague. He has not seen her since the operation in Buenos Aires.

'I hear you've been reassigned,' he says.

'Yes. I went off-piste.'

'I don't blame you. I'd have done the same.'

'Not very professional. But, thanks all the same.'

Carmen looks about. 'Nice place you found.'

'It is. I often come here, for the view, mostly. I live around the corner.'

'Are you still with the organisation?'

'No. They've let me go.'

'About time.'

The waiter returns with her order and a glass of sparkling mineral water. She sips her tea and Kantor offers the plate of baklava.

'Try one of these. They're made on the premises.'

She pops one in her mouth. 'Mmm, they're good.'

'When did you get back?'

'Three months ago. They've given me a desk job until they work out what to do with me.'

Cars pass along the corniche and people stroll down the boulevard. Waves murmur as they tumble on the shore and a breeze floats in from the sea. It is autumn and there is a tang in the air.

'Glad to be home again?'

'Yes, I am.'

Kantor pauses as he tries to find the right words, while cars go by and people walk up and down the boulevard and waves crash white along the beach.

'Look, I wanted to see you because ...'

'I know. You don't have to apologise.'

'I do.'

'It couldn't be helped. You were doing your job. It was my

fault. I should have been there.'

They sit for a while not saying anything and sip their drinks and listen to the sounds of the ocean.

'There is something else.'

'What?'

Kantor checks to make sure no one is eavesdropping, but they are alone. He speaks in a low voice.

'Edelweiss is alive.'

Carmen looks at him blankly, although he can tell it is the first time she has heard this.

'The man didn't die when he jumped. He was badly injured but he survived.'

'Is he at the Vatican?'

Kantor is expressionless. 'No, he's here, in Israel.'

This time Carmen cannot hide her disbelief but she regains her composure.

'Why ... ?'

'The government cut a deal. They knew they'd never be able to get near him again so they came up with a plan and persuaded the Pope to hand him over in exchange for their silence. The pontiff agreed as long as they didn't harm him.'

Carmen is stunned. She raises her cup and drinks her tea, now stewed and tepid. She has another pastry to take away the taste.

'He'd like to meet you.'

'Where is he?'

'At a military base in the Golan. He helps run a school there. I can give you the location.'

'Why would he want to see me?'

'I don't know, maybe he feels guilty.'

'He's not the only one. I include myself, by the way.'

'So, how about it?'

Carmen considers for a moment.

'Isn't access restricted?'

'It is. But they don't know that you know. You've got your ID and security pass?'

'Yes.'

'Then they won't ask any questions.'

'Okay, give me the name of the place.'

Kantor tears off a corner of his paper napkin, writes it down and passes it to her. She reads the note then screws it up and drops it into the glass of mineral water. The drink fizzes and the paper unravels and disintegrates. Carmen gets up to go and the agent also rises.

'I appreciate it,' and she kisses him goodbye.

Kantor watches her walk away until she vanishes in the crowd, just another man in awe of a woman's beauty.

The old Roman road to Haifa is long and straight and recedes into the distance. On one side are kibbutzim and on the other lies the Mediterranean. The baby in the carrycot beside the driver is asleep. Carmen looks at her slumbering daughter with pride and affection. She is so consumed with love for the child that sometimes she cannot believe the little girl is actually hers. Often, she gets up in the middle of the night to make sure the baby is there, that this is not a dream which will evaporate on waking. Carmen wonders how she could be blessed with anything so perfect. The child looks just like her father. She has Ariel's fine features and his deep blue eyes. She even has his smile.

It is a warm, sunny day and Carmen has the vehicle's windows open. She is surrounded by orange groves and a scent of citrus is borne on the wind. At a roundabout near Haifa she takes the road north to Acre. Before she reaches the ancient biblical port she turns east and drives towards Karmiel and the border. As the gradient increases, the car meanders through olive-clad hills, passing farmsteads and pale flocks of sheep that graze on the terraced slopes. A shepherd calls out and, with a bleat and a clanking of bells, his flock follow him to fresh pasture. It is not long before Carmen reaches the Golan's southern checkpoint.

Once her credentials are verified, she enters the security zone. The area is strewn with radar stations and anti-aircraft batteries and there are scores of tanks and armoured cars. Overhead, a pair of F-15 Eagles scream as they patrol azurite skies. The surrounding hills are dotted with newly constructed towns and villages as Israel populates the area with settlements. In time the residents will no longer be unwelcome immigrants amongst the Druze but natives born in the region. The Golan belongs to Israel and, despite the efforts of the Assad regime in Damascus, it will never be returned to Syria. Not if Carmen has anything to do with it. She fought here alongside her comrades only a few years ago and many of them shed their blood and died, their bodies laid out in regimented cemeteries. Now it will be her home. She has asked to be reassigned to military intelligence and the agency has agreed.

After an hour Carmen approaches Camp Filon. It is so secret that it does not appear on any maps, nor is the place signposted. At the entrance she is stopped by a tanned and fit-looking soldier. It is Friday and he wears a kippah instead of a helmet.

'Afternoon, ma'am. Your ID and pass, please.'

'There you are,' she says and hands them over. As the lance corporal looks at her papers she notices the medal ribbon on his uniform. He is a Yom Kippur veteran like her and she wonders which unit he served in. They might even have been comrades.

'What's the purpose of your visit?'

'I want to put my daughter's name down for the kindergarten.'

The soldier peers across at the sleeping child.

'Cuteness!' and the man grins. 'Perhaps my boy and her will be playmates.'

'How old is yours?'

'Just had his first birthday. He's starting to walk now, or toddle, I should say. How about yours?'

'Only five months.'

'Great. Well, have a nice day,' and the soldier salutes and opens the barrier.

She enters the camp and drives to the school, parking in the forecourt. Carmen releases her daughter from the cot and carries her down a path shaded by cork oak. Instead of bullets snapping and whistling through the air, there is a sound of birdsong. As she nears the school she can hear a shrill cry of voices and children playing.

The man she has come to see is waiting for her.

Ignacio gets up from a wooden bench and using a pair of crutches, he walks stiffly towards his visitor. He seems different from the photographs she had pored over during the assignment in Buenos Aires. His nose is broader and his cheeks have been filled in. But it is not only the plastic surgery. He has also put on weight and has a flowing beard, like a desert father, or a prophet.

'Hello ...'

'Hi ...'

'Thanks for coming.'

'Not at all, glad to be here.'

They stand for a moment, neither knowing what to say. Carmen realises something else is different about the doctor.

'Your eyes, they're brown.'

Ignacio laughs softly.

'The one thing they couldn't change. I use contact lenses.'

He indicates the bundle in his visitor's arms.

'And who's this, may I ask?'

Carmen jiggles her child, which wakes and starts to cry.

'This is Evita. Say hello, sweet pea.'

'I should have known. And who's the daddy?'

'Have a guess.'

'My God, that's wonderful! Can I hold her?'

'Please do,' and she hands him her fretful daughter.

'Shush, now,' Ignacio says as he takes the girl. He starts to soothe her with a lullaby and the baby quietens.

'She looks like Ariel.'

'I think so, too.'

'You don't know how lucky you are. I'd love to have a kid.'

'There's plenty of time.'

Ignacio appears pensive.

'Time's not a problem. It's my injuries ...'

'I'm so sorry. I didn't know.'

'It's Okay. I survived. Ariel didn't,' and he hands the child back to her mother. 'She's lovely.'

Birds sing amid the oak trees and a lizard darts from its hiding place and goes rustling through the shade. A voice calls out.

'Rabbi, are you coming to teach? Everyone's waiting.'

'Sure. I'll be with you in a minute.'

The boy runs back to tell his classmates and the two of them are alone again.

'What are you teaching?'

'The Torah.'

The visitor is surprised.

'But you're Catholic.'

Ignacio gives a shake of his head.

'No, not anymore. I've converted – I'm Jewish.'

Carmen rocks the baby in her arms.

'Atonement.'

'Or, as we say in Hebrew, Yom Kippur.'

The air begins to burn with an incredible brightness as the souls of the six million rise up from the death camps and march towards the gates of heaven. They advance across the sky like a host of angels, singing hosanna after hosanna. There is not an army in the world that can stop them. Trumpets sound and the gates open wide and they are received into the Bosom of Abraham where the righteous dead await Judgement Day.

And the night will be no more. They will need no light of lamp or sun,
for the Lord God will be their light, and they shall reign for ever and ever.